"If you will trust me, I'll protect Daisy."

Jacob watched the emotions wash across Lilly's soft features. She wanted to trust him but something held her back.

"Thank you." The words sounded tight in her throat.

He offered her a smile. "I won't let you down."

If someone was going to hurt Daisy, they'd have to go through him. He'd vowed to watch over the little girl and he'd do just that.

Jacob realized then that his promise included Lilly. If anyone hurt Daisy, they'd also be hurting Lilly. His instincts told him that she was a kind person. Her sympathy for him when he'd told her about his upbringing had been sincere. Jacob knew he'd not let either Daisy or Lilly be hurt.

He just prayed he'd not lose his heart in his desire to protect them both. Jacob had no intentions of falling in love. Women couldn't be trusted not to abandon those they claimed to love the most. His birth mother had proven that. No, he'd harden that part of his heart and still keep his promise.

Rhonda Gibson lives in New Mexico with her husband, James. She has two children and three beautiful grandchildren. Reading is something she has enjoyed her whole life, and writing stemmed from that love. When she isn't writing or reading, she enjoys gardening, beading and playing with her dog, Sheba. You can visit her at rhondagibson.net. Rhonda hopes her writing will entertain, encourage and bring others closer to God.

Books by Rhonda Gibson

Love Inspired Historical

Saddles and Spurs

Pony Express Courtship
Pony Express Hero

The Marshal's Promise
Groom by Arrangement
Taming the Texas Rancher
His Chosen Bride
A Pony Express Christmas
The Texan's Twin Blessings
A Convenient Christmas Bride

Visit the Author Profile page at Harlequin.com.

RHONDA GIBSON

Pony Express Hero

⬧ **HARLEQUIN**® LOVE INSPIRED® HISTORICAL

Recycling programs for this product may not exist in your area.

LOVE INSPIRED BOOKS

ISBN-13: 978-0-373-28362-0

Pony Express Hero

This edition published by arrangement with Love Inspired Books.

® and TM are trademarks of Love Inspired Books, used under license. Trademarks indicated with ® are registered in the United States Patent and Trademark Office, the Canadian Intellectual Property Office and in other countries.

www.Harlequin.com

Printed in U.S.A.

And they that know Thy name
will put their trust in Thee: for Thou, Lord,
hast not forsaken them that seek Thee.
—*Psalms* 9:10

To my brother, Marty McConnell,
for all the good times we shared growing up
and the support you have shown me as an adult.
I'm proud to call you my little brother and best friend.
As always, thank You to my Lord and Savior
for allowing me to write books for Him.

Chapter One

Mud Springs, California
Summer 1860

A scream tore through the early-morning air. Instantly alert, Jacob Young reined in his horse and pushed back his hat, scanning the area for trouble. His horse shifted beneath him, its movements telling him it, too, sensed something was wrong.

Then Jacob saw her. A child, no more than three or four years old, in bare feet and a white nightgown. He squinted, searching intently for her parents, but found no one. Why would a little girl be in a ravine by herself at this early hour of the morning? The sun had barely begun to top the horizon.

His gaze moved to the other end of the ravine. A cloud of dust rose like steam from a kettle. Icy fear twisted around his heart as he saw what had the little girl scrambling up the small hillside. Cows, hundreds of cows, thundered down the gorge toward her. The rumble of hooves pounded the ground along with the continual terrified screams from the little girl.

Stampede.

Jacob kicked his horse's flanks and shouted, "Hiyah!" The horse's sturdy legs tensed—then, like a shot, they raced down one side of the ravine toward the small figure that seemed so very far away. He leaned over the horse's neck, urging him to go faster and faster. They were close but so were the cows. A flicker of apprehension coursed through him. Would he make it in time?

The child stumbled and fell, losing ground she'd already gained. Frantically she glanced behind her. Jacob was close enough now to see that fear, stark and vivid, glittered in her eyes. She spotted him racing toward her and stopped trying to climb the ravine; instead she turned and ran in his direction. Clear brown eyes looked up at him expectantly. A solid wall of cattle closed in on her.

Jacob leaned over and grabbed her around the waist. Thankfully she weighed no more than a half bale of hay or Jacob felt sure she would have unseated him. He pulled her up and plopped her in front of him in one swift move. Her fingers clutched his arms and she pressed back against him, turning her head sideways to hide her eyes from certain disaster. His arms wrapped protectively around her tiny waist as the horse swung away trying to outrun the thundering, bellowing cattle. If need be, he'd shield her with his body, should the horse fail in its attempt to get them to safety.

His heart beat so hard and fast in his chest it felt almost painful. The cows continued down the ravine and the dust rolled, causing him to cough. The horse managed to get up the canyon wall just before the cattle pounded past them.

The little girl shuddered. He tightened his hold, offering comfort the only way he knew how. She sneezed and rubbed at her eyes. Jacob slowed the horse to a walk.

"Honey, are you all right?" He loosened his grip on the child.

She wiggled around to face him. "Uh-huh." Big brown eyes looked up at him. Her heart-shaped face was covered in dirt and muddy trails traveled down both cheeks where her tears had run into the collar of her now very soiled nightgown.

"What are you doing out here?" he asked as he wiped at the dirt on her face with a handkerchief from his pocket.

She shook her head and her blond braids slapped the sides of her little face. "I don't know. I went to sleep and when I woke up I was here."

The sound of hooves pounding the ground had Jacob twisting in the saddle and looking over his shoulder. A young man and woman raced toward them. Fear and relief warred for a place on the woman's face.

"Daisy! Are you all right?" the young woman called.

Jacob felt more than saw the little one nod, her hair rubbing against his chin. Her name fit her. Her golden hair resembled the color of a yellow daisy, her brown eyes the button in the center of the flower. Jacob was thankful he'd come along when he had, but anger twisted in him like a volcano on the verge of erupting.

When the woman and man got close enough, Daisy answered, "I'm all right. Lilly, he saved me." Her big brown eyes drank in Jacob's face.

The woman pulled her horse alongside Jacob and reached for the child but Jacob was having none of it.

"Where were you? Why was she here by herself? What kind of mother lets a child wander off alone at this time of the morning?" Jacob's heart demanded he say more but the child in his arms tensed and placed her hand against his heart. He took a deep breath and reined in his temper.

"Now see here." The man bristled at Jacob's words but the woman held her hand up and silenced him. Tears glistened on her pale heart-shaped face.

"I've been looking for her since early this morning. I have no idea how she got here… I don't know how she opened the door to get out of the house." A hot tear rolled down her cheek. She swiped at it with a trembling hand. "I would never intentionally let her wander off, nor would I want her hurt in any way."

With an odd twinge of conscience, Jacob handed Daisy across to the woman. It surprised him to see her wearing men's trousers. Her pretty blue eyes ran over the little girl as her arms gathered her in a tight hug. Golden hair hung over one shoulder in a tight braid, reminding him a little of his adoptive mother, Rebecca.

The woman whose name he now knew to be Lilly looked to be about his age, twenty, maybe a year or two younger than himself. Jacob realized he was staring and said, "I'm not sure why she is out here by herself but the cattle almost did her in."

Before Lilly could speak the man beside her interrupted. "And I'd like to know what you're doing on Johnson soil, mister."

Jacob leaned against his saddle horn, aware that his hands still shook. "My name is Jacob Young." He pushed back his hat and met the other man's eyes.

"Lilly, the cows came running toward me. I almost got runned over," Daisy said, laying a small hand against Lilly's cheek.

Lilly stopped running her hands over the child and looked over Daisy's head. "Thank you for rescuing her." She hugged the little girl close to her. "I'm Lilly Johnson and this is my sister, Daisy."

"You still haven't told us what you are doing here," Lilly's companion said. Ice-blue eyes scowled at Jacob.

Jacob didn't care for the man's tone but he assumed that he was Daisy's father so thought it best to answer him. "I'm the new stock tender for the Pony Express. I was headed to the Johnson ranch to let the owner know I'd arrived."

Lilly stopped fussing over the little girl and straightened in the saddle. "I'm the owner of the ranch, Mr. Young."

"Then I'm assuming Mr. Roberts, the Pony Express superintendent, told you I was coming."

"He did." She nodded to the man beside her. "This is Sam Hawkins. He's the foreman of the ranch but your job is totally separate from the ranch, so the two of you won't really have much time to spend with each other."

Lilly directed her gaze back to the little one in her arms. Her worried voice questioned her sister. "Daisy, what made you come this far from the ranch house? You know you aren't supposed to leave the house or the yard without an adult."

The little girl's eyes filled with tears. "I didn't, Lilly."

"Then how did you get out here?" Lilly asked, her voice shaking as her hands smoothed the hair from Daisy's forehead.

Daisy looked confused. "I don't know. I was sleeping and woke up here." She shrugged as if it were all a mystery to her.

Worry and fear entered Lilly's face and eyes. She looked to Sam.

He shook his head as if to say, *Not here*.

Her head swiveled in Jacob's direction. Clear blue eyes looked him over. "Follow us and I'll show you the barn and tack room, where you will be staying." She spun her horse around and headed for home.

Jacob couldn't shake the feeling that something was dreadfully wrong. Little Daisy had said twice that she'd been sleeping in her room and then woke up out here in the ravine. How had she gotten here?

Sam didn't seem too concerned as he rode with Lilly and Daisy. If anything the man had been angrier to find him with Daisy than relieved that the little girl was all right.

Jacob told himself that it was none of his business. His business was to work on the ranch while searching for his birth mother to find out why she abandoned him when he was ten years old. He might need to remind himself of that fact quite often if things were as off-kilter on the Johnson ranch as they seemed.

He thought about the little girl's caramel-brown eyes. They looked nothing like Lilly's pretty blue ones. Lilly had said they were sisters but other than hair color, they didn't look much like they were related. He shook his head, reminding himself once more to mind his own business. He had his own family problems to deal with and didn't need to add another family's to his.

Still, Daisy reminded him of his adoptive sister, Joy, and he'd fight to the death to protect Joy. And deep down, Jacob knew he'd watch over Daisy in the future, too. How could he not?

Lilly's insides quaked. Daisy had been so close to being killed. If the Pony Express man hadn't shown up, she hated to think what would have happened.

Jacob Young had said he was the new stock tender. The last one had been an older man and had been nice enough but she really hadn't paid him much mind. Come to think of it, she'd seen the Pony Express riders exchange horses by the barn and then continue on. She'd really not paid much attention to them, either—her first order of business had been to take care of Daisy and the household along with any ranch business or financial things that Sam brought to her attention.

If she was honest with herself, she'd stayed away from the men because she didn't want their attention. The last thing she needed was to fall for a man who was only interested in her family ranch—a ranch that belonged to both her and Daisy.

Her father's last wife and Daisy's mother, Gertrude, had taught her that people weren't always who they first presented themselves to be, especially if they thought you had land or money. Gertrude had treated her like a servant when her father was out of the house or away on business, but was sweet when he was present. Her stepmother had told Lilly many times that should her father die, Lilly would be on the first stagecoach to a boarding school. If Gertrude hadn't died first giving birth to Daisy and leaving Lilly without a stepmother and her father without a wife, Lilly would be in a boarding school now or working someplace far from her beloved ranch.

Looking back she probably should have told her father about Gertrude's true nature, but her love for him had stilled Lilly's tongue. He'd often told her he'd married Gertrude so that she could be a mother to her. Lilly shivered, as her stepmother had been anything but a true mother.

After lunch, as Lilly made her way across the yard and to the barn, she wondered how Daisy had gotten out in the ravine. The little girl's feet hadn't been scuffed up like they should have been if she'd walked barefoot all the way out there. She didn't want to think about it but Lilly felt sure someone had taken the girl from her bed and carried her off. But why leave her in the canyon?

"You are deep in thought."

Lilly stopped several inches away from Jacob Young. What he'd said was true. She'd been so deep in thought that if he hadn't spoken, she would have run into him. "I was."

He stepped out of the barn door. "I'm sorry to have disturbed you." Jacob pulled one of the Pony Express horses out of the barn with him.

"No, I'm the one who is sorry. I snapped and it wasn't because I'm irritated with you. If anything, I'm very grateful to you." She offered him a smile that she hoped he'd recognize as a peace offering.

Jacob looked back at her and returned her smile. "No harm done." He walked the horse several feet away from her.

The sound of a bugle blared through the air. A few seconds later, Lilly made out the Pony Express rider and his horse. In less than five minutes, the rider had exchanged horses and was back on the trail.

Jacob pulled the tired horse back into the barn. He passed Lilly and led the horse into one of the many stalls. He closed the door behind the animal while staying in the stall. "If you want to share your thoughts, I'm a pretty good listener."

Lilly walked to her mare's stall. "I was just thinking about Daisy and how she got into the canyon this morning." She pulled a saddle blanket off the nail on the wall and spread it out over the horse's back.

"I've been thinking about that, too." Jacob took the saddle off the horse while he talked. "Has she ever walked in her sleep?"

"No, she's a heavy sleeper but she's never walked in her sleep," Lilly answered as she tightened the cinch under her horse's belly. She stood. "And even if she had walked that long way, her feet would have been cut up from the rocks and plants along the way."

"And I take it they weren't?" He leaned against the stall door.

Lilly shook her head. "No, they were dirty but not hurt in any way, which I'm grateful for. Normally Daisy sleeps until I wake her after my morning ride. Only this morning, something led me to go check on her before I left." She sighed and leaned her forehead against her horse's neck. "I'm so glad I did." Lilly straightened and looked at him.

They stood staring at each other for several long minutes, both deep in thought. Who would want to hurt her little sister? Lilly didn't want to suspect any of her men of trying to harm Daisy, but she felt a chill travel down her spine. Suddenly she reconsidered taking her daily ride.

Suspicions gnawed at her. Had someone taken Daisy while she'd been saddling her horse for a ride? Everyone on the ranch knew her routine. Or had they crept in earlier while she'd slept in the next room? Goose bumps formed on her arms at the scary thoughts.

She began to unsaddle the horse. "Sorry ol' gal, I can't risk leaving Daisy alone."

Jacob walked over to her. "I can take her out for you, if you'd like."

Lilly looked at him. What did she know about him? That Mr. Roberts had said he was coming to be the stock tender and that he'd saved Daisy this morning. "Thank you, but no. Maybe I'll take her out later today." She patted the mare's nose.

He nodded and stepped around her. Jacob pulled the saddle from the little mare's back and said, "You know,

I believe Daisy when she says she didn't walk out there on her own."

Lilly nodded. "So do I." She sighed as she put the saddle blanket away.

He returned to the Pony Express horse and began brushing it down. Lilly walked to the barn door and stepped out into the sunlight. What was she going to do?

Lilly entered the house and checked on Daisy again. After lunch, the morning's activities had caught up with Daisy, so Lilly had put her down for a nap.

The little girl slept on her side, curled into a ball. Her blond hair spilled over the pillow, her little lips slipped up into a smile as she dreamed. Lilly's heart went out to the tiny girl. They were all that was left of the Johnson family. Lilly couldn't lose Daisy, too, and would protect her with all she had. But would it be enough? What did she need to do to ensure the child's safety?

Lilly walked over to the all-wood window that was partially open to let in fresh air. It might be uncomfortable for Daisy but Lilly shut the opening. She looked around the room for something to stop the window from being opened. Finding nothing she went to the wood box in the kitchen. Judging a piece of kindling to be about the right length, she returned to Daisy's room and placed the stick between the bottom lip of the window and the top of the window casing. She pushed against the wood and shook it. The piece of kindling held firm. There. That should stop intruders with evil intent.

She chewed her lower lip. Fear threatened her peace. Lilly knew she had to get to the bottom of this or Daisy would never be allowed out of her sight.

The Johnsons had never locked their doors before. But now, well, she couldn't take the chance that someone would slip in and steal Daisy again. Lilly vowed she would keep Daisy safe at all cost.

Chapter Two

Jacob mucked out the stall and leaned on his pitchfork. He didn't like where his thoughts had been all morning but he couldn't shake his gut feeling. Daisy and maybe even Lilly were in danger.

His gaze moved to the fifteen-year-old boy who took care of the Johnson horses. Upon his arrival, the young man had shown him where everything was and even his room off to the side of the barn. Jacob called to him now. "Caleb?"

"Yeah."

"How many men work this ranch?" Jacob continued working as if the question were of no importance.

"Well, let's see. There's Sam, he's the foreman. Then there is Cook, Edward, Asher, Lewis and myself. We're the regular hands. During the cattle drive, Sam hires others. Usually drifters." Caleb sat with a saddle in front of him. As he talked he rubbed oil into the leather.

"So six," Jacob muttered.

"Yep, six." Caleb shook his head. His black bangs

fell into his eyes as he picked up a bridle and began to work oil into the thick leather. "How do you like the tack room?"

Jacob stopped and wiped sweat from his brow. "It's not as nice as the one we have at home but it's livable."

Caleb laughed. "Yep, that's what ol' Ike used to say." He deepened his voice. "It's livable."

Jacob thought about the tack room. It was a spacious room and the front part nearest the stalls was used for saddles, bridles and all other manner of things needed to work the farm. His portion of the room had a small woodstove, a bed, an end table and a tall chest of drawers with a cracked mirror and washbasin resting on top. Jacob decided that the next trip to town he'd buy a couple of blankets, some rope and maybe a pillow.

Going through the chest of drawers he noted that the previous stock tender had used the top two drawers for sugar, coffee, salt and several other cooking items. He didn't look forward to cooking his own meals, especially in a room with little air flow. He felt his stomach protest not having eaten since the night before.

"Cook said to tell you, if you'd like to have meals over at the bunkhouse, he'll set a plate for you," Caleb said as if reading his mind, or possibly because his stomach rumbled.

Jacob grinned. "That's right nice of him."

Caleb nodded. "Cook is nice enough. Just don't be getting into his sweet cakes. He doesn't share those."

A soft laugh sounded from the doorway. "No, he doesn't share those," Lilly said as she entered.

Daisy danced into the room behind her. She wore

a light blue dress with what looked like cowboy boots meant for a boy. From the looks of the footwear, she'd not had them long. "Look, Caleb. Lilly let me wear my boots today. We're going riding," she said, holding her foot up for Caleb to see.

"That's wonderful, little Miss Daisy," Caleb answered. He stood and walked toward the tack room. "I'll get your saddle for you, Miss Lilly."

"Thank you, Caleb," Lilly called after the boy. She pulled her saddle blanket from the wall and walked to her horse's stall.

Daisy looked shyly at Jacob. "I get to ride with Lilly today."

Jacob leaned on his pitchfork and smiled at the little girl. Her hair was done in pigtails. "I heard. That's exciting."

"It is. We are going to check the fences. That's important work. Huh, Lilly?"

"Yes, it is," Lilly answered. She rubbed the horse's nose.

"Want to come?" Daisy asked Jacob.

He looked to Lilly and she shrugged.

"That would be fun. Are you sure you don't mind if I tag along?" The thought of getting out of the stuffy barn appealed to Jacob.

Both Lilly and Daisy shook their heads.

Jacob quickly went to saddle up his own horse.

Daisy followed. "I wish I had my own horse."

"You don't?" Jacob asked.

"No. Lilly said that I might get one for my birthday."

"When is your birthday?" Jacob asked, pulling the cinch under the horse's belly.

The little girl sat down on a bale of hay. "In two months."

Jacob nodded. "And how old will you be?"

"I will be five years old," Daisy said, pulling straw from the bale.

She spoke very well for a four-year-old going on five. Jacob thought about his adoptive sister, Joy. She wasn't a big talker, unlike Daisy, who was even now telling him that Lilly said this year she might have a birthday party and everything.

Jacob listened to her continued chatter as he finished up. He looked over the stall toward Lilly. The woman actually stood there smiling from ear to ear. Had she been watching to see how he'd respond to Daisy? And if so, why?

The thought that she might see him as a future husband stopped his hand as he started to lead the horse from the stall. The last thing he needed was a woman pining away for him. No matter how pretty she was or how blue her eyes, he had no intention of becoming romantically involved with her. Women couldn't be trusted. He'd learned that when his own birth mother deserted him. Jacob shook his head—he realized he was letting his imagination get the best of him. He didn't know Lilly, how could he think she'd see him as a future husband? Come to think of it, no one had said she didn't already have a man.

Caleb had named off six men that worked the ranch but hadn't mentioned a husband for Lilly. He watched as

Lilly smiled at Daisy. Without having to ask, he knew Lilly was still unwed and wondered why. She was pretty enough and in most folks' eyes should have been married a few years ago. So why wasn't she?

"Come along, Daisy," Lilly called to her little sister.

Daisy skipped off to join Lilly. She took Lilly's hand and glanced over her shoulder to make sure Jacob followed. Her little pigtails bounced as she left the barn.

"She is a cute little thing, isn't she?" Caleb said from the tack doorway.

Jacob nodded. His mind worked with questions. He pushed away the ones regarding Lilly's marital status and focused on Daisy. Could Caleb have been the one to take the girl from her bedroom? If so, why would he do such a thing? His gut usually told him what type of person a man was when they first met. For instance, he hadn't cared much for Sam Hawkins on sight. But he'd not had that gut reaction with regard to Caleb.

Caleb pushed away from the door and returned to his oil and leathers. "I have a sister a little older than her. I miss her a lot. Daisy is like a little sister to me and I'll hunt down any man that is out to hurt her." Anger filled the young man's voice and the warning was clear. Hurt Daisy and I'll hurt you.

No, Caleb hadn't been the one to take the little girl from her bed. Still, Jacob would keep an eye on the boy. He stepped out of the barn just as Lilly swung up into the saddle behind Daisy.

She was still in her trousers and looking as pretty as a hummingbird on a bright sunny morning. Jacob looked away. Maybe going out on a ride with them wasn't such a good idea. Still, his protective nature overrode any caution he might have felt at spending time with a pretty girl and her little sister.

Just don't let your heart get in the way of your head, he mentally scolded himself as he swung up into the saddle and followed the sisters out of the yard and across the pasture.

Lilly didn't know who she could trust. The man riding beside her and Daisy was new on the ranch and they weren't friends, at least not yet. She'd never considered becoming friends with any of the men before, except Sam. But now, with Daisy being threatened and Jacob being the only new person on the ranch…could she trust him? Tell him what she suspected? Or should she tell Sam? After all he was her ranch manager.

Daisy pointed at a rabbit that sat on a small incline. Her joy at seeing the small animal brought a smile to Lilly's face. She pulled her horse to a stop so the little girl could enjoy the sight.

Memories of riding with her father to check the fences flooded Lilly's mind. Daisy would never have memories of riding with their father. He'd died when she was a year old and too young to ride out with him. Lilly still missed him. Bitter memories flooded her tired mind. According to Sam, her father had fallen from his horse while chasing a mother cow and her calf, resulting in a broken neck and immediate death.

Jacob's horse stomped its foot, probably trying to get rid of a pesky fly, and the action pulled Lilly from her sad thoughts. She glanced his way and smiled. He'd been quiet most of the ride. They both had. Daisy talked enough for all of them.

"Lilly, can we go to the pond?" Daisy asked. The little girl tilted her face so that she could look up at Lilly.

"I suppose so," Lilly said, pulling the horse's reins to the right and gently kicking its sides. The horse moved toward the pond.

Jacob followed.

When they got to the water's edge he slid from his horse's back and let the horse drink, then helped Daisy down from Lilly's mare. Jacob sat her down on the ground and then looked to Lilly.

She refused his hand and slid from the horse on her own. Her desire to talk to someone grew. Lilly wanted to voice her fears without worrying that they'd get back to the person who had taken Daisy.

Daisy pulled off her little stockings and boots and waded in the water.

"Don't go too far out, Daisy," Lilly warned. She moved a little away from her sister and sat down.

Jacob joined her. He pulled up his knees and focused on Daisy, who splashed water with her bare feet. "Can I ask a question?"

Lilly searched his face. From his expression and tone she deduced that the question was of a personal nature. "I suppose so."

"Do you think someone is out to hurt Daisy?"

She nodded. "After this morning, what else can I think?"

Jacob turned to face her. "I know I'm new here and

you don't know me at all. I'd like to tell you a little about myself, if we have time."

Lilly knew he was trying to put her at ease so nodded. "If you are sure," she said.

"I am." He returned his gaze to Daisy. His voice continued in a low tone. "When I was ten years old my mother dropped me off at an orphanage. She didn't want to bring me to California with her. I don't know why she didn't. Maybe she was ashamed of me, maybe I was a burden she was tired of taking care of, but whatever the reason she abandoned me."

Lilly laid her hand on his arm. "I'm so sorry."

He shook his head. "I lived in that place for two years and then Rebecca and John Young came to the home. They adopted me and took me to their farm. John became like a pa to me and Rebecca a ma, even though she wasn't that much older than me. John died but before he did, he made arrangements with the Pony Express to hire his boys. There are seven of us in all. As he was dying, John told me to take care of his family. And I did."

Lilly looked at Daisy. Her father hadn't had the chance to ask her to take care of Daisy. His death had been sudden, but still heartbreaking. "I'm sorry for your loss."

Jacob's Adam's apple bobbed as he swallowed. "Then a man named Seth Armstrong came along as the station keeper. He and Rebecca fell in love and were married a couple of months ago. He's now in charge of taking care of my brothers and little sister, freeing me to look for my birth mother. I never forgot my mother and have wondered for ten years why she left me at that orphanage. So, I began making my way to California in search of her. I'm still searching for her."

Lilly dropped her hand from his arm. "Do you have any idea where she might be?" There were other questions she wanted to ask Jacob, but she started with the one that she felt was the most important to him.

"Rebecca heard that she might be living in Sacramento."

Jacob turned his warm brown eyes on her once more. "I'll ask around when I go to town, but after all these years, I'm not sure I'll ever find her."

"So how long will you be staying on the Johnson ranch as a stock tender?" Lilly asked, realizing that Jacob could leave at any time.

"Your ranch is my last stop. I can travel from here to inquire about her presence. I'm staying as long as the Pony Express will keep me hired. And, if I don't find my mother in Sacramento, I'll just have to live never knowing why she gave me up." His eyes looked deeply into hers. "I've never been in trouble with the law. I have brothers and a sister that I love very much. They might not be my blood but they found their way into my heart. Someday, I'll head back to Wyoming, where my family lives."

Lilly watched as Daisy picked up little rocks and tried to skip them across the pond water. He wasn't staying forever. He'd mentioned a sister. "How old is your sister?" she asked.

"She's five. Almost the same age as Daisy. Children

need people to watch over them, not to harm them," he answered as he also looked to Daisy.

Lilly sighed. "I'm afraid I don't know how to protect her. I don't know who to trust. I'm sure Sam would never hurt her but until this morning, I wouldn't have believed any of the men working on my ranch would hurt her, but someone tried." She crossed her arms over her knees and buried her face in the fabric of her trousers.

He laid his hand on her shoulder. "If you will trust me, I'll help you protect Daisy."

She looked up into his eyes. There was truth and sincerity in his gaze. Lilly knew Jacob hadn't taken Daisy—he'd saved her. But how much trust should she put in a stranger? Although, what choice did she have?

Chapter Three

Jacob watched the emotions wash across Lilly's soft features. She wanted to trust him but something held her back. Had she been hurt, too? He pulled his hand from her shoulder.

"Thank you." The words sounded tight in her throat.

He offered her a smile. "I won't let you down. I'll watch over Daisy as if she was my own sister."

Lilly stood. "Daisy, we need to get back to the house."

"Aw," Daisy said, picking up her stockings and boots. She dragged her feet through the dirt as she walked back to them. "Do we have to?"

Jacob laughed. Joy would have felt the same way, if she'd been here. "Yes, we have to. My tummy tells me it's getting close to dinnertime."

Daisy brightened up at the prospect of dinner. "Lilly says we're going to have fried chicken."

"That sounds wonderful." Jacob's stomach growled, as if it was in total agreement.

A giggle burst from Daisy's lips. "Mr. Jacob, your tummy is talking."

He shook his head. "Not as well as you."

Daisy handed her stockings and boots to Lilly. "Will you help me, please?"

Jacob looked to Lilly. "I'm amazed at how well she talks."

She smiled as she slipped a sock onto Daisy's foot. "That's because we have never talked baby talk to her."

"I'm not a baby," Daisy told him with a grin.

He laughed. "No, you are not." Jacob shook his head. "I'll go round up the horses."

Jacob found them both munching on grass just inside the tree line. He heard Daisy giggle and looked back to see Lilly tickling the little girl. His heart tugged in his chest at the sight.

If someone was going to hurt Daisy, they'd have to go through him. He'd vowed to watch over the little girl and he'd do just that. No man, or woman for that matter, was going to hurt that sweet child.

Lilly looked up and met his gaze. Her eyes were gentle and contemplative. He felt a curious swooping pull at his innards.

Jacob realized then that his promise included Lilly. If anyone hurt Daisy, they'd also be hurting Lilly. His instincts told him that she was a kind person. Her sympathy for him when he'd told her about his upbringing had been sincere. And Jacob knew he'd not let either of them be hurt.

He just prayed he'd not lose his heart in his desire to protect them both. Jacob had no intention of falling in love, like Seth and Rebecca had. Women couldn't be trusted not to abandon those they claimed to love the most. His mother had proven that. No, he'd harden that part of his heart and still keep his promise.

He ignored the tiny voice that whispered to him that his adopted mother, Rebecca, had been a woman of integrity. She'd not abandoned her duties even though she was very young. Lilly was also young and she'd managed to take the care of her sister seriously. Jacob pushed the last thought aside. He didn't want to admire Lilly in any way or fashion.

Lilly waited as Jacob lifted Daisy onto her horse, then she mounted up behind her. Jacob paused while she settled into the saddle then climbed onto his horse, shifting until he was comfortable. He treated her like a gentleman treated a lady. It was hard not to be impressed when his manners toward her and Daisy were so thoughtful. There wasn't a lot of gallantry found this far west of the Mississippi so Jacob's actions were like a warm summer's rain during the hottest part of the day. Lilly realized she wanted to trust him. Could she afford to?

He'd opened his life up for her to view. Had he expected her to do the same? Tell him about her childhood? How her father had married a woman who was supposed to love her but had only despised her? Share how they'd both died and how Daisy had been her responsibility since she was born? Loneliness and confusion mingled together in one huge surge of yearning. How she longed for someone to share her life with—

the joys, sorrows, even the mundane everyday living. Right now her future looked vague and shadowy. *Lord, please*, she thought in silent prayer. *Send my other half, my partner. Someone I can trust to love me for myself and not for the ranch. I'm tired of doing this alone.*

As they returned to the house, she listened to Daisy chatter about the birds, flowers, tall grass and other things that flitted through her young mind. Jacob laughed at her funny expressions and words. Almost without a second thought, Lilly decided to trust him, and to do so she'd need to share a part of their life, too.

Caleb met them as they arrived at the barn. "Miss Daisy, the cat had her kittens. Would you like to see them?"

Daisy squealed and leaped into the boy's arms. "Oh, yes!" She waited for him to lower her to the ground and then clasped his hand. "Where are they?"

He kneeled down beside her. "In the back stall but you can't go running in there. She's a new mama and might be nervous. We have to go in quietly and not talk too loudly. Also, don't touch the babies today. We'll hold them when they are a little older and their mama isn't as skittish as she is today. All right?"

Her blond head bobbed her agreement.

Caleb stood. "Miss Lilly, would you like to see them, too?"

Lilly smiled. "Not right now." She watched them walk hand in hand to the barn. Was Caleb trustworthy? Had the young man taken her sister into the ravine? As she climbed down from her horse, she gnawed at her bottom lip.

Jacob took the reins from her hands and smiled. "Can you believe that boy threatened me this morning?"

Her face went from worry to shock.

An easy laugh spilled from Jacob. "Oh, not how you're thinking. But in his own way. Caleb told me that anyone who hurt Daisy would answer to him. In other words, don't hurt her because I love her like a little sister."

Lilly felt the emotions drain from her body. She'd gone from confusion, to worry, to shock in just a matter of minutes. At this rate she'd be emotionally exhausted by nightfall.

He pulled the horses over to the large water trough beside the barn, his shoulders hunched and powerful. They were broad and maybe strong enough to support the dread and fears that filled her heart as she worried about Daisy.

"Thank you for sharing your past with me." She rubbed her horse's neck as it drank from the fresh water. "I grew up on this ranch. It's all I know and all I want to know." Lilly thought about her little sister in the barn.

Jacob leaned against the barn and smiled. "Sounds like a nice childhood."

She grinned. "It was. Mama died when I was about Daisy's age. I remember her soft smile, warm smell and gentle hugs."

"I'm sorry for your loss." Jacob had crossed his legs and now rubbed the toe of his boot against the other. She wondered if he looked at the boots to avoid seeing sorrow in her eyes.

"Thank you. Then when I was ten, Papa decided I

needed a mother's touch and married my stepmother."
She laughed and heard the bitterness in it. "I know he
meant well, but she was not mother material."

"And now, your childhood isn't sounding so nice."
His warm brown eyes, gentle and contemplative, looked
into hers, inviting her to continue.

"Oh, it was nice. But, I grew up at the age of ten. Gertrude made sure of that. When Pa was away, I cooked,
cleaned and was treated like the hired help." Lilly fell
silent as the memories took over. She hated those years
of her life.

His silence reminded her that Jacob still listened patiently. "But five years ago, all that changed. Gertrude
had Daisy. She died shortly after that but left Papa and
me with a beautiful baby. Daisy has been my life ever
since. I love her as if she was my child instead of my
sister." She realized how silly that must sound to him
and giggled. "Well, you know what I mean." Lilly felt
heat fill her face.

Jacob remained silent; his hat shadowed his face so
Lilly wasn't sure of his expression. Had her story made
him think that she'd been too silly in her love for Daisy?

He must have sensed her watching him because
Jacob looked up again. A spark of some indefinable
emotion crossed his features, but he spoke in a gentle,
soft voice. "I'm sorry. Did your father leave after your
stepmother died?"

Lilly realized he must have assumed that he'd abandoned her and Daisy like his mother had him. "No, he
had a riding accident that broke his neck and killed
him instantly." Sorrow filled her heart. Even after four

years she still felt her loss cut through her like a two-edged sword.

"So you've been taking care of Daisy and running this ranch on your own?" He pushed away from the barn.

Lilly nodded. "Yes, with Sam's and Papa's lawyer's help." Did knowing her father was dead change his view of her? Would he, like so many others before him, now see her as wife material? Making himself a ranch owner in the process?

Apparently unaware of her thoughts, Jacob tugged his horse around and walked toward the barn. Lilly followed with her own mount. He stopped just inside the barn door. He placed a hand against the barn, his demeanor stiff and tense. His jaw clenched as if he was holding raw emotion in check. She placed her hand on his forearm.

"What is it, Jacob?"

"Did I mention earlier that my mother's name is Gertrude?"

Lilly's breath caught in her lungs. Her fingers clenched around the fabric of his sleeve. She swallowed hard and tried to think of something to say. He seemed to have the same problem. Lilly's heart told her Gertrude was the same woman. She walked past Jacob toward her horse's stall. "Gertrude is a common name for women born during that time."

Lilly began to remove the saddle from the horse. Trying not to sound strange, she asked, "Jacob, what is your last name?"

He looked at her as if she were dense. "Young."

She swallowed. "I mean before you were adopted."

Jacob grunted as he pulled the saddle from his horse's back. He carried it to the tack room and placed it on a sawhorse. He adjusted it three or four times, finally latching on the saddle horn in a tight-fisted grip. "My birth name is Fisher."

Lilly felt as if her knees might give out from under her. Her stepmother, Gertrude Fisher, was Jacob's mother. That made him Daisy's half brother. Strange and disquieting thoughts raced through her mind. Would he want to take Daisy away from her? Or would knowing she was his own flesh and blood make him want to protect her more? And, would he think he could protect her better by taking her away? Icy fear wrapped its ugly fingers around her spine.

She could tell him that half the ranch belonged to Daisy, but should she? New fears and questions twisted her insides. Would that make him less inclined to take Daisy away? Or would it make him want to take the ranch? Was he the type of man who would woo her to get his sister and the ranch?

Did he somehow already know all this? Had he secretly been checking things out, with plans already formed? And she had let her guard down. Her emotions had ruled that Jacob could be trusted, but what had emotions always proven to her? That they certainly could not be trusted. She had eagerly accepted Gertrude, longing for a mother's touch and love, but that had led to years of loneliness and disappointment.

Chapter Four

Over the next few days, Jacob got to know his new home better. He now knew the barn and everything in it as if he'd lived there all his life. He met the other men of the ranch and took his meals with them. Rode the fence lines and learned where the ravines were located.

Since the ranch wasn't a Pony Express home station, but a way station where the riders exchanged horses to deliver the mail, there was no station manager. Jacob was free to come and go as he pleased as long as he was ready when a new rider came in needing a fresh horse.

He helped out where he could and kept an eye out for the Johnson women. Lilly and Daisy were never apart. He'd watched them puttering around the house, in the garden, washing clothes out by the well and playing tag on the side of the house. Lilly always seemed alert to their surroundings and had even waved to him a few times when she caught him looking in her direction.

However, since the day she'd told him about her past, Lilly had stayed away from the barn. According to Caleb it wasn't like her not to take her horse out for a ride at least once a day. Jacob assumed it was because of her worry over Daisy that kept her close to home. Still, he didn't think it was good for her or her horse.

As he put the recently returned Pony Express horse into a stall, Jacob realized that the last time she'd spoken to him had been after their short ride to the river. She'd asked him his last name and then hurried from the barn as if her biscuits were burning in the kitchen. Had he said something wrong? Something that had disturbed her? Made her think he was a danger to them? Or had she simply decided to be cautious? He knew now that Daisy was her only living relative. He could understand Lilly's strong desire to want to protect the little girl.

He closed his eyes and inhaled the warm scent of hay from the barn. Jacob had to admit that he missed his family. His adoptive mother, Rebecca, would be calling them all in for lunch about now. His rowdy brothers would be pushing and shoving to be the first inside. He missed the way Joy, his sister, ran to him and begged to be swung about in the air.

"Jacob? Is now a bad time?"

Lilly's soft voice broke through the memories and his eyes snapped open. She stood to the side with her hands buried in a long skirt that touched the straw-covered floor of the barn. Since he'd arrived he'd never seen her in a dress or skirt, and the sight took him by surprise. To cover it, he cleared his voice. "Not at all. I was just… putting the horse away."

She grinned a knowing smile. "Good. I was wondering, since the Pony Express rider just left, if you'd have time to go with Daisy and I to Mud Springs?"

Daisy stood behind Lilly. She peaked around her sister. "Pleeeease."

Jacob nodded. "Mud Springs?" He'd not heard of that town when he'd come through so perhaps it was a small town between the ranch and Sacramento.

"That's the old name. About five years ago the town folks renamed it El Dorado. We're still used to it being Mud Springs." She pulled her braid around to her left shoulder and played with the band at the end. Her blue eyes looked up at him inquisitively.

Jacob recognized the town name El Dorado. "I'd be happy to go. Let me tell Cook so he doesn't expect me for lunch."

Caleb stood up from where he'd been kneeling in the back stall. "I'll tell him for you," he offered. Caleb grinned at Daisy. "Want to see the kittens while Jacob gets the wagon ready?" He shot a mischievous grin at Jacob.

Daisy's blond braid bobbed as she nodded. She looked up at Lilly. "Can I, Lilly?" Weariness laced the little girl's voice as if she feared her sister would say no.

"Yes, just remember they are still very little."

"I will." Daisy skipped the short distance to Caleb.

Jacob had missed the little girl's voice and happy nature. He grinned. "I better get the wagon." He started to leave the barn but stopped when he heard Lilly call out.

"Caleb?"

The young man popped his head up. "Yes, Miss Lilly?"

"Will you keep an eye on Daisy? I'd like to go fix a picnic lunch for the trip." She nibbled at her bottom lip.

Jacob's eyes met Caleb's. He nodded to the young man.

"I'll watch out for her," Caleb agreed. "Don't worry, we'll stay here in the barn and watch the mama cat and kittens."

She nodded. "I'll be quick." Lilly turned and saw Jacob. "Do you need help with the wagon?" she asked, tugging at her braid.

"No, I can take care of it," he answered.

Lilly walked toward him. When she was at the door he said, "Caleb will take good care of her and I'll be right outside."

"I know." Still she worried the tip of her braid. Then she turned toward the house and marched smartly away.

Jacob moved to the side of the barn where the wagon sat.

A heavy Irish accent drifted to Jacob. "Need help with getting that pulled to the front of the barn?" Asher asked.

Jacob glanced over his shoulder at the broad-shouldered man. Asher seemed good-natured. His red hair and green eyes made him very recognizable. He answered, "That would be nice."

The big man grabbed the tongue of the wagon while Jacob pushed from behind. Within a minute they had the wagon standing in front of the big barn. The two men continued to work together until the horse was hitched up and ready to go.

"I could have gotten the wagon pulled around but

your help made it much easier. Thanks." He grinned at the Irishman.

"Happy to help. I suppose I should feed the hogs. I can hear their squeals from here." He walked away.

The hog pens were farther away from the house. Asher scooped up two slop buckets as he passed the bunkhouse and then disappeared around the corner.

Jacob grinned. He liked Asher and couldn't imagine that he'd harm man or beast. Still, he'd get to know him better before he trusted him or anyone else on the ranch other than Caleb. He walked back into the barn, where Caleb sat with Daisy on a bale of hay. "What are you two doing?" he asked. Then he saw the small fur ball in Caleb's hands.

"Looking at the kitty," Daisy whispered. "This is the one I want to keep."

The kitten was still small and its yellow fur wasn't very thick. "Aren't you going to keep them all?" Jacob asked as he sat down across from them on a large bucket.

She shook her head. "No, Lilly only keeps two kitties on the ranch at a time."

Caleb grinned. "The other two will go to the Lawrences, they own the farm to our right."

The mother cat chose that moment to let her disapproval come through. She meowed loudly. "Sounds like you better put that baby back," Jacob said as he stood and stretched.

He looked forward to this trip to town. Even though he'd come through it on his way to the Johnson ranch, Jacob planned to ask again about his mother. The sooner he found her, the sooner he'd have answers to his questions and get on with his life.

Knots filled Lilly's stomach as she hurried back to the barn. The wagon looked ready to go. She placed the basket full of food and a couple of Daisy's favorite toys behind the seat. Lilly inhaled deeply. Anticipation of Jacob's reaction ate at her. Lilly tried to ignore the feeling, knowing she was doing the right thing.

She'd prayed earnestly, asking God what to do with the new knowledge that Jacob's mother and her stepmother were one and the same. Lilly didn't want to tell him because she feared he'd want to take over Daisy's upbringing. She also feared he'd think the ranch belonged to him, too. But, after much prayer, Lilly felt it wouldn't be right to keep the truth from Jacob.

The thought of him continuing his search for his deceased mother saddened her. Knowing would be better for him than not knowing. This was something she had to do. She released the pent-up air.

Lilly walked the short distance to the barn and stepped into the doorway. Jacob stood. He stretched out his back and flexed his wide shoulders. She quaked at what his reaction might be to the news she'd been holding onto for the last few days.

Jacob had given her no reason to fear him and yet she did. Lilly knew the fear wasn't for herself but for Daisy. Not that he'd hurt her, but that he'd take her away.

Jacob turned as if sensing her nearness. "About ready?" he asked.

Lilly nodded, unwilling to speak in case her voice

gave out on her. She had to get these emotions under control.

Daisy ran around Jacob and looked up at her sister. "I know which kitty I want." She bounced around like a happy puppy.

"You do?" Lilly smiled as the little girl's braid flopped about her shoulders.

"Uh-huh. The orange one." Daisy grabbed Lilly's hand and pulled.

Lilly stood her ground. "Daisy, what have I told you about pulling on people?"

Daisy dropped her hand and her head. "Not to."

"That's right. Where were you going to pull me to?" Lilly asked, as she tried not to smile at her sister's antics.

Daisy looked up at her with big eyes. "I was going to show you my kitty." Her bottom lip pouted out.

Lilly kneeled down beside the little girl. "I think that is very sweet but I also think we should leave the kittens alone for a few more days." She saw Daisy inhale and a protest form on her little mouth. Lilly interrupted quickly. "It won't be that long and you don't want the mama to hide them, do you?"

"No." The dejection in the little girl's voice tugged at her.

She stood. "I tell you what, when we get to town you can buy a small sack of lemon drops. How does that sound?"

The bouncing began again. "Come on, Mr. Jacob." Daisy ran around Lilly and started climbing into the wagon.

At the sound of his warm chuckle, Lilly shook her head. It amused her that he found Daisy comical now, but just wait until he had to deal with one of her crying spells. Then he wouldn't be laughing. She followed Daisy to the wagon.

Jacob hurried around her and offered his hand to assist her up. Surprised by his speed, she lay her hand in his. Lilly told herself that it was because of the skirt and her fear of catching the tips of her boots in the hem that she allowed him to help her.

His warm, callused palm held tightly to hers as she raised herself into the wagon. "Thank you." Lilly sat down and made sure her skirt covered her legs. The warmth of his touch remained on her hand, making the other feel cool.

Within moments he was on the seat beside her. He looked over his shoulder at Daisy, checking to make sure she remained seated in the back of the wagon, and then quirked a brow at her. "Everyone ready?"

"I am." Daisy smoothed the yarn on her rag doll's head.

Lilly nodded. She folded her hands in her lap and stared straight ahead, wishing he wasn't quite so nice because she had to figure out how to break the news to him. She couldn't quite fathom what that had to do with anything, but then these days her mind was a crazy mixture of hope and fear; hope that she was wrong that someone wanted to hurt Daisy and fear that someone truly did.

Jacob gently slapped the reins over the horse's back and clicked his tongue to get her to go. The wagon lurched and the wheels ground the dirt as they took off. Lilly tried to choose which of the several ways she'd thought through on how to broach the subject of his mother.

She could hear Daisy talking to her doll and the little wooden horse that she'd brought along to play with. Should she say something in front of her little sister? After all, Daisy and Jacob shared the same mother. Lilly had no idea how Daisy would feel. Could someone that small—that young—even understand what it meant? Would Jacob want to tell Daisy himself?

Jacob's rich voice broke the silence. "This is a nice ranch. I hope you don't mind but I rode the fence lines and checked out some of the ravines on the property."

Lilly glanced at him. "No, I don't mind." She nibbled at her bottom lip.

They fell into silence once more. Daisy told her doll and horse all about the kittens in the barn. Lilly listened as she chattered about the yellow kitty and how they were going to be the bestest of friends.

She glanced in Jacob's direction and saw the soft smile on his face. He was either listening to Daisy, too, or deep in his own thoughts. Lilly looked across the pasture they were passing. It had recently been cut and the grass gathered for feed. The sounds of birds in the nearby trees chirping their happiness soothed her troubled thoughts.

In a quiet voice, Lilly said, "Jacob, I'd like to stop someplace for lunch before we get to town."

Daisy piped up from behind them. "I'm hungry."

Just as she thought, the little girl had been listening

to them. Lilly answered, "Me, too." She hadn't eaten much breakfast. Worry had consumed her and the thought of food hadn't appealed at the time.

"I could use a bite to eat, too," Jacob agreed. "If I remember right, there is a little stream up the road. Would that be a good place to stop?"

"Yes!" Daisy squealed. "Lilly and I stop there all the time."

Lilly grinned as she relived memories of wading in the cool water, first with her father and later with Daisy. She realized he was watching her expression and answered, "Yes, it's a favorite spot of ours."

At Daisy's gleeful squeal, Jacob set the horse into a trot and said, "The sooner we get there the sooner we eat."

Daisy laughed and encouraged him to go faster. As if the horse sensed the little girl's urgency it trotted faster. Lilly found herself laughing with her sister and enjoying the ride. Her hair escaped her braid and teased the side of her face. Lilly knew she'd look a sight if they didn't get to the stream soon.

Jacob pulled the wagon off the road and headed for a cluster of trees, where he stopped the horse and set the brake. He turned to smile at her. "Hope you brought plenty. I'm starved."

She pushed her hair back. "I believe I did."

"Good, 'cause I'm starving, too," Daisy said, slumping against the seat as if weak from hunger.

"Daisy, you really are a mess. You know that?" Jacob asked, jumping from the wagon as laughter spilled from his throat.

She laughed, too, and jumped from the wagon. Lilly held her breath as Daisy sailed over the side of the wagon through the air. Jacob caught her up and swung her around. In one action Daisy showed the two adults just how much she trusted Jacob. How much more would she trust him once she learned he was her brother?

New fearful thoughts entered her mind. What if Daisy wanted to live with Jacob when he returned to his Wyoming family? Would the little girl leave her? Could she bear it if Daisy did leave?

Chapter Five

Jacob watched Lilly's face as she set down the picnic basket under the tall tree he'd chosen to have their lunch below. Where had the joy gone that had filled her face minutes earlier? She gnawed at her bottom lip as she pulled food from the basket and her change in mood gnawed at him. Something wasn't quite up to par, but he'd be hanged if he knew what it was.

Daisy kneeled beside her sister and peered into the hamper. "I want a cookie." Her small hand reached inside but quickly came back out when Lilly slapped it.

"No, not now. You have to eat a sandwich first, then you can have a cookie." She pulled out a ready-made sandwich and handed it to her sister.

Daisy frowned at it. "Can I eat it by the water?" Her lower lip puckered out as if she was going to cry.

Lilly reached out and tugged at Daisy's braid. "Only if you stop pouting and drink all your milk."

Daisy sucked in her lip and nodded. She took the bottle of milk that Lilly handed her. "Thanks." Then with her sandwich in one hand and the milk in the other, she skipped away to the water's edge.

"Don't get your boots wet!" Lilly called after her.

Jacob joined her under the tree.

"I won't," Daisy called back.

He sat down on the ground beside the picnic basket. "If I eat all my sandwich, can I have a cookie, too?" Jacob hoped his teasing would bring back the joy they'd shared earlier.

She offered what he considered a weak smile. "Sure." She handed him a sandwich wrapped in cheesecloth.

Jacob took the sandwich. "Thank you." He waited until she'd finished setting out the food and drinks and then asked, "Is something bothering you?"

Lilly studied his face. What she looked for, Jacob couldn't say. He held her gaze, waiting. She looked away, tucking a strand of hair behind one small ear.

"I have to tell you something." She played with the corner of her cheesecloth-covered sandwich.

From the way she was gnawing at her lip, Jacob was pretty sure whatever she had to tell him was pretty important to her. "All right." He unwrapped the cheesecloth and pulled a piece of ham out from between the bread. Jacob hoped by acting normal it would put her at ease. He bit into the sweet ham and waited.

"Remember when I told you my father remarried?" She looked up at him.

"Yes." Jacob found himself nodding as if to assure her he remembered.

"Well, I realized the other day, when you told me your last name, that my stepmother was your mother."

She swallowed hard. "I haven't been sure how to tell you."

Her words struck him like lightning hitting a tree. A loud roar began in his head and white-hot pain hit his heart. His eyes burned as the words ricocheted through his mind. His mother was dead. A part of him wanted to grieve, the other part wanted to be angry.

To fight the grief Jacob focused on the anger. He stood to his feet. His mother had not only abandoned him as a ten-year-old, but now he also felt like she'd abandoned him once again. Now he'd never know why she'd left him at the orphanage.

"I'm sorry, Jacob. I should have told you the other day." Sadness filled her voice.

Jacob wanted to be angry with her but couldn't be. Hadn't he already thought that her stepmother and his mother might be the same person? Jacob knew that he had but hadn't wanted to believe that it was possible.

He sighed and handed her his uneaten sandwich. "Thank you for telling me, Lilly." He turned away. The stinging in his eyes was getting worse. Grown men didn't cry in front of others. "I'll be back in a few minutes." His throat felt raw as he walked down the bank of the stream away from Lilly and Daisy.

Unwanted tears streamed down his face as Jacob thought of the loss of his mother. He sat down on a fallen log beside the water's edge. Jacob had convinced himself that he'd replaced his love for his birth mother with hate, but now knew that wasn't true. She'd been his mother no matter what reason she'd deserted him. He still loved her even if she didn't love him.

"Mr. Jacob?"

At the sound of Daisy's voice behind him, Jacob wiped at his eyes. He turned slowly to face the little girl. "Yes, Daisy?"

"Are you all right? Lilly said I should leave you alone, but…" She walked around the log and saw his face. Daisy stopped and completed her sentence. "I didn't listen and snuck off." She reached up and touched his damp cheek. "Are you sad?"

He placed his hand over hers. "I am."

She climbed into his lap and laid her head on his chest. "Why?" Her little hand rested on his shoulder.

Jacob curled his arms around her small body. "I just found out that my ma is dead."

Daisy snuggled closer. "Oh, my ma is dead, too."

He tightened his arms around her as he realized that Daisy's ma and his were the same. "I know." Jacob rested his chin on the top of her head. Was that the reason Lilly had been afraid to tell him? Did she think he'd take Daisy away from her?

Jacob inhaled the little girl's soft scent. Now that he knew he had a real sister, would he be able to leave her with Lilly?

Grief and confusion washed over him. Jacob held his little sister close and silently prayed. He didn't want to hurt Lilly, but now that he knew Daisy was his flesh and blood, he'd never leave her. She was all the real family he had left.

Lilly's fears grew as Jacob and Daisy came back to camp. He held the little girl's hand in his and new determination filled his eyes. She'd seen Daisy follow him but hadn't tried to stop her.

"Lilly, I ate all my sandwich." Daisy smiled happily. "Can I have my cookie now?"

"Yes, you can." Had Jacob told Daisy he was her brother? She turned to get Daisy a cookie from the small bowl she'd brought with them.

Daisy took it with a smile. "Mr. Jacob would like his cookie, too, but he didn't eat his sandwich yet."

Mr. Jacob? Lilly looked to Jacob. Would Daisy still call him "Mister" if Jacob had told her that she was his sister? Lilly didn't think so.

"I have to finish my sandwich before I get my cookie. Isn't that right, Lilly?" Jacob raised an eyebrow in question.

"Afraid so. Daisy, why don't you take your boots off and wade at the edge of the stream while you eat your cookie? As soon as Jacob finishes his lunch we'll be heading on into town," Lilly answered.

Daisy sat down and began pulling at her boots. Her cookie clamped between her lips. Jacob reached down and pulled a boot from her foot. She managed to get the other off and drew the cookie from between her teeth. "Eat real slow, Mr. Jacob. I want to splash in the water for a long time."

He laughed. "Then you better get going."

Daisy squealed and ran for the stream's edge. Her braid swung against her back. The sound of the water splashing as her bare feet hit it brought a smile to Lilly's face.

Lilly handed him his sandwich. She'd rewrapped it

so that the bread wouldn't get dry. "I could never run like that on this ground with my socks and shoes off."

Jacob took it from her and once more unwrapped it. "She's really something, isn't she?" He took a big bite from the sandwich.

Lilly looked at him. "Yes, she is." She paused. "You didn't tell her, did you?"

Jacob shook his head. "No, I thought it might be better to wait."

What was he waiting for? What were his plans? The questions slammed against her brain. Would he tell her when he was ready to leave?

"I thought we'd keep the knowledge that she's my half sister between us." His brown eyes watched her as he chewed.

Lilly couldn't keep the tremble from her voice. "Why?"

"I wanted to tell her, but if I do she'll tell everyone else and I'm not sure I want others to know yet." He wiped at the crumbs that clung to his upper lip.

She didn't understand. Why wouldn't he want Daisy to tell others? Lilly refused to ask why again. She focused instead on nibbling the sugar off a cookie.

"If we tell her and she lets everyone know, then the person who kidnapped her the other day will have some kind of reaction. And I'm not sure if the results will be good or bad." Jacob took another bite of sandwich and looked out to where their sister now played in the water.

Lilly followed his gaze. She understood what he was saying and didn't know what the results would be, either. Would the person who had taken Daisy before try again, if they knew Jacob was her brother? Or would they do something to get rid of Jacob? Would telling put both of them in harm's way? Was there a chance that by telling everyone they might scare off the person? She turned her gaze back on him.

"You can see my point, can't you?" he asked, then stuffed the last of the bread into his mouth.

Lilly nodded. "It might be better to leave things as they are."

As he watched Daisy play in the water his features expressed awe and something else that she couldn't quite pinpoint. "I really am sorry for your loss, Jacob. I probably didn't break the news to you in the right manner and for that, I'm sorry, too."

He turned to face her. "There is no easy way of telling someone something like that. Thank you for letting me know that I don't need to search for her any longer." His gaze returned to Daisy.

What was he going to do now? He'd said that the Johnson ranch was his last stop and he'd continue to work for the Pony Express, but would his plans change now? And what were his thoughts regarding Daisy? How did one ask such personal questions?

"Lilly, would you mind telling me more about my mother's life here? Was she happy? I mean… I'm still amazed that Daisy is my sister."

His eyes were red-rimmed as if he'd been crying. It had never dawned on Lilly that Gertrude had been a loving mother to anyone. Gertrude had treated her more like a servant than a child that she was supposed to love and care for. She decided then and there that she'd never speak ill of Jacob's mother.

She sat down on the grass, mindful of the skirt she wore today. "Gertrude came to the ranch when I was eight years old. Papa was of the mind that I needed a woman's guidance."

Jacob sat down. "So he didn't love her?"

Lilly looked down at her hands. "Not at first. She came in response to a mail-order bride ad my father placed in some of the big newspapers. But after a couple of years I believe they both must have had feelings for one another." She grinned and looked toward Daisy. "How else would we have had a little sister?"

He chuckled. "Having a child doesn't require love." Jacob reached for the bowl of cookies.

"True, but Father loved your mother. A little girl of ten can see when things change in her household." She didn't tell him how much she resented the fact that her father provided for his mother's every whim, or how Gertrude used that knowledge to threaten her in her father's absence.

He nodded and munched on the cookie, which reminded her of a little boy eager to hear more. Lilly smiled. "Anyway, after three years of marriage Daisy came along."

Jacob finished off the cookie. "You both have flower names. Does that mean your father named Daisy?" He picked up a second cookie.

Lilly nodded. "Yes. He did. Daisy was born here on the ranch. Father had gone into Sacramento to talk to a man about buying more cows when Gertrude went into labor. Daisy came a little early. Anyway, we sent for a man to go get Papa and the doctor, but Daisy came very fast. Your mother passed away shortly afterward."

Memories flooded her mind like springwater off the mountain. Sam had helped deliver Daisy. He gave the baby to Lilly and told her to take her to the kitchen. Lilly had thought Gertrude was sleeping and had hurried out of the room to do as Sam said. It was while she took care of the baby that Gertrude died. She remembered returning from the kitchen with the clean baby and Sam stepped out of the bedroom looking very pale. His hands were shaking. The foreman had insisted that he would clean up Gertrude and dress her for burial before Lilly's father returned. Since there were no other women on the ranch, no one had argued.

Jacob broke into her thoughts. "Is she buried here on the ranch?" The second cookie was gone as fast as the first.

Lilly focused on his face. "Yes, she's buried in the family cemetery. I can take you to it, if you want to go there now."

He stood and dusted off his pants. "No, let's go on into town. Maybe tomorrow, we can take a trip there." Jacob snatched the last two cookies from the cookie tin. "I'll go and get Daisy."

She watched him walk away with long strides. He stopped and gave Daisy one of the two cookies. Their sister beamed up at him.

Now that he knew Daisy was his sister, Lilly knew all their lives were about to change. Thankfully, he'd be even more determined to keep Daisy safe. She just prayed he wouldn't try to take Daisy away or think he had a right to run Daisy's half of the ranch.

Chapter Six

Jacob stomped his feet at the front door to remove the dirt from his boots. Yesterday's trip to town had been uneventful since there was no reason to inquire of his mother. He'd gone with Lilly and Daisy to the general store, where they had purchased supplies.

With Lilly's help he'd bought new sheets and a pillow for his cot. He'd also purchased a couple of hand towels for his room. Daisy came home with a fresh batch of lemon drops. He'd smiled when Lilly told the girl she was limited to one a day.

The rooster crowed just as he raised his hand and knocked on the wooden door. Had his mother stood at this door and knocked also? He still ached not knowing why she'd abandoned him, but now that he knew he'd never be able to ask her why, Jacob felt even emptier. Other than Daisy he had no blood relatives.

Lilly pulled the door open. "Good morning, Jacob." Weariness filled her eyes. "What can I do for you this morning?" she asked with a note of caution.

He cleared his throat. "Well, I'd hoped to make a trip to the cemetery but didn't feel right going into your family plots without you." Jacob twisted his hat in his hands.

Her clear blue eyes studied him. "It's a bit early. Daisy hasn't had her breakfast yet."

Jacob nodded. "I forget that little girls eat later than working men." He grinned, very aware of the tension in Lilly.

Daisy pushed past her sister. "Hi, Mr. Jacob."

"Good morning, Daisy." He noted that she still wore a thin white gown much like the one she'd been wearing the morning he'd met her. With his thoughts focused on his mother's resting place he hadn't realized how early it was.

Daisy's smile brightened his mood. "Are we going to go visit Ma and Pa?" Daisy asked, tilting her head back and looking up at her sister.

"After breakfast," Lilly answered. She smoothed the curls from around Daisy's face then looked at him. "Would you like to join us?"

It was kind of her to offer, but he could tell by her pinched face that she'd rather he not. "No thanks. Cook served flapjacks for the men's breakfast and I'm afraid I might have overdone it this morning."

"Lilly's making us biscuits and gravy with sausage," Daisy said. She grinned her pleasure and then pushed past Lilly once more, returning inside the house.

Jacob laughed. "She's constantly moving, isn't she?"

Lilly smiled. "From sunup to sundown. But I wouldn't give her up for the world."

There was a warning in her voice that Jacob hadn't missed. He nodded his understanding of her unspoken statement. "When you ladies are ready, I'll be in the barn. There are a couple of other things I wanted to talk to you about this morning, too. But they can wait until later." He spun on his heels and marched across the yard back to the barn.

A tight knot in Jacob's throat begged for release. For the first time in a long time he'd awoken with a happy desire to bond with his family. He'd dressed hastily, rushed through breakfast and hurried to see his little sister and Lilly. There had to be a connection between them and he wanted to experience it, and the best way he could think of to do that was to be in each other's presence. But Lilly had squished the joy right out of his plans.

A warning voice whispered in his head. All women twisted up a man's thinking; first his mother, and now Lilly. Yesterday she'd seemed like she cared…all nice like and telling him she was sorry for his loss. Then this morning she acted as if he was the enemy. How come? He'd done nothing overnight to cause that kind of a reaction from her.

One might think he was going to cart off Daisy and never let Lilly see her again. Jacob stopped his mad stomp across the yard. His mouth dropped open. Surely Lilly didn't think he planned to take their sister away from her? Lilly was Daisy's only family, besides himself.

Jacob knew what it felt like to lose your single living family member. Little Daisy had already lost her mother and father. He would not be the cause of her losing a beloved sister.

It dawned on him that that wasn't exactly true. His father might still be alive. Father had never been around and his mother never spoke of him. Jacob started walking again. Should he try to find his father?

He entered the barn and inhaled the musky fragrance of hay and horseflesh. By pulling the doors wide open Jacob let more sunlight and much needed fresh air into the otherwise shadowed barn.

Then he answered his own question. No, looking for his father would do no good. He had no name to go on and no idea who his birth father was. His adopted father, John Young, had been the only Papa he'd ever known and he, too, was dead. Jacob told himself that he was alone and evidently unloved by his birth parents. If a man's parents couldn't love him, then who could?

A few minutes later, the Pony Express horse snorted at him as Jacob pulled him from the stall. Thankful he had a job to do, Jacob focused his mind on that as he walked the horse out to the yard for a bit of exercise.

He made a mental note to assure Lilly that he'd never take Daisy away. Jacob wanted to be a part of Daisy's life, but he'd never separate the two sisters. That would be wrong. Jacob pushed all thoughts of his birth parents and his sister from his mind and focused on the horses that were in his care.

The horse snorted and bobbed its head as they walked. The poor beast wanted more freedom and Jacob wanted that for him. No animal should be stuck in a stall all the time.

Asking Lilly for a portion of land on which to release the horses was part of his plan this morning. He had six that belonged to the Pony Express and they all needed exercise and sunshine.

An hour later, Lilly and Daisy joined him. Lilly was back in her men's trousers and a pretty brown blouse with small yellow flowers on it. Daisy wore smaller trousers and a pink blouse. They'd both pulled their hair back into ponytails today, tied with ribbons to match their blouses.

Daisy couldn't seem to wait to get to him, her ponytail bobbing as she ran to the barn, where he stood in the doorway. "Hi, Mr. Jacob!" She stopped in front of him with a wide grin. "Is Caleb here? I want to see my kitty." She tried to see past him to the back of the barn.

For a moment he'd allowed himself to think she wanted to see him. That his half sister cared for him. How foolish. Jacob reminded himself once more that he wasn't the lovable type. With a sigh he answered her. "No, he's helping mend fences today."

As Lilly joined them she heard the exchange between Jacob and Daisy and noticed his crestfallen expression. So the man hoped Daisy would care for him. It was as clear as the nose on his face. But he seemed to forget that Daisy didn't know they were related, nor had she known Jacob long enough to care. But she had accepted him and whether Jacob knew it or not, that was a big deal with children. They seemed to have a built-in sixth sense about whom they could trust and who not to trust.

"Caleb will be back later, sweetie. After we visit the

cemetery we'll come straight back here and you can
see the kittens."

"But what if Caleb still isn't here?" Daisy whined.

"If he's not back, I'll show both you and your sister
the kittens," Jacob promised. His warm voice brushed
against Lilly's ear like a soft feather.

Lilly didn't dare look at him. She wasn't sure if she
could keep her wariness of him from showing. "That
sounds like fun." She smiled at Daisy.

"Let's go." Daisy grabbed Lilly's hand as if to pull
it and then stopped. She dropped her sister's hand and
said, "Please."

"Is the cemetery far from here?" Jacob asked, tying
the Pony Express horse to a rail outside the barn.

Daisy pointed out the door. "Just over that hill."

Lilly answered, "Daisy's right. It is just over the hill
but if you are expecting a rider soon, we should probably take the horses."

"Not until this afternoon. I was just exercising him
before his big run." His gaze moved up the hillside. "We
can walk or ride. It's up to you."

She looked to the hill. If they walked, she might be
able to hold him back a little while Daisy ran ahead.
Lilly needed to know what his plans were in regard to
their sister. She'd spent all night worrying as to what
those plans might be.

Lilly knew fear wasn't from the Lord and so decided
in her heart that she'd face whatever Jacob's plans were.
"If we walk, Daisy could gather wildflowers to put on
her mother's grave." She smiled at the little girl.

"Let's walk, Mr. Jacob. I want to pick flowers for

Mama and Papa's graves." Daisy looked up at him hopefully.

Jacob's handsome face split into a grin. "Then walking it is." He motioned for Daisy to lead the way.

Lilly walked slowly as the other two hurried forward. She watched as Daisy skipped ahead. The little girl darted about looking for the prettiest flowers. She grinned as Daisy sniffed at each blossom.

Jacob glanced over his shoulder at her and slowed his pace.

When he came even with her, he said, "I think we need to talk."

Lilly nodded. "I do, too. Now that you know about your mother and Daisy, what are your plans? Have they changed?" She felt the air catch in her throat and her heart pound against her chest as she waited for his answer.

"Nothing has changed, Lilly. My plans are to continue to work for the Pony Express and get to know my sister." He looked to where Daisy tugged at a stubborn flower and grinned at her determination to uproot the plant.

She swallowed hard. "What if the Pony Express decides not to run this way any longer? Then what?"

Jacob stopped walking and turned to her. "Why don't you ask me what you really want to know?" He pushed his brown hat back on his head and waited for her to answer.

Lilly inhaled deeply. "All right. Will you try to take Daisy away from the ranch, and me?" She felt the sting of tears burn her eyes but refused to shed them. Losing Daisy wasn't an option and she would fight him, if need be.

"Never."

His strength in the way he said "never" surprised her. She waited for him to continue. When it became obvious he wasn't going to say anything more, Lilly asked, "You do realize that she owns half this ranch, don't you?"

"Yep."

Again with the one answer. Lilly sighed. "Jacob, I need you to talk to me. Giving me one word at a time isn't talking."

"No, I reckon it isn't, but will you believe me if I say more?" Jacob folded his arms across his chest and waited, chin up and jawline taut.

Lilly looked away, unable to meet his gaze. She saw Daisy almost at the top of the small hill. In a few minutes she would be out of sight. "Daisy! Wait for us!" Lilly called to her. Then she turned to Jacob. "Is your word any good?"

Jacob answered without so much as a pause. "As good as yours, I suppose." He gave an impatient shrug then leaned toward her, a determined look on his strong features. "All I'm asking for is a chance to get to know my sister. I have no intentions of taking her away from you or this ranch. And to answer your earlier question, yes, I figured she owned half the ranch since her father has two daughters. The ranch belongs to you two, I want no part of the ownership of it."

Lilly studied him, aware that Daisy waited for them at the top of the hill.

She nodded. Peace filled her as she asked the Lord if she should trust him. Instead of telling him that she felt relief from her worries, Lilly said, "I believe you."

He offered her a warm smile. "Good. I want to be a part of her life." Jacob turned toward the hill. "We better get going or she's going to come get us."

She laughed. "True."

As they climbed he asked, "Have you thought about sending her to school this fall?"

Lilly nodded. "Yes, but I'm not sure she's ready yet."

"Why not?" Puzzlement filled his voice.

"She's young and full of energy. I wonder if she'd be too active to pay attention to the teacher." Lilly knew how hard it was for Daisy to sit still. Attending church on Sundays depended on how active Daisy seemed that morning.

"Well, then wait a year. I think she needs an education, but starting her too early may not be the best thing for her." He glanced Lilly's way.

How did he know that's what she'd been thinking? Daisy would mature more in the year she spent at home and Lilly intended to work with her on being still and listening. Maybe having him around wouldn't be so bad after all. If they continued to think along the same lines, Daisy would have two people who loved her and were doing what they thought best for her.

Lilly topped the hill. The small family cemetery rested below. Tall trees shaded the graves and not far away the meadow opened up and allowed the wildlife to roam free within its grasses. It was a peaceful spot. She came here at times to talk to her papa about the running of the ranch. Lilly knew he wasn't really here, but it gave her peace and at times she needed all the peace she could get.

Daisy smiled up at Jacob. "Race you to the bottom." And then she was off and running.

Jacob took off after her.

Lilly stood where she was. Right now everything felt right. But she knew it wasn't. She hadn't forgotten that several days earlier someone had taken Daisy from her bed and left her in a ravine, where she could have been trampled by stampeding cattle.

A shiver ran down her spine. Would Daisy ever be safe? Could she trust Jacob to protect their sister? The question that troubled her the most was, why would anyone want to hurt Daisy?

Chapter Seven

Unease crept up into Jacob's hairline. He sensed more than saw someone watching them. Daisy had laid her flowers on both graves and stood looking down at them. He realized that the little girl really hadn't known either of her parents. A protective sensation raced through his veins and he looked to Lilly.

Was it his imagination or had she, too, detected someone was watching them? Her gaze darted about the area as if searching. Jacob said in a low voice, "If you two are ready, we should probably get back."

Lilly nodded.

"But we just got here," Daisy protested. "I want to play in the meadow."

Lilly's voice sounded tense as she said, "Not today."

"But…"

Jacob spoke before she could finish. "I thought you wanted to see the kittens." His reminder had the effect he hoped for.

Daisy's face lit up. "I'll race you back." She started

to turn and run but Jacob caught her around the waist and held her tight.

"Not this time." His gaze returned to Lilly. She stood with her hands on her hips, frowning at Daisy.

"Let me go." Daisy struggled in his arms. Her laughter assured him that his sister wasn't afraid of him but had assumed he was playing with her.

"I think it's time you slowed down and listened to your elders," Lilly told the protesting Daisy.

Immediately the little girl stilled. "Are you angry with me, Lilly?"

Lilly's gaze darted around once more before she focused on Daisy. "I'm not angry, Daisy. But, if you want to go to school in town you will need to slow down and listen when a grown-up tells you no."

"Oh." Her little lips trembled as if ready to go into a full-blown pout.

Jacob slowly released his hold on the little girl but took her hand in his. Lilly moved to the other side and took Daisy's free hand. Daisy looked at them both inquisitively.

"Let's see if we can walk back to the barn without dropping hands," Jacob said as if he had just created a new game.

Daisy forgot all about pouting and laughed. "Oh, that's easy." She swung her hands but continued to hold his and Lilly's tightly. "See, I can even move them."

Before Jacob could answer he saw Sam riding up on his left. It seemed odd that they hadn't noticed him before. The feeling that they were being watched evaporated like a morning mist. Had Sam been watching them? Or was there someone else who had simply left when he saw Sam coming?

"Good morning," Sam said. He pulled his horse to the side of Lilly and kept it at a slow pace. "What are you three doing out here?"

Daisy answered. "We were visiting Mama and Papa." She happily swung their arms. "I got to put flowers on their graves."

"I see." Sam shook his head as if he thought they were wasting time.

Over the last few days, Jacob had managed to stay clear of the foreman. Either the man had been busy elsewhere or had been away from the ranch.

"Did you just happen to notice us, Sam, or was there something you needed to see me about?" Lilly asked, grinning down at Daisy.

Jacob watched the tips of Sam's ears turn red. Was the man embarrassed that she'd asked why he'd sought her out? Or was he angry that she'd talked to him like his boss and not his friend?

"I need to discuss this year's cattle drive with you." Sam looked pointedly at Jacob.

Lilly's gaze slid to him as well, then she returned her attention to Sam. "What about it?"

"Do you think we should be discussing ranch business in front of a Pony Express man?" Sam asked, making it clear he thought Jacob had no business listening to their conversation.

Lilly answered. "I don't see why not." She stopped walking. "It's not like he's not going to miss the men when they leave."

Daisy almost lost her grip on Lilly's hand. She held tightly to Jacob and laughed. "I almost dropped your hand." Her face shone as she held up their two hands for Lilly to see.

"I'm sorry, Daisy. Why don't you just hold Jacob's hand for a few minutes while I talk to Sam?" Lilly said as she released Daisy's hand.

"All right." Daisy clung tighter to Jacob, not wanting to lose the game.

Lilly turned back to Sam. She crossed her arms over her chest and waited.

Sam shrugged his shoulders as if he didn't care any longer if Jacob heard their discussion or not. "I need to hire about six more men."

She nodded. "When will you be heading out?"

Sam leaned against the saddle horn and looked down on Jacob. "Next week. Soon as I get the men and the cattle rounded up."

Jacob asked. "How big is the herd?"

Sam glared down at him.

Lilly answered, "Should be about fifteen hundred head this year."

"Can we go see the kittens now?" Daisy asked.

He didn't want to leave Lilly with Sam. He couldn't pinpoint what it was that he didn't like about the man. Was he starting to care about Lilly? Was he jealous of the other man? No, that couldn't be possible. They'd only known each other a short while. Besides she was his sister's sister. There was no way he was going to get romantically involved with her, or any other woman for that matter.

* * *

Lilly answered Daisy. "Wait just a minute, sweetie, I need to finish my business with Sam first." She didn't understand Sam's reluctance to talk in front of Jacob. "Is there anything else?"

A snarl twisted Sam's thin lips. "We need a horse wrangler to handle the horses. Maybe Jacob would like to come along." His gaze met Jacob's.

She heard the insolence in Jacob's voice as he answered. "Already have a job, Hawkins."

Lilly watched Sam's eyes harden. It was obvious Sam didn't care for Jacob addressing him by his last name. Or perhaps it was Jacob's tone Sam didn't appreciate.

Sam turned his horse to leave but then looked back down at Lilly. His voice dripped with sarcasm as he said, "When you have time, Cook wants to talk to you about his supplies for the trip."

She nodded then watched Sam kick his horse hard. The gelding snorted its pain and leaped forward. Lilly frowned. Sam normally wasn't so rude to her.

Daisy took Lilly's hand into her smaller one. "Mr. Sam isn't very nice, is he?" she asked.

Lilly turned her gaze to the little girl. "He just has a lot on his mind," she answered. Was that true? Or was he upset to find her and Daisy out with Jacob?

Sam had offered to marry her shortly after her father had died. Lilly remembered assuring him that she'd be fine and that he needn't offer her marriage. Sam had warned her that if she didn't marry him, other men would try to marry her to get the ranch in their hands. He'd not asked again but sometimes she felt his gaze upon her and shivered. Sam was her father's age. She couldn't see marrying anyone her father's age.

They walked hand in hand back to the barn. Lilly couldn't shake her thoughts of Sam. He'd been right. It seemed every cowboy around had come to the ranch to offer their condolences and marriage. She wasn't about to give her ranch to any man. Besides it wasn't hers alone—it was Daisy's, too.

Jacob grinned across at her. "Are you planning on attending the cattle drive this year?"

"No, that's Sam's job. He goes on the drive and acts as the trail boss. Once the cattle are in San Francisco he sees to the sale of the cows and the return of the men and horses," Lilly answered. "My job is to see that the men get hired and then paid once everyone gets back."

Jacob nodded. "So you hire the men?"

"Lilly and Mr. Sam do it together. Last year I got to listen to them ask the cowboys questions. It wasn't very fun," Daisy answered. She swung their arms.

"I'm sure it wasn't," Jacob agreed with a grin.

Daisy looked up at him with big brown eyes. "Nope, but Lilly told Mr. Sam that I needed to learn about ranching."

"She did?" Jacob asked. His gaze met Lilly's over the little girl's head.

Daisy's ponytail bobbed. "Yep."

"We're here," Lilly said, releasing Daisy's hand. "You made it all the way to the barn without running and without dropping Jacob's hand."

Daisy jumped up and down. "That means we can look at the kittens now."

Jacob's rich laugh filled the midmorning air. "Yes, it does." He untied the Pony Express horse and then followed her into the barn.

"Jacob?"

He turned and looked at her. "I need to go see Cook. Will you keep an eye on her?"

Jacob nodded. "Always."

"Thanks." Lilly walked across to the bunkhouse. She realized that she'd enjoyed most of the morning. It hadn't been fun confronting Jacob about his plans, but after that she'd enjoyed her time in his company.

His relaxed nature and easy smile made her feel safe. Jacob's awareness of their surroundings had alerted her to Sam's presence. She'd seen him long before he'd ridden up on his horse. He'd been standing at the edge of the meadow watching them, giving them time alone to visit their family graves before approaching.

She banged on the door to the bunkhouse. Since all the men shared it, except for Jacob, Lilly didn't want to surprise them by barging in. She called out. "Cook, Sam said you need to see me."

Cook came to the door. "Come on in, lassie." He was a big man with a big belly.

"Thanks." Lilly followed him inside to his small kitchen. He waved her to sit down at the large table. Benches filled both sides and she knew that Cook was offering her the best seat in the house—his chair.

He walked over to a sideboard and picked up a piece of paper and a short pencil. "I made a list of supplies that we'll need on the drive." Cook handed it to her.

"Sam tells me we'll have extra men to feed this year so the list might seem a mite longer than past years."

Lilly read over the simple food staples on the list. "This looks fine to me," she said as she handed back the paper.

Cook studied the columns he'd written. While he looked it over, she looked at him. He was about her father's age, with silver at his temples. Green eyes filled his large face. "I'm thinking of adding a few items." He looked over the paper at her.

She stood. "You know what you need and I trust you to make sure the men don't go hungry on this trip." Lilly smiled at him. She started to leave and then turned back.

He held the end of the pencil between his teeth as he stared down at the paper. "Cook, what do you think of Jacob Young?"

His gaze rose to meet hers. "He seems like a good man. Always willing to help a body out. Why do you ask?" Cook motioned for her to sit back down while he poured her a cup of coffee.

"Sam doesn't seem to like him much."

Cook handed her the coffee. "Don't reckon he does."

"Any idea why not?" The strong coffee coated her tongue and left a bitter taste in her mouth. Lilly sat the cup down and then looked up to see his amused expression.

He patted her on the shoulder. "I imagine he feels threatened by the younger man." Cook walked to the woodstove that stood in the corner. A large pot steamed on the top.

What was the big man talking about? As far as Lilly knew the two men didn't interact. The Pony Express employee had nothing to do with her ranch so shouldn't have any dealings with Sam Hawkins, either. "Threatened how?"

Cook stirred the contents of the pot and then laid the wooden spoon down on the rim. He turned with a sigh. "Didn't Sam propose marriage to you a while back?"

Lilly tucked a wayward strand of hair behind her ear. "Yes, but that was years ago."

He wiped his big hands on the flour-sack apron around his waist. "Makes no never mind. I've seen him fire men just for looking in your direction." Cook chuckled. "It's hard to fire someone who isn't in your employ."

Sam had fired men because of her? Surely Cook was mistaken. Sam's feelings for her were no more than that of an old friend. Yes, he'd offered her marriage but that had been years ago and he'd been trying to protect her for her father's sake. Lilly decided Cook was reading more in to Sam's feelings for her than was really there. She stood. "Thanks for the coffee. I better get back to Daisy."

He waved her thanks aside. "Don't go letting the man upset you. Sam will get used to Jacob soon enough. The boy's got a good heart." Cook returned to his pot, leaving Lilly to show herself out.

She walked toward the barn with several thoughts on her mind. Did Sam really care for her romantically? If so, she'd have to discourage him. Her thoughts went to Cook's words—*the boy's got a good heart*. Had he been speaking of Jacob or Sam? Neither were boys. Cook being at least twenty years older than her father, she supposed to Cook they may seem like boys.

Lilly stopped in the shade of the barn to think and consider her conversation with Cook. She found herself comparing Sam and Jacob.

Sam was close to her father's age and had been on the ranch for years. He'd been foreman of the ranch since her father's death and was always ready to offer advice, whether she needed it or not. Cook had insinuated that Sam had feelings for her that were of a romantic nature. She had no intentions of marrying anyone, so she dismissed those thoughts as ridiculous.

She considered what she knew of Jacob. He seemed closer to her age. Cook had called him a hard worker and said he minded his own business. Jacob smiled often, but she knew his mother's desertion had hurt him deeply, even if he pretended otherwise. She'd learned he was Daisy's half brother and that he'd protect her no matter the cost to himself. Lilly shook her head. He'd never said that, so why did she feel so strongly that it was true? In reality she only knew what he'd told her.

Lilly's gaze moved to the bunkhouse. Cook seemed to believe Jacob was a good man. She'd have to believe it, too, at least until he proved differently.

Chapter Eight

Jacob watched Daisy play with the newborn kittens. The old mother cat kept a close eye on the little girl as she cleaned the other two babies. He was surprised she hadn't moved her kits. Maybe the mama cat realized Daisy wouldn't hurt the babies.

While she cuddled the kitten, Jacob rubbed oil into a bridle. His thoughts went to the cattle drive. Would Sam take Caleb on the drive? If so, he'd miss the boy's company. He'd gotten used to Caleb's chatter and good-natured teasing of everyone around him. There was an innocence about him that reminded him of his brothers back home. They were a tough lot but only in brawn. They'd never gone up against a conniving or dishonest man—those were the kind of things that could harden a boy into a man, but not in a good way. He wished he could protect Caleb, but on a cattle drive there was no way.

Lilly entered the barn. She stood in the doorway for a moment then advanced toward them. "Did you need to talk to me about something else, Jacob?"

Jacob nodded. "I wanted to see if you could spare a little pasture space for the Pony Express horses."

"How much and where did you have in mind?" Lilly looked over the stall, down at Daisy and the cats.

He hung up the bridle. "Enough for six horses to run and graze on."

"And I'm thinking they'll need a good source of water, too." She turned her pretty blue eyes on him and smiled.

"That would be right nice. I kind of hoped you'd let me use the east pasture. It's quiet and has a small pond in the center of it." Jacob wondered if she would tell him to check with Sam.

"I don't see why not. Sam should be giving me his weekly report this evening and I'll let him know I've given you permission to use that pasture. Is there anything else?"

Why hadn't Sam waited until their evening meeting to talk to her about the cattle drive? Why had he hunted for her earlier? He realized she was waiting patiently for his answer. "Oh, yes, I have one more thing. Would you mind if we stepped outside?"

She tilted her head to the side and studied his face. "All right." Lilly glanced down at Daisy. "Daisy, as soon as I'm done talking to Jacob we need to go to the house, so give all the kittens love so that they'll all be tame, not just your favorite."

Daisy smiled up at her. "Yes, Lilly. I will."

Lilly led the way to the barn door. When they stepped out into the sunshine she said, "I'm guessing you wanted to talk about Daisy."

Jacob nodded. "I would like to teach her how to ride by herself. And, if it's all right with you, I'll give her a horse of her own for her birthday."

She pulled her braid around her shoulder and began fiddling with the clasp at the end. "I don't know, Jacob. She'll only be five years old. Isn't that kind of young to give a child a horse?"

He studied her features. Was she worried he planned on spending more time with Daisy? Or was it that she feared the little girl would get hurt? "How old were you when your father gave you your first horse?" He asked because he was sure that she'd been young. Lilly rode her own mount as if she'd been in the saddle from day one.

Lilly sighed. "Five, but..." Her gaze shot to the barn.

Jacob grinned. He realized then that Lilly feared Daisy might get hurt. "I'll tell you what. You think about it and if you change your mind, let me know. And, if you want to, you can attend her lessons with her or use that time to have a few minutes of peace and quiet."

The worry left her face and she returned his smile. "Peace and quiet? Huh?"

"An hour a day. If you still have doubts about her owning her own horse, then I'll get her something else and she'll be none the wiser." Jacob wanted—no, he needed—the hour to get to know his sister.

"You can teach her but don't promise her a horse. I'm not sure if she's ready for the responsibility of caring for one yet. If she's going to own a horse, she'll also need to learn how to take care of it." Lilly looked at him as if expecting him to change his mind.

"Then she'll learn from the best. Not only have I taught my brothers how to ride, I also taught them how to care for their horses." Jacob grinned as he remembered when his stepfather, Seth Armstrong, had first come to the Young farm. He'd thought the boys unable to ride but they'd quickly shown him they knew how, even if they didn't all own a horse at the time. He chuckled at the memory.

"What's so funny?" Lilly asked.

Jacob looked at her. "I remember the look on Seth's face when he discovered that the Young men not only knew how to ride, but also how to care for their horses."

"Seth is your stepfather, right?" Lilly crossed her arms over her chest.

He nodded. "He's a good man."

"I'm sure he is."

A look he couldn't quite decipher crossed her face. As quickly as it appeared, it vanished. Had it been loneliness? Was she missing her own father? After all, they'd been to the man's grave site only a little while ago.

A flush filled her cheeks. "Well, if there is nothing else." She waited but not quite long enough for him to answer and then continued, "I'll get Daisy and head to the house. We've baking to do."

"No, that was all I wanted to ask you." He walked with her back to the barn. "Do you want me to wait until tomorrow to move the horses out to the pasture?"

Lilly entered the barn. "Yes, I don't see any reason why you can't have that pasture, but I want to make sure before we start moving livestock. Sam will know if there are any weeds that can harm the horses out there."

Jacob had already walked every inch of the pasture and knew it was safe but held his thoughts. If she needed to talk to her foreman before making a decision, that was fine by him.

"Daisy, time to go," Lilly called.

He expected their sister to whine but instead the little girl came around the stall. She brushed hay from her hair and dress.

Daisy held one hand to her tummy and said, "I'm ready."

"Come along then." Lilly turned to leave the barn.

Jacob continued to watch Daisy. Did her tummy hurt? Was that the reason she had her hand over it? The little girl took small steps toward the door. She kept her right palm clasped over her belly. Maybe she was sick. He was about to ask when the mother cat let out a yowl.

Daisy looked back over her shoulder. The panicky look on her face said it all. He bit back a chuckle. He quickly glanced around to see if Lilly saw what he did but Lilly had already left the barn.

"Daisy?"

Her eyes met his. She answered in a broken whisper. "Yes, Mr. Jacob?"

"Daisy. Why do you suppose the mama cat is upset?" Jacob watched her shrug her small shoulders.

"I don't know." She turned around again to leave.

The mama cat came from the stall and trotted to Daisy. She rubbed her body around Daisy's legs and made frantic yowling noises.

Daisy looked down on the tabby. "Go away." She hissed at the mama cat.

Jacob leaned against a stall door. "You better put the kitten back. She'll follow you all the way to the house if you don't." He crossed his arms over his chest and tried to steady his features into a stern look, even though inside he laughed at the little girl's quandary.

With a sad sigh, Daisy ducked her head as she walked back to the stall. He heard scuffling noises and then she returned.

She made to dash from the barn but his firm voice stopped her. "Do you want the mama cat to hide her babies from you?"

Daisy shook her head. "No."

He pushed away from the stall and walked to where she stood. Jacob kneeled down in front of her. "Then you better leave them with their mama from now on."

Her bottom lip began to tremble. "I just wanted to play with it some more."

"I know, but you knew you weren't supposed to take it from its mama, right?" He hated seeing her lip quiver but knew he had to be strong.

"Uh-huh."

"Daisy. Lilly and I want to be able to trust you but if you are going to be sneaky and try to disobey us we won't be able to." He looked into her brown eyes that reminded him so much of his mother's eyes.

"I won't be sneaky no more." She reached out and touched his shoulder. "Are you going to tell Lilly on me?"

"No, you are going to tell her what you tried to do."

He knew it would be hard for the little girl to do so, but she had to learn.

Daisy's eyes filled with tears and she whispered, "I don't want to."

Jacob patted the hand on his shoulder. "I know, but if the mama cat decides to hide her babies from us, Lilly will want to know why. It will be better if you tell her now, so that she won't be disappointed later."

Her little chin thrust out. "Mama might not move them."

"No, but you still tried to take one knowing it was wrong. It's better to confess what we've done as soon as possible. Otherwise it will eat at you and you'll feel very bad."

Daisy's eyes grew wide. "It will?"

He stood up just as Lilly returned to the barn. "Yep, so get it over with and you'll feel better."

"All right, Mr. Jacob." Daisy lowered her head and walked to Lilly. She took her sister's hand.

Lilly looked at him with a confused expression. Jacob smiled at her. He didn't want to tell on the little girl so didn't answer the puzzled look. Her gaze moved down to Daisy.

Lilly watched a tear streak down Daisy's cheek. "What's going on in here?" She looked to Jacob again.

"Daisy has something to tell you, don't you, Daisy?" Jacob answered. When the little girl nodded, he went to the tack room to leave them alone.

Lilly kneeled in front of her little sister. "What do you need to tell me?"

Daisy wiped at the tears that seemed to flow like a river down her cheeks. "I wanted to take my kitty to my room but Mr. Jacob saw me and made me take it back to its mama."

Jacob returned from the tack room carrying a Pony Express saddle and bridle. He stepped around the two of them and proceeded to a stall that housed one of the Express horses. If he was interested in their conversation, he didn't let it show while he worked.

"You took it from its mother? How?" Lilly asked. She studied Daisy's face, trying to ignore Jacob's shoulder muscles as he hoisted the saddle onto the horse's back.

Daisy wailed. "I stuffed it under my shirt."

"What?" Lilly couldn't believe her ears. "You put a baby kitten under your shirt?"

"Uh-huh!" Daisy's tears continued to flow.

Lilly stood and took her hand. "Thank you, Jacob, for catching her. I'm not sure what has gotten into her but I'll make sure she doesn't do that again." At Jacob's nod, she headed out of the barn.

"Are you going to spank me, Lilly?" Daisy looked up at her sister.

Lilly didn't want to spank the girl. Her father believed in the saying "spare the rod and spoil the child," or something like that, but Lilly didn't feel that sneaking a kitten from the barn was worthy of a spanking. "No, but you are not allowed near those kittens until they are at least four weeks old." At her words, Daisy howled as if Lilly had spanked her.

Lilly pulled Daisy up the porch steps and looked

to the barn to see if Jacob had heard the little girl and come running. Thankfully he was nowhere to be seen.

Once they were inside, Lilly sent Daisy to her room. She told her to pick up her toys. She knew that Daisy would play for a long time before actually cleaning her bedroom.

With a sigh, Lilly went into the kitchen and poured herself a cup of coffee. She took a sip of the mild brew and then began to gather up what she'd need to make bread for the week. Thoughts of the day filled her mind as she worked.

Jacob had been very attentive to both her and Daisy. He'd done the right thing in stopping Daisy from bringing the kitten to the house. Still, Lilly wished she'd have noticed what her sister was up to. Yes, Daisy was Jacob's sister, too, but it didn't feel right him scolding her.

How much more would he take on as Daisy's big brother? Was she ready to allow some of the responsibility of Daisy's upbringing to fall on Jacob's shoulders? She'd told him he could teach the little girl how to ride a horse on her own. Had she done the right thing?

Lilly sat down at the table and bowed her head. "Lord, please help me as I go through these events that I know will be life-changing." Having Jacob in their lives had already brought about some change. How much more would it bring?

Chapter Nine

Jacob grinned as Daisy hung on to the saddle horn for dear life. If he didn't know better he'd have thought she'd never ridden a horse before. "Are you in the saddle good?" he asked, resting a hand on her knee.

"Uh-huh." She sounded breathless.

"Good. Now I'm going to walk around the corral. Just relax." Jacob slowly walked the horse in a circle. He saw Lilly hanging clothes beside the house and knew she watched their every movement.

After a few trips around the yard Daisy said, "This is fun." She smiled brightly at him as she hung onto the saddle horn. Her little knuckles were no longer white but seemed more relaxed.

"Riding a horse can be fun but you have to remember that the horse has feelings and can be dangerous." He stopped walking the horse and smiled up at her. "Did I tell you that this horse's name is Gingersnap?"

Daisy shook her head. "Like the cookie?"

"Yep, and Gingersnap likes her neck rubbed." He

reached up and patted the little mare's neck. He'd chosen Gingersnap because she was older and more patient than the other horses in his care.

She leaned over the saddle and stroked the mare's neck. "Like this?"

Jacob moved to the side of the horse in case Daisy lost her grip. "Yes—see, she likes that." He pointed at the way her ears were perked up.

Daisy sat up. "Is Gingersnap a Pony Express horse?" She fingered the horse's black mane.

He reached up and helped Daisy down. "She is. She's very fast and very smart."

The little girl looked up at the horse. Her voice came out small, but was full of awe. "She sure is big."

To a little girl Gingersnap probably did seem big. To Jacob she was the smallest of the bunch and the tamest. There was no other horse on the ranch that he'd trust to Daisy, except maybe his, but she was too small to ride the big gelding.

Jacob handed the reins to Daisy. "Here, lead her around the corral."

"By myself?" she squeaked.

He laughed. "No, I'll be right beside you."

"Oh." She paused, looking up at the horse. Then took a step forward. Daisy watched over her shoulder to see if the mare would step on her.

Jacob fell into step beside her. "This isn't very hard, is it?"

A grin split her face and her big brown eyes shone with happiness. "No, I like Gingersnap. I wish she was my horse."

"Well, maybe someday you will have a horse of your own." Jacob saw Lilly walking toward them.

"Look, Lilly, I'm walking Gingersnap," Daisy called to her.

Lilly nodded. "I see that." She leaned against the fence and watched them walk around the corral several times. When they came even with her again, she said, "You are doing a good job, Daisy."

The little girl beamed at the praise. "Thanks. Mr. Jacob is teaching me."

Jacob laughed. "Mr. Jacob" sounded so strange to him and yet he knew that having Daisy call him "Mister" was Lilly's way of making sure that the little girl showed proper respect without being too personal with him. He said, "She's a good learner."

Daisy smiled wider. "Thanks." She pulled her little shoulders back and continued marching in front of Gingersnap.

When they came even with Lilly again, Jacob stopped Daisy and Gingersnap. "Let's call it a day, ladies." He took the reins from Daisy's hands and then led the horse out of the corral.

Daisy shut the gate behind them. "I wish I could walk her some more."

"You can tomorrow," Jacob answered. "Now you have to come with me to the barn so I can show you how to take the saddle and reins off." He stopped beside Lilly. "Would you like to join us?" Jacob hoped she'd tell him what the final decision was on the pasture.

"I would love to." Lilly pushed away from the fence

and took Daisy's hand in hers. "Remember, Daisy, to be very careful around the horse."

He didn't know if she took the little girl's hand to prevent her from running ahead or to restrain her so that she could offer her warning. Jacob continued into the barn and listened to the sisters' conversation.

"I will, Lilly. Mr. Jacob said to always be aware of what your horse is doing. He said they are smart animals but they are still animals and to pay attention to them." Daisy took a deep breath and then continued. "Mr. Jacob said that Gingersnap is a Pony Express horse and is very fast. Did you know that?"

Jacob put the mare into the stall and turned to see what Lilly thought of him teaching Daisy on a Pony Express horse. She met his gaze.

"No, I didn't, but I'm sure he thought it was the best horse to teach you on." Lilly released Daisy's hand and allowed her to join Jacob in the stall.

Aware that Lilly watched their every move, Jacob showed Daisy how to take off the saddle and saddle blanket. Then he taught her how to brush the horse's ginger-colored coat. Daisy talked nonstop and asked lots of questions. When they were finished he made sure he stood between Daisy and the horse, then turned to where Lilly lounged patiently on the opposite side of the stall door. "Well, what do you think of our lesson?"

She nodded. "I think Daisy did a good job paying attention and being aware of the horse."

He pulled on Daisy's ponytail. "I do, too."

Lilly stepped back and opened the door for them to

exit. Daisy skipped past them. She stopped in the center aisle and looked longingly to the back stall.

Jacob followed. He wondered why she didn't ask to go see the kittens. His gaze moved to Lilly. She looked at Daisy and shook her head. Then it dawned on him that Lilly must have taken her kitten privileges away as a form of punishment.

"I spoke with Sam last night and he agrees with you that the Pony Express horses need more room to exercise and graze. So you can move them out there whenever you like." Lilly extended her hand to Daisy. "Daisy, would you like to go out on a ride with me?"

Daisy seemed to forget all about the kittens. "Yes!" she squealed.

Lilly's sweet laughter filled the barn. "Are you sure you're not tired of horses?" she teased.

"Nope, I like them." Daisy skipped to the stall that held Lilly's horse.

Jacob walked into the tack room and pulled Lilly's saddle from the long bench that rested against the back wall. Her laughter had warmed his heart. He didn't think he'd ever heard her laugh with so much joy. Jacob hated to admit that he enjoyed the sound of it. He carried the saddle back to the stall.

Caleb entered the barn and strolled toward him. "I'll do that, Jacob." He took the saddle and continued to the horse's stall.

Lilly opened the door to the stall but prevented Caleb from entering. "I'll take that, Caleb. How can I expect Daisy to take care of the horse she's learning on and not take care of my own mount?" She held out her hands for him to place the saddle into.

Caleb looked to Jacob. It seemed Lilly had never saddled her horse before. The boy didn't know what to do.

Jacob nodded at him. "Let her have it, Caleb."

When the boy started to protest, Jacob held his hand up and said, "She's your boss, give her the saddle."

Reluctantly Caleb did as he was told. Lilly had already placed a saddle blanket over the horse's back and now made quick work of getting the saddle in place. "Relax, Caleb, it's not like I haven't ever saddled my horse before."

Jacob noticed that Daisy watched her sister. Was that why Lilly had insisted she saddle her own horse? Probably. He pulled down the bridle and handed it to Caleb.

"Are you going with us, Mr. Jacob?" Daisy asked.

He looked to Lilly. She didn't do anything to encourage him so he shook his head. "Not this time. I need to move the Pony Express horses out to the pasture behind the barn."

Disappointment filled her face. "Oh."

Lilly led the horse out of the barn. Caleb and Daisy followed. With Caleb's help, Lilly and Daisy were soon trotting out of the yard and up the hill toward the cemetery.

Jacob missed them immediately. He'd enjoyed his time with Daisy and the sound of Lilly's unguarded laughter. For a few brief moments they felt more like family and less like strangers.

Daisy was family, but Lilly wasn't and never would be. He told himself to stop thinking of Lilly and her sweet laughter. *Focus on your sister and getting to know her better but leave Lilly alone.* Jacob prayed that was possible.

Lilly followed the fence line. She listened to Daisy talk about her morning and how wonderful Jacob and Gingersnap were.

"Can I have my own horse, Lilly?" Daisy asked as her arms tightened around Lilly's waist and she laid her head against Lilly's back.

She ignored Daisy's question as she noticed that a couple of logs that made up the fence were unnotched. Lilly pulled the horse to a stop and looked around. It looked as if a few head of cows had found their way through the crisscrossed log fence.

"What's wrong?" Daisy asked behind her.

Lilly pointed to the hole in the fence. "See the fence?"

Daisy leaned to the left and looked around her. "Uh-huh. It looks broke."

"It is broke," Lilly confirmed. "Hang on to the back of the saddle, I'm going to get down and look."

"All right. I'm holding on to the saddle," Daisy said.

Lilly swung her leg over the horse's neck and slid off. She tied the horse's reins to the fence and then walked to the disjointed logs. Cow tracks marred the ground between the fence's gaps. It looked as if several head had found their way out. The thought that other cattle might get out prompted Lilly to try to fix the fence. She pulled and pushed on the logs but couldn't get them to fit correctly.

"Do you want me to help?" Daisy asked.

She wiped at her sweaty brow. "No." Lilly thought perhaps she'd made it worse instead of better. "I think we need to find one of the men to fix it." She climbed back on the horse, hating to leave the open fence line.

"Where are the men today?" Daisy asked.

Lilly looked over her shoulder at her little sister. "I don't know for sure."

"Mr. Cook or Mr. Jacob might know," Daisy suggested as she rewrapped her arms around Lilly's waist.

The pasture that Jacob was moving the horses into was closer than the bunkhouse. Lilly turned the mare in that direction. "You're probably right. Maybe Jacob is in the pasture by now."

She felt Daisy's head nod against her back. As Daisy pointed out wildlife and wildflowers, Lilly worried about the fence and her lost cattle. The fence needed to be fixed quickly. "Hang on, Daisy, we're going for a little faster ride."

Lilly gently set the mare into a gallop. Daisy laughed and squealed behind her as they raced across the open land. The wind whipped at their hair and for a few moments Lilly allowed herself to feel carefree.

Jacob came into view. He stood by the gate and was releasing four horses into the pasture. His shoulders looked wide against his tan shirt and his hat was pushed back on his head. It was obvious that he'd heard her coming and had stopped to see why she was galloping toward him. Or had he been expecting her? Did he already know about the fence? And if so, why hadn't he said something?

Chapter Ten

Jacob shaded his eyes. Something was wrong. He felt it deep in his belly. Lilly's horse covered the ground at a fast clip. He watched her blond hair bounce behind her. Tiny arms surrounded her waist and he released the air in his chest. For a brief moment he thought something had happened to Daisy.

She slowed the horse to a trot and then down to a walk. When she got within talking distance, Lilly asked, "Jacob, would you go back to the ranch and tell one of the men at the bunkhouse that the west fence is down?"

"Lilly says our cows went out the hole," Daisy said from behind her.

He studied Lilly's face and then asked a question of his own. "And what are you two going to do?"

Lilly sat up straighter in the saddle. "Go make sure no more of my cows get out." She turned the reins on her horse but he stepped forward and grabbed the halter.

"Why don't I go look at the fence? It might be safer if you two told Sam or one of the other men to come help me," he suggested, looking pointedly at Daisy and raising his eyebrows.

For a brief moment Jacob thought Lilly was going to refuse. Then she glanced over her shoulder and sighed. "You're right. I'll send Caleb or Cook out to help you if Sam isn't near the bunkhouse."

He released his hold on the bridle. She turned the horse toward home. Jacob walked to where his own horse was tied and mounted. Within a few minutes he found where the fence had been knocked down.

Jacob dismounted and began repairing the fence. His horse neighed, alerting him that someone was arriving. He stopped notching the logs into place and looked over his shoulder.

Sam slid off his horse with a grunt. "Looks like you about got that fixed."

"About," Jacob agreed as he lowered the log in his hand into place.

Sam kneeled and examined the cow prints. "Looks like about three head of cows got out." He stood.

Jacob wiped the sweat from his brow. "Need help tracking them?" He watched the older man's face. Cold eyes returned his gaze.

"Don't reckon I do. This is ranch business and you are not a ranch hand." He pulled himself into the saddle and turned the horse around.

Jacob watched as he took the horse back a ways and then turned him to run toward the fence. Its hooves cleared the fence with no trouble. Sam stopped and leaned in the saddle to look down at the ground. Without a word of thanks for fixing the fence, Sam carried on about the ranch business as if Jacob wasn't there.

He'd met men like Sam before. Sam was older, probably in his early forties. He liked everyone to know where they stood. Working with different men all the time, Sam had to let them know he was the boss. Jacob knew he'd have to earn the older man's respect. He picked up his horse's reins and climbed aboard.

Sam had one thing right about Jacob and that was that he worked for the Pony Express, not the Johnson ranch. He wheeled the horse around and headed back to the barn. There were still two more horses to move before dinnertime.

When he arrived at the barn, Lilly motioned for him to come to the house. He slid from his horse's back and walked to her. Jacob assumed she wanted to know about her fence.

She surprised him by saying, "Jacob, I've decided that Daisy and I should have dinner in town tonight and was wondering if you'd like to go with us." Lilly rested a skirt-covered hip against the porch rail.

"Isn't it kind of late in the day to go to town?" he asked.

Lilly answered with a grin. "No, I thought we'd go to Orange Grove. It's only five miles away and is kind of small but has a great boardinghouse that serves a nice dinner."

Jacob had heard of Orange Grove but hadn't been there. "How soon do you want to go?" he asked, checking his watch. He'd hoped to move the two horses to the pasture and he had a rider arriving within the hour.

"As soon as your rider comes through." She smiled, obviously pleased that he hadn't said no.

Jacob nodded. "I'll hitch up the wagon." He decided to wait until morning to move the other two horses.

Just as he turned to go back to the barn her voice stopped him. "No, we'll take the horses. That will be faster."

Why was she in such a big hurry to get to town? She'd said she wanted dinner but Jacob felt there was more to it. He nodded. "I'll be ready to go as soon as Bob exchanges horses."

"Thank you." Lilly returned to the house.

Lilly showed Daisy her paper advertisement. "What do you think of this?" she asked. Lilly hadn't liked being forced to stay at the house while the men fixed her fence and looked for her cows. As the owner of the ranch, Lilly felt she needed to have the freedom to work on it. Daisy was still too young to wag all over the pastures. She braced herself for the argument she knew Daisy would start once she realized Lilly planned to hire a nanny, and that the woman's main job was to take care of her.

Daisy took the paper and twisted it. She looked at the letters and then to Lilly. "What does it say?"

"'Nanny wanted,'" Lilly answered as she took the paper from her sister. "'Must be dependable, trustworthy and like children. Apply at the Johnson ranch.'"

The little girl tilted her head sideways. "You want a nanny? What's a nanny?" Daisy wrinkled her nose as if the word smelled funny.

"A nanny is a woman who comes to your house and helps out," Lilly answered as she folded the paper and put it in her purse.

Daisy's eyes narrowed. "How does she help out?"

Lilly waved her hand. "Oh, she cooks, cleans the house and does laundry. That kind of stuff." She raised her head to find Daisy standing in front of her with her little arms crossed over her chest.

"Are you getting her so she can watch me?"

"Yes, she will be here to help me keep an eye on you, too." Lilly gathered her small handbag and walked around Daisy toward the door. "Jacob will be here in a moment to collect us. Come along." She didn't give Daisy time to protest as she opened the front door.

"I don't want a nanny," Daisy declared as she followed.

Lilly sighed. "Well, like it or not you and I need one."

"Well, I don't like it," Daisy wailed. She stomped her little boot-covered foot.

Jacob strolled up to the house pulling two horses behind him. "What don't you like?" he asked.

Daisy's lower lip pooched out. "Lilly is going to get me a nanny."

Lilly watched his reaction. To his credit Jacob didn't miss a beat. "Do you know what a nanny is?"

He handed Lilly the reins to his horse. A little surprised, she took them. Then he walked to where Daisy still stood on the porch. Jacob picked her up and carried her to his horse.

Daisy's arms went around his neck. "It's a lady who watches me. Lilly said she's a lady who will help out around the house, but I know Lilly just wants to go ride her horse and leave me at home," she answered.

Jacob placed her in the saddle. "I've heard that most nannies like to play and have tea parties." He took the reins from Lilly's hands and swung into the saddle behind Daisy.

Daisy tilted her head to look back at him. "You have?"

"Uh-huh." He put both arms around her small waist and waited for Lilly to mount.

Lilly managed to get on the horse and keep the skirt wrapped around her legs so that she would be decent. She noticed that Jacob hadn't looked her way until he was sure she was situated comfortably on the horse.

When he did glance her way Jacob said, "I wondered how you were going to ride in a dress."

Daisy spoke up. "It's not a dress, it's a skirt." The sass was back in her voice.

Jacob ignored Daisy's rude behavior and smiled at Lilly. He motioned for her to lead the way. Lilly did as he indicated, happy to be away from her fussy sister for a few moments. She listened as their conversation continued.

"Mr. Jacob, tell Lilly not to get a nanny."

Since she was in front of them Lilly couldn't see Jacob's face when he answered, "I can't do that, Daisy."

"Why not?"

A long pause filled the air and just when Lilly had decided Jacob wasn't going to answer Daisy, he said, "Well, it's like this, I'm not Lilly's boss and neither are you. I'm sure that your sister is doing what she thinks is best. You talking ugly to her isn't going to make her change her mind."

Lilly heard the stubborn, sassy tone as Daisy said, "I don't think it's best."

Jacob chuckled but Lilly didn't hear his normal warmth. "Maybe not but I don't think you're being very nice to your sister or respecting her wishes." A long pause filled the afternoon air around them. Even the birds seemed to be holding their songs as they waited to see what Daisy would say to his reproach.

She glanced over her shoulder at them. Daisy faced forward with a frown on her face. Jacob held her loosely in his arms. He gently kicked the horse and brought it alongside hers.

Daisy looked at Lilly. "I'm sorry, Lilly," she said in a low voice.

Lilly smiled at her little sister. "It's all right. Just don't make a habit of it." Her gaze met Jacob's smiling one.

He offered Daisy a quick hug. "That's from Lilly. She can't reach you right now but I'm sure she'd like to give you that hug."

Daisy giggled. "Your whiskers tickle."

Jacob laughed. "So tell me about this Orange Grove. I've never heard of it before."

"It's a small town. Has a boardinghouse, a small general store and a church that I like to attend," Lilly answered.

"That's it?" he asked.

Lilly nodded. "There is a nice group of people that

live there, too. I'm hoping one of the ladies needs a job and can come to the ranch."

A little while later, they entered the small town. Orange trees surrounded the outside edge, explaining the name. Lilly pointed her nose into the air and sniffed, the fragrance of oranges taunting her with a hint of what the area would smell like when the fruit was fully ripened and ready for the harvesters.

Lilly guided her horse down the street to the boardinghouse. "I think we should eat first and then I'll take my sign to the general store." She stopped in front of a two-story house and slid from her horse. Green shutters cased each side of two sets of double windows, with a wooden door in the center. A covered porch ran the length of the house and four cane-bottom rocking chairs invited the weary traveler to sit a spell. Whitewashed pickets and a rail added a bit of charm and if one didn't look too closely they wouldn't notice that the pickets were rough-hewn and not quite straight.

Every time Lilly saw this house she longed for smooth planks on the outside of her own ranch house instead of rough logs, but smooth planks had been a luxury they couldn't afford when her parents had built their home.

She stepped around her horse and lifted her arms. Jacob handed Daisy down to her. The town was quiet, just as she'd expected it to be. This late in the day, everyone was home having their dinner or working in their orchards.

"This seems like a nice quiet town," Jacob said as he tied the two horses to the hitching posts.

Daisy took his hand in hers. "It is. Lilly said we can have strawberry pie if we eat all our dinner." She took Lilly's hand in her other hand. "Isn't that right, Lilly?"

Lilly swung Daisy's hand gently. "I said you can have strawberry pie. Jacob can have whatever he wants."

The little girl released their hands and hurried up the front walk. She stopped at the door and waited for them. Lilly stepped around her sister and entered the boardinghouse.

Thankfully the dining room wasn't very full, which to Lilly's way of thinking meant they'd be eating in no time. She looked forward to savoring someone else's cooking for a change.

"Lilly!"

She turned at the sound of her name. "Hello, Marge." The two women hugged.

"Come on in and have a seat," Marge said as she scooped Daisy up into her arms. "Girl, you are growing up so fast. Pretty soon I won't be able to carry you."

"I'll be five soon," Daisy said with a proud grin.

Marge was an older woman who had always been there for Lilly and Daisy once their father had passed on. She and her husband owned the boardinghouse. "I know you will." She set down Daisy and indicated that they all sit at the square table in front of her.

"What brings you into town?" Marge asked once they were seated. Her gaze raked over Jacob and her eyes asked for introductions.

Lilly spread her skirt around her legs and then answered. "I'm looking for some help out at the ranch."

"What kind of help?" Marge handed them both sheets of paper with food and prices listed on them.

Daisy took the paper and frowned. "Lilly is looking for a nanny for me," she sadly told Marge.

"Is that right?"

The little girl answered, "Uh-huh."

Lilly decided to take the conversation back. "Marge, I'd like for you to meet Jacob Young. He's the new stock tender for the Pony Express out at my place."

The older woman leaned back and studied his face. "Well, how do you do, Mr. Young?"

He laughed. "Please, call me Jacob. Everyone else does."

Daisy giggled. "I call him Mr. Jacob." She patted the paper.

"Nice to meet you, Jacob. What would you like to drink?"

He looked at the menu in his hand and said, "I'd like a cup of coffee."

"Lilly?" Marge turned to her.

She smiled. "I'll have a glass of water and Daisy will have milk." Lilly liked Marge and knew that by stopping here for dinner, Marge would make sure everyone knew she was looking for a nanny for Daisy.

"Be right back with those drinks. You folks take your time looking over the menu." She left them alone to decide what to eat.

Jacob scanned the paper and then laid it down. "How's the meat loaf here?" he asked.

"It's good. I like the roast beef with mashed potatoes," Lilly answered absently, looking to see if Marge had added anything new.

"I always get a chicken leg," Daisy said, mimicking Jacob and laying her paper off to the side.

Marge returned with their drinks and took their orders. "This nanny you are looking for, Lilly, do you want a young woman or an older one?"

"Age doesn't matter. I just need someone who is trustworthy and dependable." Lilly looked to Daisy, who was slurping her milk from a spoon.

Daisy looked up and added, "And likes children. I'm a children."

Jacob's warm laughter spewed from his lips.

Marge laughed, too.

Daisy grinned in confusion.

And Lilly felt a warmth begin in her stomach that seemed to travel to her heart. She told herself to ignore it. Jacob wasn't handsome, he wasn't smart and his laughter didn't thrill her down to her toes. Lilly reprimanded herself for lying. Jacob was handsome, smart and his laugh, well it made her feel happy. Happier than she'd been in years.

Chapter Eleven

Lilly stared at the woman in front of her in disbelief. "So, it's your opinion that children should be kept separate from adult company except on special occasions?"

"That's exactly right. A child should have expectations to live up to. If they desire to be in the company of adults, they should work to achieve that purpose. It gives them something to look forward to, a goal to attain. It educates them as well as teaches them discipline."

"But she's my sister, Mrs. Crump. I can't imagine closing her off in a room the biggest part of the day and visiting her only at certain times."

The woman actually frowned at Lilly as if Lilly could benefit from the same kind of treatment. She sighed. Who knew hiring a nanny could be so difficult. This was the second woman she'd talked to; the first lady had wheezed and coughed her way through their talk, occasionally sipping from a small, flat container. She called the homemade concoction "the recipe," but from the smell, Lilly wondered if a little corn mash wasn't the main ingredient.

And even now a third woman sat in her parlor, waiting for a chance to speak to Lilly about the job. Her three boys were having a high old time climbing on Lilly's porch rails to see which one could jump the farthest.

"Mrs. Crump, thank you so much for coming this morning. I appreciate the effort, but I have ideas that differ from yours and I'm afraid it just wouldn't work. I have a bag of goodies for you. I know the ride out here was an inconvenience and I hope this will make up for it. There are a few jars of apple butter and home-made soup from last year's garden and a loaf of fresh baked bread."

She handed over the paper bag, a moment of pride stealing through her at how pretty it looked. Very seldom did Lilly get to indulge her feminine talents, but last night she'd braided stands of welt together for handles and added a pretty bow. For the final touch, she cut out a bluebird from an old copy of the almanac and pasted it on the front.

It worked like a charm. All three ladies loved the gift and showed no signs of upset at not being hired as Daisy's nanny. Once the yard finally cleared of wagons, she heaved a sigh of relief and headed across the yard to the barn. She could hear squeals and laughter and figured Daisy and Jacob were in the paddock behind the barn. Instead of going through the barn, she decided to walk around it, knowing that Jacob was teaching Daisy to ride.

As she continued on, her thoughts turned to the fact

that finding a nanny for Daisy was proving to be harder than she'd anticipated. She slowed her steps. Was there no one she could trust to watch her little sister so that she could run her ranch? With each step her aggravation grew. Lilly loved Daisy, but also needed to be available to work the ranch. She couldn't depend on Sam and the men to fix every little problem. Lilly didn't want to ask Jacob to help with the ranch, he might get used to it and see himself as a partial owner. No, that wouldn't do. But, could she trust Jacob to help her care for their sister?

Jacob ran in front of Gingersnap, leading her, his hand securely on the bridal bit. The little mare trotted after him. Daisy squealed with laughter as she tried to balance with one hand on the saddle horn. Her blond hair had come out of its ponytail and hung down her back.

His job was to keep Daisy occupied while Lilly talked to the three women who had come out to apply for the nanny job. He'd been surprised to see how quickly they'd arrived.

If anyone had asked him the day before if he thought anyone would apply for the job of nanny, he'd have told them no. The little town of Orange Grove didn't look like it had three single women in it. Of course, no one said the ladies were single. Maybe they were married and had children of their own for Daisy to play with.

Would Lilly hire a married woman with children? She'd said age didn't matter, but what about their marital status. He concentrated a moment on what Lilly might consider a proper nanny, his thoughts taking him away from what he was doing at the moment. He slowed down to a walk.

Caleb laughed out loud from where he stood with a bucket of water that he'd brought from the stream to fill the water trough. He poured the fresh water into the wooden trench. "I saved a little for you, old man." He waved Jacob over to the shade of the barn.

"I want a drink," Daisy said from her perch atop the horse.

Jacob led her over to Caleb. "What was so funny and who are you calling 'old man'?"

"You."

"Boy, I can outwork, outlift and outride you all day, so what are you talking about?"

"Uh-huh. Then why're you looking worn out?" Caleb held the bucket up to Daisy.

Daisy took the pail and raised the rim high to drink.

Jacob frowned at Caleb. "I'm not worn out," he protested.

"Then why did you quit running with Gingersnap?" Caleb countered.

Daisy squealed as the weight of the water shifted to the front, then ran from the bucket in a rush, dousing her head and face with cool water that seemed to take her breath away. She turned loose of the bucket, then made a mad grab for it, lost her grip on the horse and tumbled over the opposite side.

Jacob's breath caught in his throat. He rushed around the horse and caught her, just before she hit the ground. Water covered Daisy from head to toe. Caleb quickly grabbed Gingersnap's reins, speaking soft words and stroking her nose, keeping her calm during the ruckus.

Jacob expected tears from Daisy but she looked at him with a big grin and said, "You caught me."

Caleb nodded. "He sure did." His eyes were huge as he looked down on Jacob and Daisy.

He slid her down on the ground. "Are you all right?" Jacob asked, putting the bucket on the ground and running his hands up and down her arms.

"I'm all right."

Sam crossed the yard. His gaze looked amused. "Good catch, Jacob. Caleb, I need a word with you." He motioned for the boy to follow him to the water trough.

Jacob looked at Daisy. "Ready to get back on the horse?"

She nodded. "I didn't mean to fall off."

"I know you didn't." Jacob picked her up and sat her on the horse's back. He handed her both reins. "I'm going to walk around for a few minutes first and then we'll try trotting again."

"All right." Daisy's gaze moved to where Sam and Caleb stood talking.

He adjusted her stirrups and patted her on the leg, thankful that Daisy hadn't been hurt in her fall.

Worry lined her face as she whispered, "Is Caleb in trouble?"

Jacob looked to where the two men stood. Sam spoke in a lowered voice and Caleb's features said he wasn't happy with what he was hearing. "Don't know, let's continue your lesson."

At her nod, he began slowly walking beside Daisy

and the mare. After several quiet moments, Jacob clicked his tongue and then ran beside the horse while holding onto her bridle. She trotted along beside him.

Gingersnap seemed to know exactly what they were doing and kept pace with him. Her ears twitched as if listening for a new command.

Daisy sat straight in the saddle. Her little face focused as she clung to the reins instead of the saddle horn. Pride built in Jacob's heart for the little girl.

"Whoa," he said, gently pulling on the bridle so that the horse would slow back to a walk. "You are doing good, Daisy." She wasn't talking to him, chattering like she normally would. Had her fall earlier scared her more than he'd thought?

Jacob searched her face and realized she wasn't looking at him, but over his shoulder. He turned to see Caleb enter the barn with his shoulders slumped and his head down. His gaze swiftly searched out Sam. The older man was walking back to his own horse that stood grazing a few yards away.

"I am tired of riding Gingersnap," Daisy said, looking down at him.

He knew instinctively that Daisy wanted to go check on Caleb. "We'll take a short break and then I need to go get another horse from the new pasture." Jacob reached up and pulled her from the horse's back.

As soon as her feet were on the ground, Daisy ran for the barn. Jacob tied Gingersnap to the water trough and then followed slowly. He didn't want to get into the other man's business but like Daisy he was concerned for Caleb.

Jacob heard Daisy say, "I'm glad you aren't going, Mr. Caleb. I would miss you for a whole week if you went."

"Thanks, Miss Daisy, I would have missed you, too." Caleb sat on a bench just inside the barn door.

Daisy saw Jacob standing in the doorway. "Mr. Sam says Mr. Caleb has to stay behind and he don't get to go on the cattle drive this year."

Again Jacob didn't want to interfere with the ranch business. "That's too bad," he said instead of asking why not.

The little girl laid a hand on Caleb's leg. "How come you can't go?"

Caleb looked to Jacob. "He said I need to keep an eye on things around here."

"Like me?" Daisy asked.

Caleb smiled at her. "No, like the horses and the barn."

"Oh." Daisy looked longingly back to where the kittens were.

"Daisy and I are going to the small pasture to get a Pony Express horse. Want to come?" Jacob met Caleb's gaze.

"Thanks for the offer but I need to get the saddles oiled and make sure all the equipment will be ready for the drive." Caleb stood.

Jacob clamped a firm hand on the boy's shoulder. "That's an important job, too, Caleb." He squeezed to assure Caleb that he thought he was doing a good job.

"Thanks, Jacob." He swallowed hard. His young Adam's apple bobbled.

From the corner of his eye, Jacob watched Daisy edge closer and closer to the farthest stall that held the kittens. "It's true. Someday, I'll own a ranch and I'd be honored if you'd work for me." He smiled at the boy to let him know he meant every word of it.

"Daisy!" Lilly's sharp tone had all three of them spinning around.

She glared at them with burning, reproachful eyes. What had gotten into her? Had one of the women she'd been talking to said the wrong thing? Or was it that Daisy had almost reached the newborn kittens?

Daisy ran to her. "Are the ladies all gone?" she asked innocently.

"Yes, they are. What were you doing?" Lilly's gaze raked over the little girl.

Jacob couldn't help comparing Daisy's messy appearance with the perfect way she'd looked earlier in the day. Her hair, which had been pulled up neatly into a ponytail, now hung about her shoulders in a damp mess. Her pants were dirty with splotches of moisture on them. To a woman's eyes, she must have looked a sight.

"I was just looking around the barn," Daisy answered.

"You aren't fooling anyone—you were inching your way toward those cats. Do I need to keep you at the house all day?"

Daisy's lips trembled and her brown eyes flooded with unshed tears. "Why are you so mad, Lilly? I didn't do nothing wrong."

The anger washed from Lilly's face. "I'm sorry,

Daisy. I shouldn't take my frustrations out on you."
She kneeled down to hug Daisy. "Yuck! You are soaked.
How did you get so wet?"

Caleb hid his grin by ducking his head just as Lilly
turned her attention on him and Jacob. Jacob wished
he could hide so easily. Her gaze demanded answers.

Daisy giggled. "I dumped water on my head and fell
off the horse."

Why did children have to tell everything? Couldn't
the child have held her tongue? No, Daisy was already
into a full-blown explanation of their morning. Lilly's
eyes bored into his as their sister talked. Jacob sighed.
From the look on Lilly's face, he had a lot of explaining to do.

Lilly listened to her sister as she stood. Daisy and
Jacob had had quite the morning. But she couldn't
focus on Daisy's story. She could still hear Jacob saying, "Someday, I'll own a ranch and I'd be honored if
you'd work for me." Did he think he'd own her ranch
before much longer? That worry, along with the ladies'
visit first thing this morning, had her wound up tighter
than a pocketwatch. At Daisy's pause, Lilly said, "I see."

"Daisy and I were about to go to the small pasture
and get one of the Express horses. Want to come?" Jacob
asked.

"I..." The sound of wagon wheels crunching on the
road stopped her answer. She sighed. "Need to see who
this is first."

Sunlight hit her eyes as she exited the barn. Aware
of the other three following her, Lilly looked to see

who had arrived. A young woman with long brown hair pulled up into a fancy hairstyle, where part of it was up and part of it hung down her back, climbed down from the wagon. She wore a red velvet dress and fancy button-up shoes. She looked around the ranch until her eyes fell upon them.

She sashayed across the yard like she owned it. When she got within speaking distance, the woman held out her hand. "I'm Willow Springs. I came in response to your advertisement over at the Orange Grove general store."

Lilly took her hand. "I'm Lilly Johnson, this is my sister, Daisy. Come on up to the house, I have a pot of tea made and we can discuss the job."

Willow kneeled down in front of Daisy. "I hope I get the job, Daisy. I like little girls." She tucked a strand of Daisy's hair behind her small ear, then stood. She turned to Lilly with a wide grin. "I'd love a cup of tea."

Lilly looked to Jacob, who nodded his head.

"Daisy and I are heading to the small pasture." He laid a protective hand on her shoulder. "Isn't that right?"

"Yep, I get to ride Gingersnap." Daisy pointed to the mare.

"Good. I'll see you both in about an hour." She turned toward the house and heard the gentle swish of Willow's skirt as she followed.

Willow didn't strike Lilly as someone looking for a nanny job. When she'd first seen her, Lilly thought she was a woman of ill repute. But then she'd seen her eyes. They weren't hard or cold. They were hopeful and warm.

She opened the door to the house and motioned for Willow to enter. "The kitchen is off to the left."

Willow entered the kitchen and moved to the table but didn't sit down. "This is a nice house." Her gaze moved around the pantry and seemed to drink in every detail.

"Please, have a seat," Lilly said, indicating one of the kitchen chairs.

"Thank you." Willow pulled out the chair that gave her the best view of both doors. She sat down. "You've already decided that I don't get the job, haven't you?" She held her hands in front of her with the palms together.

Lilly placed a small tea bag in each cup and poured hot water in them. "No, I haven't decided anything, yet." She placed a cup in front of Willow and then sat down, too.

Sugar and cream sat in the center of the table. Lilly had given three different ladies a cup of tea and talked to them about the job she had advertised. The first one had been too old to watch an active little girl and Lilly had felt sorry for her, but had to tell her she couldn't offer her the position. The second had been a widow who was more interested in housekeeping than in taking care of a little girl. The last one might have worked out, if she hadn't told Lilly she'd be bringing her three boys all under the age of ten with her and expected to have rooms at the ranch. "Please, help yourself to the cream and sugar."

"Thank you." Willow reached for the sugar. Her hand

shook and all the confidence she'd shown earlier seemed to have fled her now.

Lilly sipped her weak tea. She set down the cup and asked, "Why do you want to work here, Mrs. Springs?"

The young woman put down her cup. "Please, call me Willow. Mrs. Springs is too formal and is what folks call Ma in church." She smiled as she stirred the tea into her cup. "I need a new start and I like children."

Lilly sat back in her chair. She wrapped her hands around the warm cup. "I'm glad you like children. Daisy can be a handful." She wanted to ask what Willow meant by saying she needed a new start. But how could she ask such a question without seeming rude?

Willow's green eyes bored into hers. "Mrs. Johnson, can I be honest with you?" She leaned forward.

"If I am to call you Willow then I hope you will feel free to call me Lilly and yes, I expect you to be perfectly honest with me." This woman was more forward than anyone she'd ever met.

Her chest rose as she took a deep breath and then pressed on. "Lilly, my husband, God rest his soul, died in a mining accident a few months ago. I've been trying to take care of myself and as a last resort had gone into town to see if there was a saloon I could work at. I've never done that kind of work, but I'm desperate. Then I saw your advertisement and thought maybe God hadn't turned His back on me yet." She picked up her teacup and took a small drink.

It seemed to Lilly that the other woman was trying to build up the courage to say more. "I'm glad you did. Tell me, what are you willing to do as a nanny to Daisy?"

A small smile touched Willow's lips. "Well, I will help her get dressed, fix her meals, but most importantly, I'll play with her and make sure she stays out of harm's way."

Lilly could just imagine what Willow's first impression of the little girl had been. Daisy had been soaked with mud and dirt all over her clothes. Her hair hung in damp ringlets around her shoulders, not in the ponytail Lilly had pulled it up into that morning. "What if I told you that I don't want you to let Daisy out of your sight?"

"I'd say you are a wise woman. Children Daisy's age can get into a lot of mischief, if not watched properly."

"You seem to know a lot about children. Do you have any children?" Lilly watched sorrow flood Willow's eyes before she shut them. When she reopened them, they were clear.

"When my husband died, he had our three-year-old son with him. They both died in the cave-in." Willow looked down into her cup.

Lilly's heart ached for the young mother who had lost her husband and son. "I am so sorry."

Willow looked up. "Thank you, but it wasn't your fault. But I do need the job." Her moist green eyes met Lilly's.

She saw honesty and raw pain in the green depths. Lilly decided of the four women who'd applied for the job, Willow was probably her best choice. "I have one more question for you and if you don't want to answer, you don't have to. It won't sway my decision one way or the other."

The young woman nodded. "All right."

She swallowed. "How old are you?"

Willow laughed incredibly. "That's the question?"

Lilly felt foolish but wanted to make sure that this woman wasn't too young to watch Daisy. She nodded. "Yes."

"I'm twenty-five. How old are you?"

It was a fair question and one Lilly didn't mind answering. "I turned twenty in February." Her stomach growled and Lilly realized it was almost time for lunch. "The job pays ten dollars a week, plus a room and your meals. If you want the job, it's yours."

A big smile graced her pretty face. "Before I allow you to hire me, I have one more thing I have to show you. I'll be right back." Willow left the room in a hurry.

Lilly wondered what she had to show her. The thought that she should follow the other woman had her standing up, but then Lilly realized that if the woman was going to work at her house, she needed to trust her to come back and reveal her secret.

Lilly picked up her teacup and set it in the washtub. She heard the front door open and close again. She turned from the washbasin to see Willow return to the kitchen. Within her arms she held a baby wrapped in blankets.

"I'll understand if you don't want to hire me, now." Willow cuddled the baby against her in a protective manner. "This is my son. His name is Gabe, short for Gabriel."

How could she not hire her? Willow had a baby to care for and had already said this position was her last resort. Lilly stepped closer. "May I hold Gabe?" she asked, looking down on the sleeping infant.

Willow handed her son over to Lilly. "He's the reason I am desperate. I love Gabe so much I'll do anything to provide for him."

Lilly cuddled the baby close. Memories of holding Daisy like this when she was just a few months old caused her throat to swell. He snuggled within his blanket. Light brown hair covered his little head and long eyelashes rested against his cheeks. She looked up at Willow. "I still want you to take the job. Would you like to see your room now?"

A tear slipped down Willow's cheek. "Thank you. Yes."

Lilly wasn't sure what the future held for all of them. But she did know that God had put each of them in each other's paths. Still, she couldn't help but worry about what Jacob had said about the ranch. Was he planning on taking over her and Daisy's ranch? Or was he planning on buying his own? She'd heard him offer Caleb a job. How many of her other men had he offered jobs to? If he was talking about her ranch, then he was about to have the fight of his life.

Chapter Twelve

Jacob held his hat in his hands as Lilly formally introduced him to Willow Springs. The young widow was nice to look at, but he reminded himself that women couldn't be trusted and he'd have no interest in her. His concern was for the Johnson women. Well, Daisy wasn't a woman yet, but she would be someday and he was going to be there for her. "It's nice to meet you, ma'am."

"Oh, we'll have none of that 'ma'am' business. I am Willow." She juggled the baby in her arms. "And this is little Gabe."

He didn't know what to say to that. Calling her Willow seemed inappropriate but he called Lilly by her Christian name. Jacob felt confused and a little embarrassed.

As if she sensed his mood, Lilly said, "It's good that we all call each other by our first names since we are friends, or soon will be once we get to know each other better. This is a ranch after all."

Jacob nodded, thankful that Lilly had given her permission. Now all he wanted to do was get back to his barn and horses.

"Jacob, would you and Caleb please bring in the boxes of Willow's things?" Lilly motioned for Daisy to come to her. "As for you, young lady, I believe you'll need a bath before bedtime."

Daisy clapped her hands and giggled. "With bubbles?" she asked.

Willow touched the top of her head. "Is there any other way to take a bath?" She dramatized her voice and made Daisy giggle even more.

"We'll have to see if we have the right soap to make bubbles. I'm not sure if you used the last of it last time you took a bath," Lilly answered. She walked to the door and held it open for Willow and Daisy to enter.

Jacob and Caleb walked to the wagon. There were two boxes, one large and the other of medium size. "I'll take the big one," he said, pulling it toward him.

Caleb did the same to the smaller box. "She doesn't have much stuff, does she?"

"Do you have more than this?" Jacob asked playfully.

Caleb frowned. "No, but I'm not a woman. They usually have wagons full of stuff, not two boxes."

Jacob shrugged his shoulders. "Well, maybe she likes traveling light." He led the way up the porch steps.

Lilly stood at the door and opened it for him. "I'll show you to Willow's room."

Caleb followed him inside and looked around. Jacob got the impression that this was the young man's first time in the house. They walked through a large sitting area with a fireplace. A large window overlooked the yard. The kitchen sat off to the right. They entered a long hallway. Four doors led off the hallway and Jacob assumed they were bedrooms.

"Lilly, can we show Mr. Jacob and Mr. Caleb my room, too?"

Daisy skipped in front of them.

"Is it clean?" Lilly responded as she opened the second door to the left.

Daisy looked down. "No."

Lilly looked at Jacob and grinned. "Do you still want to show it to them?" she asked Daisy.

"Ummmm." Daisy scuffed her boot against the floor. She looked up. "Maybe they can see it next time."

Lilly motioned for Jacob to take his box in first. The room was bigger than his tack room. It had a full-size bed with a green-and-white quilt on it. A tall armoire stood off to the right of the bed and there was a dresser to the left. A cabinet with a built-in washbasin sat under the window. He set the box beside the dresser, assuming that clothes filled the container.

"Just set yours on top of his, Caleb." The young boy did as he was told and left the room.

"Thank you both for carrying those in. I could have gotten them but appreciate that you did it for me," Willow said.

"Our pleasure," Caleb said before Jacob could respond. He noticed that the boy's neck and cheeks turned a soft red before he ducked his head.

Lilly frowned and Willow smiled knowingly.

"I made a spice cake earlier. Would you both like a slice before you go back to work?" Lilly asked, leading them back down the hall and toward the front of the house.

Caleb recovered from his embarrassment and said, "I'd love some. Cook tries to bake, but, well, he's not very good at it."

Jacob laughed. "Well, then it's a good thing for you that you're not going on the cattle drive."

The young man sighed as he entered the kitchen. "I'm not much of a cook, either. I'll be begging Cook to fix me a meal by the time he gets back."

Jacob started to comment but Lilly spoke before him. "From what I gather from Sam, you two will be the only men left on the ranch when they leave. How about you two have your meals here at the house." She slid dessert plates in front of both of them and added three more around the table.

"We wouldn't want to put you out," Jacob answered, shooting Caleb a look that he hoped the boy would understand.

Daisy came to stand beside his chair. "I don't want you to go hungry, Mr. Jacob." She laid a small hand on his shoulder.

"Oh, Daisy, stop being so dramatic. They aren't going to starve." Lilly laughed as she set the cake in the center of the table. She looked for Willow. Not seeing the other woman, she stepped out of the kitchen and called down the hallway, "Willow, come join us for dessert."

"They might starve, Lilly," Daisy said, turning big brown eyes on Jacob. "Can you cook, Mr. Jacob?"

He tweaked her nose. "I can open a can of beans. So I won't starve."

She wrinkled her nose. "Did you hear that? He's gotta eat beans." Daisy looked at Lilly like it was all her fault that Jacob could only open a can of beans.

"I said they can come up to the house and eat with us." Lilly walked to the coffeepot and poured four cups. Then she looked at Daisy. "Would you like a glass of milk?"

Daisy climbed into the chair closest to Jacob. "Yes, please."

Willow entered the room. Her green eyes looked at the small table. Her only choice was to sit down by Caleb. "Is there anything I can do to help, Lilly?"

Lilly placed a hot cup of coffee in front of Jacob. She motioned for Willow to sit down. "Go ahead and start serving the cake while I get the rest of the drinks."

"Where's the baby?" Daisy asked.

"He's sleeping." Willow picked up Daisy's plate and put a small slice of the cake on it.

Daisy looked down at her dessert. "He needs a bed, huh?"

Willow quickly dished cake onto Jacob's plate and then Caleb's. "Yes, but for now he can sleep with me."

Lilly sat a glass of milk in front of Daisy and a cup of coffee in front of Caleb. "Would you have preferred milk, Caleb?"

Jacob wondered if Lilly was politely reminding the boy that he was fifteen years old and too young for Willow.

Caleb shook his head. "Nope. Coffee is fine."

Lilly picked up Daisy and then sat back down with Daisy on her lap. She hugged the girl and then said, "Thank you, Willow."

Willow smiled at her. "I should be thanking you. This cake smells wonderful." She bowed her head, reminding everyone that they should say grace.

Jacob listened as Lilly thanked the Lord for sending Willow to them and for the food that they were about to eat. Her soft voice spoke with respect. When she said "amen," everyone echoed her.

Caleb immediately dug into the cake like a starving hound dog. Jacob shook his head and then turned his attention to Lilly. "Daisy and I went to the small pasture and got one of the Pony Express horses. She's riding really well on her own."

Daisy smiled around a mouthful of cake.

"You have a Pony Express station here?" Willow leaned forward in her seat. Her green eyes sparkled with interest.

"It's a relay station. The men exchange horses and keep going," Jacob answered.

Willow smiled. "That is so exciting. I can't believe how fast those men can get mail from one end of the country to the other."

Lilly nodded. "It really has been interesting."

Jacob wondered what Lilly meant by that. As far as he could tell she hadn't shown that much interest in the Pony Express. His gaze searched hers. She smiled that sweet smile that caused his stomach to do somersaults.

"So how many of the men on the ranch work with the Pony Express?" Willow asked, pulling his attention from Lilly.

"Just Jacob," Caleb answered. "The rest of us work for Miss Lilly." He shoved the last bite of his cake into his mouth.

Willow smiled. "And what is it that you do on the ranch, Caleb?" She took a dainty bite of her cake and focused her full attention on the teenager.

He leaned back in his chair. "I'm a stable hand. I take care of the horses, the stalls and the equipment, and make sure that all the horses stay healthy." Caleb tilted the chair back on two legs.

Jacob hooked his boot over the bottom rail of Caleb's chair and forced it back down on the floor. He tried not to make it obvious what he was doing but the look on Caleb's face told all. Jacob finished his cake and then stood. "Thank you for the cake and coffee. We best get back to work, right, Caleb?"

The youth stood also. "Yeah, Sam wants that equipment oiled and ready to go by day after tomorrow." Caleb walked to the door with a swagger.

As Jacob closed the door he heard Daisy ask, "What was wrong with Caleb? Did he hurt his back when Mr. Jacob made him sit in his chair right?" He chuckled. Out of the mouths of babes.

Caleb must have heard her, too. He hurried to the barn.

Jacob followed. He wondered if he should talk to Caleb about Willow. It was obvious to all that the boy was smitten with her. Should he warn Caleb that Willow was too old for him? Or that she was a woman and couldn't be trusted?

Lilly felt as if she'd worked in the field all day. Her arms ached and her back cramped. Willow had helped her strip the beds, but Lilly had insisted that she and Daisy get to know one another better while Lilly did the laundry. It had been a while since all the bedding was done at the same time. And then she'd washed hers and Daisy's clothes.

The sun was setting as she pulled in the last sheet. Movement by the barn caught her attention. She squinted to make out who stood in the shadows. A moment later Sam stepped out of the darkness and walked toward the bunkhouse.

Lilly released the air she'd held in her lungs. What was wrong with her? She'd lived on this ranch all her life and had never been fearful. Now she jumped at shadows.

"Are you all right?"

She twisted around and gasped. "Jacob, you scared the wits out of me." Lilly hugged the sheet close to her chest.

"That wasn't my intention. I saw you staring at the barn and wondered what was wrong and then you started panting and I thought maybe you were feeling sick." Jacob crossed his arms over his chest.

"I'm fine. I just thought I saw something." She took a step toward the house and then stopped. "Was there a reason you were lurking behind me?"

Jacob laughed. "I wasn't lurking."

"Then what were you doing?"

He sobered. "I was waiting for you to get done with the wash. I wanted to ask you something."

In the fading light she could see that his features were no longer teasing. His tone had changed, as well. "What did you want to ask?"

"Would you mind if we talk a little farther away from the house?"

She looked over her shoulder, where light spilled from the kitchen door. Willow and Daisy were setting the table for their evening meal. Did he not want them to hear their conversation? "All right."

Jacob walked to the garden spot and circled to the far side, where a large tree stood. He leaned against it and said, "I think this is far enough."

She noticed that he positioned himself so that he could still see inside the kitchen. "Jacob, what is this about?"

"I wondered what you knew about your new nanny." He braced a booted foot against the base of the tree.

Lilly walked over to him and handed him one end of the sheet. If he had time to lean against a tree, he had time to help her fold the sheet. "I know she's a widow. That her husband and three-year-old son were killed in a mining accident. That she's alone other than Gabe, who she had two months ago. She seems to like Daisy and needs the job."

He worked with her to fold the sheet. "Is that all?"

She finished folding. "So far. Do you know something I don't?"

"I know that Caleb is smitten with her." He brushed a hand across the back of his neck as if it hurt.

Lilly smiled. "I know that."

He grinned back. "Yeah, I suspect you do."

"Why are you asking about Willow?" She tucked the sheet under her arm and watched his expression. Jacob might not know it, but his expression often gave his thoughts away.

Weariness filled his face. "I just worry that we don't know enough about her."

"Jacob, I knew that there was a good possibility that I wouldn't know the woman who applied for the job of being Daisy's nanny. I promise I'm not going to leave Daisy in her full care until I'm positive that she is safe for Daisy to be with. Right now I have no reason to doubt that she's a struggling widow who needs a job." She hoped her words would reassure him. Daisy was her sister and she wouldn't let anything happen to her, if she could prevent it.

He nodded. "I'd like to keep giving her riding lessons and maybe start a little schooling with her."

Darkness now fully covered them. She couldn't make out his face. "What kind of schooling?" Caution filled her voice.

He chuckled. "I just want to teach her to read."

"You don't think she's too young for reading?" Lilly hadn't thought of teaching the little girl reading.

Willow had pointed out that Daisy could do a few chores around the house. Now Jacob wanted to teach her to read. Lilly felt as if they were going to force Daisy to grow up too fast. She knew what it was like to lose your childhood and she didn't want that for Daisy.

"No, she'll be five in a couple of months."

His answer surprised her. "I don't know, Jacob." Her voice quivered.

Jacob placed a hand on her shoulder. "What's wrong, Lilly?"

Had he really heard the fear in her voice? Everything was changing so fast. She didn't want Daisy to grow up. "I'm tired. Let me think about it." Lilly started back to the house.

"Can I at least read to her at night before she goes to bed? I'd like to spend more time with her." Jacob put his hand at the small of her back.

Was he afraid she'd trip in the dark? Or did he think touching her would make her want to do as he asked? She had to admit that his hand on her back had her emotions running amok. Lilly tried to ignore her feelings and focus on what was best for Daisy.

Chapter Thirteen

Jacob removed his hand from her back when they got close to the kitchen door. Lilly still hadn't answered him. Disappointment rested upon his shoulders like morning dew on grass. With Willow taking care of Daisy, Jacob feared he'd see less and less of the little girl. He'd just found out he had a real sister and it felt as if she was being taken away from him.

Lilly stopped in the doorway and looked out at him. "This is really important to you, isn't it?"

He offered what he hoped looked like a soft smile. "You have no idea."

Lilly studied him. "No, you're wrong. I believe I understand more than you know. It's late. If you want to read with her tomorrow night, I can't stop you."

Jacob reached out and pulled her back down the back steps. He lowered his voice and growled, "Lilly, I'm not going to force my way into Daisy's life." Then he stomped off.

Old hurts ate at him. Voices in his head whispered

he wasn't good enough to read to his sister. They reminded him that women couldn't be trusted.

He stopped by the same tree he'd leaned against moments earlier. Jacob forced the unpleasant thoughts away.

Lilly hadn't done anything to him to cause such hurt, other than think he wanted more from her and Daisy than he actually did. He was very aware she feared he'd take their ranch from them, or at least try to. He'd never do that. But his knowing it didn't give him the right to become angry with her. He'd messed up.

Jacob sighed, bowed his head and softly prayed. "Lord, I shouldn't have spoken to Lilly like that. I meant what I said but the way I said it and stomping off was wrong. Please help me face her tomorrow and apologize. I know I was wrong but I'm not good at admitting when I'm wrong. I'm going to need Your strength tomorrow when I talk to her."

A gentle clearing of the throat pulled him from his prayer. He groaned inwardly, then turned to face the woman behind him. He raked his fingers through his hair. He spoke in a soft voice. "You followed me?"

"You seemed upset."

Darkness had settled around them like a black cloak. Jacob couldn't see her face and knew she couldn't see his. "I was. I'm sorry I was rude."

"I'm sorry, too."

Jacob shifted. "What do you have to be sorry for?"

Her voice sounded tired. "I overheard you offering Caleb a job and assumed you were talking about this ranch. I should have talked to you about it but instead got scared."

"I see." He rubbed his hand across his eyes. "I don't want your ranch and I don't want to take Daisy from you. I'm hoping that I can buy some land close by. As for Daisy, well, I just want to be a part of her life." He heard her deep sigh.

"I know. But, Jacob, no one knows you are Daisy's brother so how are we going to explain why you are reading her a bedtime story?"

He hadn't thought about that. She was right. It would look strange if the new man on the ranch was suddenly reading to Daisy every night. "You're right. Forget I mentioned it."

"No, let's give it some thought. Maybe we can come up with something."

Jacob wished he could see her better. Maybe if he moved closer to her he would be able to see her expression and know what she might be thinking.

Just as he took a step toward Lilly, Willow called from the kitchen door, "Lilly! Dinner's ready."

She called back. "Be right there."

He knew she needed to get back to the house. "Go on, Lilly. We can talk more tomorrow."

"Good night, Jacob."

"Good night."

He walked to his room. His conversation with Lilly ran through his mind. She'd commented on him wanting to be with Daisy more, but had avoided talking about the ranch and her fear that he wanted it. What would he have to do to convince her?

Jacob thought for several long minutes. He'd been putting money away. Perhaps now was a good time to look for a place of his own. After all, now that he had a sister living here, shouldn't he stay here, too? Would Lilly realize he didn't want her ranch if he had a farm or ranch of his own?

"Willow, I'm going to run out to the barn for a few minutes." Lilly pulled her hat off the hook and hurried outside. The cool morning breeze brushed her hair across her forehead.

She'd prayed for a solution to Jacob's problem. He wanted to read to Daisy, but it would look funny if he came to the house. Lilly entered the warmth of the barn with a smile. She'd come up with the perfect solution.

"Good morning, Miss Lilly. Do you want me to saddle your horse for you?" Caleb asked.

"Not this morning, thank you. Is Jacob around?" She searched the barn but saw no sign of him.

"No, he headed out early this morning to take care of the Pony Express horses." Caleb went back to oiling the saddle he'd been working on when she'd entered the barn.

Lilly decided she didn't want to wait for Jacob to come back and if she went to the pasture where he was, they could talk without anyone overhearing them. "I believe I will take my horse for a little ride this morning."

Caleb started to put his rag off to the side but she stopped him.

"I can saddle the horse, Caleb. You keep working, I'm sure Sam will be by shortly to check on your progress." Lilly knew that Sam expected his men to do as he said and in a timely manner.

As she worked, Lilly realized that Sam didn't come around as much as he had in the past. The only thing that had changed was Jacob's arrival as the new Pony Express stock tender. Was he the reason Sam no longer came around? Lilly realized that she hadn't told Sam about Willow, or even confided in him that she'd hired the nanny.

Jacob's arrival had changed things on the ranch. After her father had died, Sam had made sure to talk to her every day. That stopped the day Jacob arrived. Lilly wondered why as she pulled herself into the saddle.

"If Willow calls for me, will you let her know I'll be back shortly?" she asked Caleb.

He nodded. "Yes, I'll tell her."

Lilly noticed that his eyes lit up at the thought of talking to Willow. "Thanks." She walked the horse out of the barn, but as soon as they were clear of the yard, Lilly gave the mare her head.

It felt good to gallop the mare toward the pasture. She'd missed these quiet moments. Lilly allowed her mind to think. She knew that the men would be leaving on the cattle drive the next day. Had Sam had time to hire the extra men he'd mentioned? In the past he'd come to the house and given her an update, so why hadn't he this time? She decided she'd find Sam after breakfast and have a nice long talk with him.

Jacob was closing the gate when Lilly arrived at the back pasture corral. His brown eyes searched hers as he waited to see why she'd come. "Good morning," he said, untying the reins to his mount.

"Good morning. I can't stay long but I think I have a solution to our little problem." Lilly smiled down at him.

"Which little problem?" he asked as he pulled up into the saddle.

Lilly frowned. "We have more than one?"

"You tell me." Jacob laughed and turned his horse to face her.

She blew her bangs out of her eyes. "I'm talking about you spending more time with Daisy."

He waved his hand. "It was a stupid idea to want to read her a bedtime story."

"No, it wasn't. I've been thinking. The men will be leaving for the cattle drive tomorrow and you and Caleb will begin having your meals at the house. How about after supper you read to Daisy?" Lilly leaned on the pommel of her saddle and smiled at him.

"What about after they come back?"

His gaze searched hers, leaving Lilly feeling flushed. "Well, by then Daisy will be so happy that you are reading and eating with us that I'm sure she won't want you to stop and since you are family, I don't see why you have to."

Jacob grinned. "I know that I'm her family and you know that I'm her family, but no one else at the ranch knows."

"Yes, but now that Willow and the baby are in the house, it's not like you and I will be alone and it will be natural for everyone to continue with the routine that we set up while the men are away." She sat back in the saddle. Her horse stomped its hooves, as if to tell her it was time to go now.

"Thank you."

Lilly nodded. "You're welcome. I better get back, I told Willow I wouldn't be but a minute. I thought you were at the barn and then Caleb said you were out here, so I've been gone longer than planned or expected." She knew she was rambling, but for some odd reason, Lilly felt butterflies in her stomach.

She turned the horse and headed back to the barn. That was odd, Lilly thought as she rubbed her fluttering stomach. Jacob had never made her feel skittish before. Was it because that was the first time they'd ever been alone? Or was it because she'd opened up her home to a man and she'd never done that before.

Whatever it was, Lilly vowed that it wasn't because she found Jacob handsome and kind. Nope, she wasn't allowing him or any other man into her heart. She had a sister and ranch to protect.

So why did she find herself looking forward to when the other men would be leaving on the cattle drive?

Chapter Fourteen

Jacob and Caleb watched as the men drove the cattle off the ranch. The young man sighed, drawing Jacob's attention. Jacob turned his horse and headed back to the barn.

"I sure would have liked to have gone with them," Caleb said beside him.

A smile touched Jacob's lips. "Not me. Sleeping on the cold ground at night and eating cattle dust all day isn't my idea of fun. It's hard work."

Caleb sulked in his saddle. "Yeah, but the other men would respect me."

Jacob stopped. "You would think that's true, but it's not."

The young man looked puzzled but didn't argue.

"Do you want to know how to earn their respect?" Jacob pulled his horse to a stop.

Caleb nodded. His face said that he dreaded the answer.

"Work hard at what you've been asked to do. Your

job is to keep things running smoothly in the barn and any odd jobs that Sam or Lilly ask you to do. Isn't that right?" He pushed his hat back farther on his head.

"Yep." Caleb studied him, waiting.

"And Sam has given you the added chores of taking care of all the cattle that were left behind."

Caleb nodded, looking gloomy.

"Well, instead of feeling sorry for yourself, do the jobs given to you and do the best that you can do. Make sure that every head of cattle on this place is taken care of and that the barn is in tiptop shape when Sam returns. If there is anything extra you can do for the men while they are gone, do that, too. Then they will see that you are a hard worker and will start treating you like one of them." Jacob waited for Caleb's nod and then proceeded to the barn.

He worried about Caleb's silence as they rode together. Had he pushed the boy too far? Asked too much of him?

When the barn was in sight, Caleb said, "You're right. There are a lot of things I can do to help the men out."

"Such as?"

"Well, they will have to sleep on the cold hard ground, right?"

Jacob nodded.

"I suspect they'd enjoy clean sheets and a soft pillow when they get home." A grin split his lips. "And I'll clean up the bunkhouse so that it shines. Cook will appreciate that."

Jacob couldn't contain his grin. Thankfully Caleb

had taken his words to heart and planned on earning the men's respect. "Now that's the way to go about it."

Lilly called from the front porch, "Jacob, Caleb. When you get your horses taken care of come on up to the house, please."

Jacob waved to her to let her know he'd heard her.

"What do you think she wants?" Caleb asked as he slid off the back of his horse.

Jacob swung out of the saddle. "Don't know. But, she wants us both so it can't be all bad. Right?"

Caleb shrugged. "Oh, well, at least I'll get to see Miss Willow." He grinned and then started leading the horse into the barn.

He had to talk to the boy. Jacob sighed and followed. He led his horse to its stall. "Caleb, don't you think Willow is a mite too old for you?"

"How old do you think she is?" His young voice went a little off-key on the last two words.

Jacob smiled and thanked the Lord those awkward days were behind him. "I'd say she's at least five years older than you, possibly more. Plus, she has a baby. Are you ready to start a family?"

Caleb seemed to consider his words as the two of them unsaddled their horses and put them away. "No, I'd not considered the baby."

"So the age difference doesn't bother you but her having a baby does?" Jacob closed the stall door and shook his head.

"I don't think age should matter. If two people really care about each other, age isn't important," Caleb said with conviction.

Jacob laughed. "Is that right?"

"Yep, look at you and Miss Lilly. I bet she's a lot younger than you."

The laugh died. "There is nothing between Lilly and I."

"No?" Caleb wiggled his eyebrows. "You sure?"

"Of course I'm sure." Jacob frowned at the boy.

Caleb was the one to laugh this time. "If you say so." He took off at a run toward the house.

"I do say so," Jacob yelled after him.

More laughter filled the morning air.

Where did Caleb get the idea that he was interested in Lilly? Had he seen them the other night talking alone at dusk? Or even worse, had Jacob said or done something to give him cause to suspect they might enjoy each other's company?

Jacob worried that others might read too much into his and Lilly's relationship. He made a mental note to keep things between him and Lilly on the unromantic side. After all, she'd just break his heart and leave him.

Lilly met him on the front porch. "I thought you might like breakfast since the men headed out so early," she said in way of greeting.

"That's very nice of you, but we ate earlier. Cook made a batch of biscuits before they headed out."

Jacob now felt uneasy in Lilly's presence. When would the two of them ever feel anything but awkward around each other?

She giggled. "That didn't stop Caleb from accepting my offer of pancakes, bacon and hot coffee."

Jacob felt a smile tug at his lips. "No, I reckon it

didn't." He told himself that perhaps he should go inside and keep an eye on the boy. "I suppose I wouldn't mind having a cup of coffee, if you can spare it."

"Good. I have something I want to ask you." She opened the door and slipped inside.

He followed her to the kitchen, where Caleb was happily devouring a plate full of fluffy pancakes. "You should try these, Jacob. Miss Willow can sure cook."

Willow stood beside the stove with a smile on her face. "Thank you, Caleb."

Jacob pulled out a chair and sat down. His gaze moved to the clock on the sideboard and he realized there would be another Pony Express rider passing through in about an hour. Hopefully Lilly would ask her question and then he'd be able to get back to work.

Lilly walked over to the coffeepot, poured cups for herself and Jacob, then returned to the table. "Jacob, I wanted to ask you if you'd like to help me with the garden. My stepmother always cared for the garden and with Willow here to take care of Daisy, I was hoping to try my hand at raising a few vegetables."

Caleb froze in place with his fork suspended halfway to his mouth and looked from Jacob to Lilly. His eyes sparkled with laughter.

"I'll be happy to help, if I can," Jacob answered as he tried to ignore Caleb. That boy was going to embarrass them all, if he didn't hurry up and get out of there.

The next morning, Lilly chewed on the end of her pencil, struggling to remember the things to put on her list. The next few weeks, months even, would be too busy for unplanned trips to town, so her list of needed items must be thorough and complete. If she could just remember that one elusive thing. She should have written it down. She was wasting valuable time—time she could spend away from the house doing chores that had been neglected while she cared for Daisy.

Her excitement grew as she dreamed of the vegetable garden she had planned. It would be the best for miles around. She intended to get all kinds of seeds and whatever plants she could find. Why, if they planted enough, maybe Daisy could have a small vegetable stand in town one or two Saturdays.

Lilly could hardly wait to plant things near the house to make it look better. Plants. Fertilizer. Excitedly she wrote the item on her list. That's what she'd been missing. Fertilizer.

She folded the list and put it in her apron pocket, which hung by the door, then reached for the bag she'd packed earlier.

If she thought of anything else while cooking supper, she'd jot it down, but right now she had an appointment with clear blue skies and fresh air.

She met Jacob near the barn entrance and couldn't help the smile tilting up the corners of her mouth. He pulled a wagon behind him, loaded with shovels, hoes, rope and buckets. He had on a straw hat and his shirt hung open, revealing a white undershirt and suspenders. "You have plans involving dirt and sweat or something?" she teased.

Evidently, his spirit of adventure and hard work matched her own if the twinkling in those dark eyes and the lopsided grin were evidence. "Or something." His voice held a hint of questioning. "I'm not sure what the boss lady has lined up for me today, but I plan to meet the challenge."

"Are you sure I'm not taking you away from your Pony Express job?"

"Not at all. No rider expected today. I am at your service, little lady."

"Then let's hike on down to the pond." Lilly set off at a fast clip.

"Whoa! Hold on there." Jacob grabbed her arm to slow her down.

The warmth of his touch took her breath away. Or was it just the excitement of getting started. "Yes?"

"I need to know what you're planning to do so I can make sure we have all the tools we'll need. We don't want to waste time making trips back to the barn for items we can take now."

Lilly grimaced at the wait, but knew he was right. "Well, I want to uproot some of the flowering shrubs and place them in front of the porch." She knew that would put a stop to little boys climbing on the railing and jumping to the yard, like the ones last week with one of the nannies. "And I'd like to move several vines of blackberries up near the chicken coop. I know some of them will die, but if we move enough of them we should get a good crop. I like for Daisy to pick berries but don't like her being so far from the house. And her mother had such a talent for growing things."

"She did?"

Lilly heard the interest in Jacob's voice, then she remembered that Daisy and Jacob had the same mother. This was something good she could share with him. "Yes, Gertie could grow some of the finest vegetables and the flowers…oh, my, each year was better than the one before. Why, the sunflowers were over Papa's head."

His voice sounded thoughtful. "Maybe that's why I love growing things. I could have inherited it from her."

"You love planting?" Lilly didn't know a man around who enjoyed planting as much as she did. This was something else she could admire about Jacob Young.

"I always had a garden back in Wyoming. We had so many mouths to feed and money was scarce at times. There's nothing quite like planting a seed and watching it triple in yield."

"Like the story in the Bible about sowing one bad thing but reaping many sorrows," Lilly said, shrugging. "Or something to that effect."

One thing she truly was sorry about was the lack of spiritual training she'd had. Her dad had read the Bible often, just not to her, and Gertie had cared more for dime novels than she had the Bible. Occasionally Lilly and Daisy attended the church in Orange Grove and that's where she'd heard an inspiring sermon on reaping what you sowed.

"Anyway, it went something like that. I really should read the Bible more." Embarrassed, she looked back to the wagon full of tools, hoping he'd get them back on the subject at hand.

Jacob looked at her funny and she felt crimson creep

up into her cheeks. "Lilly, would you like to know more about the stories in the Bible?"

She quirked an eyebrow at him, uncertain of his meaning. He lifted the wagon handle and headed to the path behind the house. She fell in beside him, surprised at how excited she was for his explanation.

"I mean…" He paused, pointing to briar extending into the path.

She stepped over it, careful it didn't snag on the big-legged pants she wore.

"I could read chapters from the Bible each night before bedtime. It's important that a house be built on God's word. I learned that lesson a few months ago from my stepfather."

Lilly's heart leaped into her throat. How she had longed to have a spiritual home. One that provided happiness, a safe haven, wisdom and faith. She had read several of the Psalms to Daisy, but she had no clue how to interpret the scriptures. If Jacob could do that one of her greatest desires would have been met. "I would love that, Jacob. When can we start?"

"Well, if you don't kill me today," he teased, "we could start tonight."

They studied the shrubs along the trail and chose four smaller ones of more manageable size. Jacob dug around the roots of one, while Lilly tackled the other. After about an hour, they found a spot looking out over the lake and settled down for a rest under a wide-branched fir tree. Lilly reached into the bag she'd packed and removed a jar of cold milk and two slices of raisin bread. She had dried the fruit last year and this had been the last of it. She poured milk into the cup that closed the jar, then handed the jar to Jacob.

He accepted the milk and bread eagerly. "Do you have a picture in your mind of how you want the yard to look or where you want the plants placed?"

Lilly closed her eyes and pictured the yard. "I want the shrubs in front of the porch so when they bloom it will add a bit of color to the house. The honeysuckle vines I'd like to plant near the clothesline. The smell will waft all over the yard from that location." She opened her eyes and continued. "When I put bluing in the clothes you can smell it at the barn, the bunkhouse and inside the house."

His gaze was locked on her. "You don't ever wish you had someone to do the wash, or to clean the house and do the cooking?"

Lilly thought about that a moment and suddenly realized that Gertie had done her a great favor by making her work around the ranch. "No. I like taking care of the ranch and my family. Your mother taught me well. I realize now that she gave me the best gift she could by showing me what work meant and how to accomplish by myself the things I wanted done."

His heartfelt chuckle washed over her like warm honey over hot biscuits. Then he said, "You sound surprised."

In a way she was surprised. During Gertie's reign nothing seemed right or good. "Well, when Gertie was handing out chores, I wasn't seeing the possibilities like I am now. I thought she was being ugly to me."

His voice lowered and he asked, "And was she?"

Lilly studied Jacob's lowered profile a moment before she answered. "I don't want to hurt you, Jacob, but Gertrude wasn't very pleasant to me when Papa wasn't around. She wasn't a very nice person." She stayed silent a moment, but the silence was tense and Lilly couldn't stand to think she had hurt him. "Please don't be upset with me."

He turned to her the expression on his face one of perfect peace. "Lilly, my mother left me on the steps of an orphanage. I've learned myself that I could never do that no matter the circumstances. I held out hope that there was a unique reason for it, but in my travels the stories I've garnered from place to place enlightened me as to just what type of woman she was."

They sat quietly for a moment, each lost in their own thoughts. When next Lilly glanced his way, she found him in a deep sleep, his hat sideways and his chin resting on his chest. She studied him at leisure, noting the strong jaw, relaxed in sleep, and the thick hair that swept over his brow. She knew the broad shoulders had taken a lot of the burden from her own and it felt wonderful to have someone to share the responsibilities of raising Daisy.

But could she really trust him if he meant to take her ranch? She worried her bottom lip with her teeth. Today had been perfect so she chose not to clutter it up with negative thoughts. Instead she quietly stood and stepped behind the tree he propped against.

Taking a piece of grass, she drew it along the exposed part of his neck. He grunted but didn't wake. She ran it around his ear and he swatted at it but slept right on. She could barely squelch the giggles threatening to erupt. She twitched his nose and a hand snaked out faster than she could move and yanked her from behind the tree into his lap. She squealed and rolled to her feet then took off running around the side of the lake.

Lilly heard him one step behind her and then he grabbed her around the waist, lifting her high off the ground, swinging her around and around. They both collapsed onto the ground, out of breath, laughing, his hand holding hers.

Once he'd caught his breath, Jacob teased, "That will teach you not to bother a man while he's resting from a hard day's work."

"Oh, I could have done a lot worse. I entertained some mighty unusual ideas to wake you up." Immediately Lilly realized how that sounded and her face burned in shame. Jacob was having none of it. He threw back his head and laughed heartily as he pulled her to her feet.

"I wouldn't mind being awakened by a pretty girl with a soft kiss, but if I'm a judging you right, you were thinking more along the lines of dousing me with a bucket of cold water, right?"

Lilly clamped her teeth over her bottom lip, refusing to admit he was right on target. Her expression gave her away and he caught her in a quick hug. She looked deep into his brown eyes and for a moment wished he'd kiss her. It would be nice to have a real first kiss. Realizing where her thoughts were going, Lilly pulled away. "We have a lot more work to do." She stood and walked back to their resting spot. She picked up the bag, repacked it and wished he would have kissed her instead of offering a friendly hug.

After a couple of hours of hard work, they headed back to the house. The wagon was loaded with shrubs, blackberry vines and three honeysuckle vines. They were hot, sweaty and in high spirits.

They pulled the wagon close to the porch and sat side by side on the steps. The screen door squeaked and Willow joined them on the porch. She handed a glass over Lilly's shoulder. Lilly sighed as her hand wrapped around the cool tumbler. She gulped at the cool liquid. Ahhh, blackberry tea.

"This hits the spot," Jacob said.

"Thank you, Willow. A cool drink was just what we needed." Lilly sniffed the air. "What's that wonderful smell?"

Willow sat on the other side of Jacob and extended a plate toward them. "Corn fritters."

Lilly took one then reached for another just as Jacob picked up two. She smacked at his hand. "That one was mine."

"Not so. I'm bigger then you and need more food." He pulled his hand back with a laugh as she tried to take the second one from him.

"Children, children. There's enough for everyone," Willow proclaimed but the glimmer in her eyes proved she, too, enjoyed the camaraderie. "We never had much stock in our kitchen, so I've not had much practice creating different recipes, but Walter always loved my corn fritters."

"I can understand why. These are delicious." Jacob crammed the last bite in his mouth then spoke around it. "Walter was a lucky man."

"Willow, do you like to cook?" Lilly hadn't asked before. She had been intent only in finding a nanny for Daisy.

"I love to cook, bake and garden. My specialty is sugar cookies." She set the plate on the porch floor behind her. "I hope you'll let me share kitchen duties, Lilly. I want to earn my keep but that kitchen of yours keeps calling me, tempting me to try new dishes. I even love to clean up in there. Walter and I lived in one room and the woodstove was my only means of cooking. Mostly beans and cornpone. Occasionally he'd kill a squirrel or rabbit and then I'd make gravy."

"You're making my stomach growl," Jacob said, patting his stomach. Willow grinned. "Nothing like a good pan of squirrel gravy."

Lilly felt an overwhelming sense of rightness. This was the type of fellowship she'd longed for all her life. Just this simple talking back and forth, no underlying messages, no fake pretensions and suddenly all the lonely places in her heart held no shadows.

Only the shadow of fear for Daisy remained. She squared her shoulders. She would fight for her family, for this peace, for happiness for those she cared for.

Realizing it had gotten quiet, Lilly declared, "Willow, you are more than welcome to create to your heart's content. I made a list of needed supplies and it's in my apron pocket by the back door. Feel free to add to it anything you wish." She stood and brushed crumbs from her pants leg, noticing the dirt and grime clinging to the fabric and on the sides of her boots. "Mr. Jacob, as Daisy calls you, I think it's time we got back to work." She looked around. "Speaking of Daisy, where is she?"

Daisy chose that moment to join them, a pencil in her mouth, her face scrunched up in a frown. "Miss Willow, is this right?"

"It sure is. You are doing a good job," Willow answered. She hugged Daisy around the waist.

Lilly stared in awe at the paper Daisy handed Willow. Daisy had printed her name several times on the page. The letters were uneven and outside the lines Willow had drawn, but the writing was clearly legible.

"You did this, Daisy?" Jacob took the paper from Willow so he and Lilly could see it clearly.

"Mmm-hmm."

"It's a very good job, Daisy," Lilly remarked, watching Daisy blossom with their praise.

"She's an eager student. Until I learn my way around the ranch, I needed ways to occupy her in the house. Come to find out, she loves writing so we're starting on her letters. Lilly, do you think we could add a pack of colors to the market list? I wouldn't mind seeing what she can do with pictures."

Lilly felt both excited and sad. She'd planned on working with Daisy in the winter months after she turned five, but this was good, too. Her little sister was growing up. "I think that's a wonderful idea, Willow."

"Will you teach me words in the book Lilly reads to me at night?" Daisy leaned against Willow's shoulder, obviously comfortable with the woman. Lilly saw that Jacob noticed, too.

He stood, then stepped over to the wagon and removed a shovel. Willow followed Daisy into the house, their happy chatter pleasant to Lilly's ears.

"I never would've thought it would take half the day to uproot a few shrubs and dig up a couple of vines. What in the world took you so long?" Caleb stood with his hands on his hips, staring at them as if he wanted to thrash them.

Lilly felt pure laughter build up in her chest. She clapped a hand over her mouth, but one look at Jacob and she could hold it no longer. She laughed, bending over and clasping her legs. Jacob laughed loudly and grabbed Caleb around the shoulders.

"Were you worried about us, Caleb?"

Caleb shrugged out of Jacob's hands. "Why, yes, I was. I couldn't leave the ladies here by themselves to go and look for you. How was I to know you weren't broken and bleeding somewhere?"

Lilly sobered instantly. "Oh, Caleb. I hadn't thought of that. We're sorry."

Jacob looked between Lilly and Caleb. "I guess we'll need to work out a signal every hour or so to let those here at the house know we're doing good, at least till we feel there's no more need for caution."

Lilly saw the tenseness leave Caleb's shoulders. The young man cared for them. Willow cared for them. This was what love looked and felt like. She finally had family again.

Her gaze moved to Jacob. Would he consider himself

a part of her family? Did she see Jacob that way, too? He was Daisy's brother. Lilly tried to convince herself that was what she felt for him, nothing more.

Chapter Fifteen

Jacob felt his presence before he actually saw and heard Sam. He continued to comb the Pony Express horse and waited. The men had been home a couple of days and Jacob had expected this visit much sooner.

"You didn't waste any time moving into the house, did you?" Sam sat atop his horse and looked down on Jacob. Jacob didn't have to look at the other man's face to know he was scowling.

Jacob grinned to himself and then asked, "Are you asking me if I've moved into the house? Or is that just your way of trying to figure out what happened while you were away?" He ran the comb over the silky coat and waited.

"You know what I mean. Caleb tells me you took all your meals in the house and that you now spend your evenings with Lilly and Daisy." Sam shifted in the saddle.

Jacob released the horse and allowed it to return to the others. He turned to face Sam. "I take it you don't approve." He could have reminded Sam that Caleb had been with them but decided not to involve the boy.

"No, I don't." His words came out hard. Just as Jacob suspected, Sam glowered with anger.

Jacob folded his arms over his chest and said, "You know, that might bother me if you were my boss, but since you aren't, it doesn't."

Sam spit on the ground, narrowly missing Jacob's boot. "All it will take is a few words from me and Lilly will send you packing."

His thoughts ran over the past week and the closeness he and Lilly had shared. She actually seemed to care about him. "I don't think so," Jacob responded.

The thought that Sam might come between their newfound feelings sent heat waves through his gut and into his face. He kept his anger in check, knowing that Sam was just looking for a reason to get in a fight with him and then report back to Lilly.

Sam laughed without humor. "Mighty sure of yourself, aren't you?"

Jacob wasn't going to play this game any longer. "I know that Lilly and I understand one another. You can say anything you want, what have you got to lose?"

"It's more like what do you have to lose. As soon as she realizes that this ranch is what you're after, she'll send you packing faster than a miner after gold." Sam sat up straight. "I'll make sure of that."

Jacob watched the older man with narrowed eyes. Sam appeared smug, certain that Lilly would do anything he told her to. How many times had she fired men based on Sam's word?

An evil grin twisted Sam's face and he turned his horse to leave.

As Jacob climbed into the saddle he remembered something his stepfather had told him. "When a man accuses another man of something, usually it's because that's exactly what he wants to do or has done." Did Sam want Lilly's ranch? Was the older man worried that Lilly might find Jacob attractive? Or see him as a future husband?

He followed Sam back, allowing the man a good lead. Sam rode his horse to the barn and called for Caleb. Jacob watched as he tossed the reins to the young man and then stomped off to the bunkhouse. Not only was the man arrogant, but he was also rude.

Jacob shook his head. He dismounted and walked his horse into the barn. His gaze sought out Caleb. The boy was tending to Sam's horse with a frown.

"What's the sour face for?" Jacob asked.

Caleb looked over the horse's back. "You wouldn't understand," he answered.

Gone was the carefree young man that had allowed himself to relax while the other men were gone. "Try me." Jacob busied himself taking the saddle and bridle off his horse.

Caleb carried Sam's saddle to the tack room. When he returned he said, "No matter what I do, Sam doesn't like me." He sighed. "Now I just sound childish." Caleb led the stallion farther into the barn to stable him.

When he returned, Jacob said, "Honestly, I don't think Sam likes anyone. I wouldn't let it bother me."

"That's because he's not your boss and he can't fire

you." Caleb scooped fresh grain into a feed bucket and disappeared down the hall again.

Jacob waited for his return then asked, "Have you thought about becoming a Pony Express rider?"

Caleb grabbed a pitchfork and began mucking out a stall. "I thought about it, but it's too dangerous. I want to be a farmer, not a rider."

"What kind of farmer?" Jacob thought about all the time he'd spent with Lilly lately, working in her yard and vegetable garden. Growing things came naturally to him. Spending time with Lilly and Daisy made it even more enjoyable.

When she'd said a small garden, that's what he'd expected—a small plot—but she'd gone all out. He'd plowed rows and rows of dirt. Planted seeds and watered until he'd fallen into bed exhausted. But at least they wouldn't starve this winter, that was for sure.

Caleb grinned. "You'll laugh."

"Maybe," Jacob admitted.

The boy leaned on the pitchfork. "A pig farmer." He looked off into the distance. "I like pigs and think I could make lots of money raising them."

"You might have something there," Jacob said seriously. "Would you rather take care of pigs or these horses?"

Caleb laughed and began his work again. "Pigs. But what I want doesn't matter. Sam says I'm a stable boy so I'm a stable boy."

Jacob knew Asher wasn't a fan of the pigs he had to feed every day. He didn't say anything to Caleb but decided to mention to Lilly that the boy would like to work with the pigs. Was there enough of a job for Caleb to work solely with the swine? He'd ask.

The dinner bell clanged at the house. Jacob smiled at Caleb. "Time to eat. Ready?"

Caleb shook his head sadly. "I've been reminded I'm the hired help and will be taking all my meals with the other men from now on." He continued mucking out the stall.

Jacob was sure he knew where the reminder had come from. "I see. I'm sorry to hear that."

Sadness filled Caleb's voice. "Me, too. I'm going to miss the ladies' cooking."

The triangle sounded again. "Well, I better go or she's going to come get me." Jacob turned to leave.

"Nothing was said about you slipping me some dessert later," Caleb called behind him.

Jacob laughed. "You got it."

He hurried from the barn and headed to the washbasin beside the back door. The smell of fried chicken drifted in the air. Jacob glanced toward the bunkhouse as he opened the kitchen door. Sam stood watching him. Jacob knew he shouldn't do it, but he smiled broadly and waved at the older man before entering the house.

"You really shouldn't infuriate him." Lilly stood at the table. The window on the opposite side faced the bunkhouse. She watched Sam out the window. "He came by to see me today."

Willow tried to hide her smile as she helped Daisy into her chair. She got the girl seated and then began filling her plate with a chicken leg, mashed potatoes topped with a generous glob of butter and a large spoon-ful of green beans.

Daisy scrunched up her nose. "I don't like green beans."

"They are good for you," Willow answered.

Jacob answered Lilly. "I had a talk with him this af-ternoon also."

Lilly nodded. "Maybe after Daisy's story you can tell me all about it." She indicated that he should take his place at the table.

"Where's Caleb?" Daisy asked, looking toward the back door as if she thought her friend would enter at any moment.

"He's having dinner in the bunkhouse tonight," Jacob answered, pulling his chair close to the table.

Lilly was the last to be seated. A frown marred her pretty features. She said a quick blessing over the meal and then began dishing food onto her plate.

"Daisy, eat the green beans first that way you can eat the good stuff last." Jacob made a show of getting a big spoonful of green beans and taking a big bite of them. They were very good. Seasoned with bacon and salt, just the way he liked them.

Daisy followed his example. Only instead of enjoy-ing the beans she made the worst face he'd ever seen on the little girl.

"See, they aren't so bad," Jacob said then turned his head away to hide his smile.

"I think we should give them to the pigs," Daisy said as soon as she swallowed.

Jacob laughed. "Speaking of pigs, did you know that

Caleb plans on being a pig farmer someday?" He directed his question to Lilly.

She shook her head. "No, if he likes the pigs why isn't he taking care of them instead of Asher?"

He shrugged. "I don't know but he'd be very good with them and I know Asher isn't a fan of the pigs."

"They smell bad," Daisy said, sniffing at her beans.

"The beans or the pigs?" Willow asked, frowning at the girl.

Daisy curled her lip. "Both."

"Eat your beans, Daisy," Lilly ordered. "What do you think? Should I have Sam change the two men's jobs?"

Jacob picked up a biscuit and buttered it. "What else does Asher do?"

"He takes care of the pigs, chickens and the milk cows." Lilly motioned for Daisy to take another bite of the green beans.

"Almost done with them, Daisy," Willow said encouragingly as she took a bite of her potatoes.

Over the last week, Lilly had grown to value Willow. She seemed to know just what Daisy needed and when. Daisy liked Willow and often times Lilly would find them playing tea party in Daisy's room.

Jacob caught her attention. "I would want my men to be happy in their jobs. Caleb takes care of the horses and barn, but I don't think he's very happy. Asher doesn't seem to enjoy feeding the pigs, either. Maybe you could let them trade places for a few days and then see if they like the new work or if they want to go back to their old jobs," he offered.

Lilly nodded. "I agree."

"It will also give Caleb the chance to discover if pigs are really what he wants to raise." Jacob used his biscuit to get the remainder of his butter off the plate.

Willow grinned across the table. She covertly indicated that Lilly should look at Daisy's plate. "I'm about ready for dessert."

Lilly glanced at her sister's plate. Daisy had finished off her green beans and most of her other food. "Daisy, you ate all your beans. Good girl."

Daisy smiled. "Can I help Caleb with the pigs, Lilly?"

"No, they are too far away from the house," Lilly answered as she pushed back her chair and walked to the sideboard, where a large carrot cake, compliments of Willow's cooking skills, sat waiting to be sliced.

"Since I can't help Caleb, when can I play in my fort?" Daisy asked with a pout. She realized dessert was about to be served and shoved the rest of her potatoes into her small mouth.

"The fort?" Willow asked.

Lilly smiled. "That's what she calls the area under the rosebush. I haven't let her play out there in a while."

Daisy swallowed with a gulping sound. "Please, Lilly."

"If Willow wants to go out there with you, I'm okay with you going."

"Yay! We can take our tea party out there," Daisy said, looking at Willow with a wide smile.

"Sounds like fun." Willow pushed back her chair. "I'll get us fresh coffee."

As Lilly passed out the cake, Willow refilled the coffee cups. Daisy picked up her fork. "Can I have some more milk?" she asked.

Was it her imagination or did Jacob seem more reserved? Lilly handed him his dessert. "I hope you like carrot cake." She smiled. "Willow and Daisy made it."

Jacob returned her smile. "Then I know I'll love it."

"I got to put the icing on." Daisy licked a big glob of icing from her fork.

Lilly sat back down. She watched Jacob take a bite of the cake. His face lit up with pleasure.

"You ladies are wonderful cooks," Jacob proclaimed. He winked at Daisy. "This icing is so rich."

Lilly listened as Daisy and Jacob chatted. The little girl told him about the new rag doll that Willow made for her. She also shared that they had another tea party today.

As soon as Daisy's cake was all gone, Willow said, "All right, Daisy. Let's go put on your nightgown so Jacob can read you a story."

Daisy jumped from her chair. "I want to hear the story about those men that had to go sleep in the lion's house again," she said, hurrying out of the room.

"She's talked about that one all day." Willow grinned as she left the room.

Lilly collected the dinner plates. She wasn't surprised when Jacob gathered the cups and Daisy's glass. "Why didn't Caleb come to dinner?" she asked.

A hardness filled his voice. "Sam told him that he has to have his meals with the other men."

Lilly filled the washtub with hot water from the back of the stove. She shaved soap off the bar and swished the water around before adding the dirty dishes. Sam couldn't tell the men where and when to eat. She'd have to speak to him about that. "You don't like Sam much, do you?"

Jacob stopped scraping food into the slop bucket. His brown gaze met hers. "I don't like him at all."

"Why not?" She washed the cups and set them in the rinse water.

Jacob set down the bowl he'd just emptied and picked up a tea towel. "He's arrogant, rude and a bully."

Lilly pursed her lips together to avoid smiling. When she'd gotten control of her facial muscles she said, "Thanks for being so honest."

He dried a mug and set it to the side. "Look, I know he's your foreman and I really don't have much to do with him. But, today he came out to the Pony Express pasture and gave me a warning."

"I see." She continued washing the dishes. "What kind of warning?"

"Well, first off he let it be known that he didn't like me coming to the house for my meals. Then he insinuated that I am after your ranch." Jacob picked up a plate and began drying it.

Lilly knew Sam was protective of her and Daisy. Maybe if she explained to Jacob how Sam had sort of stepped into her father's boots, he'd understand. She took a deep breath. "Sam has been on this ranch for as long as I can remember. Since Papa's death, he's made sure that suitors and cowboys passing through didn't get any ideas about marrying me and taking over the ranch. Maybe he was just offering a warning, not a threat."

He nodded. "Perhaps."

She smiled. "Remember I told you he'd come by to see me, too?" Lilly waited for him to nod again. "He wanted to warn me not to get to close to you. Sam seems to think that you are after the ranch, but I set him straight."

"Oh, how did you do that?" Jacob asked.

Lilly heard her uncertainty in her voice. "I told him we have talked about that and that you have assured me you are going to buy your own ranch or farm." She focused on the dishes instead of looking at him.

She'd enjoyed their time together over the last several weeks and couldn't seem to forget the warmth of his hug. But, thanks to Sam, once more she felt leery of his motives.

Jacob was a good man and a hard worker. But, Sam's words that Jacob might be putting on a front had her gut twisted tighter than the strings on a turkey's legs right before roasting time. How many times had she asked herself if Jacob was too good to be true?

Chapter Sixteen

Jacob heard the note of hesitation in Lilly's voice and wondered if she was still concerned that he wanted her ranch. He simply said, "I'm glad. How did he take that bit of news?"

She laughed nervously. "He said 'time will tell.'"

Jacob decided he'd take a trip into town in the morning and see if there were any farms or ranches for sale in the area. The sooner he bought his own place, the sooner she could take her mind off him stealing her ranch. "Sam's right about that." Jacob dried the last dish just as Daisy came running into the kitchen.

Willow had braided the little girl's hair. It bounced behind her like a small rabbit. "I'm ready, Mr. Jacob."

Jacob put down his towel and grinned. "So am I."

Willow handed him the Bible and smiled. She had the baby in the crook of her arm. "I thought Gabe might like to hear the story, too. If that's all right?"

He would have liked for it to have just been him and

Daisy, but Jacob wasn't about to stop Willow from listening to God's word. "Of course he can listen."

"I want to hear about the lions again." Daisy climbed into his lap.

Jacob inhaled the little girl's fragrance. "You smell like vanilla," he said, tickling her.

She giggled. "That's cause I put some behind my ear this afternoon."

"You put icing behind your ear?" Lilly asked. She leaned down and looked behind Daisy's ear.

"Uh-huh," Daisy answered.

Jacob felt Lilly's hair brush his cheek as she sniffed at Daisy. It felt as velvety soft as it looked. The impulse to reach out and touch the silky strands almost overpowered him. Thankfully, Lilly stood up.

Willow shook her head. "You keep putting sweet stuff behind your ears and the ants are going to crawl in bed with you and gobble you up." She smiled to take the sting from her words.

Jacob positioned Daisy on his knee and then opened the Bible to the book of Daniel. He read the story of Daniel in the lion's den. As he read, Jacob roared like the lions and shouted for joy when the king saw that the lions' mouths were closed. He enjoyed reading to them all and ended with a smile.

At the end of the story, Willow announced it was bedtime. She tucked Gabe close to her and waited for Daisy to say good-night to Jacob and Lilly.

Daisy hugged Jacob and whispered in his ear, "I love you, Mr. Jacob." Then she scurried from his knee, hugged Lilly good-night and ran out of the room.

Willow followed, carrying a sleeping Gabe.

Those were the sweetest words Jacob had ever heard. He stood. "Thank you for the meal, Lilly. Would you mind if I took a slice of cake to Caleb? I'm sure the boy would enjoy it as much as I did." His intention was to leave as quickly as possible and savor the joy Daisy's words had given him.

Lilly put two large slices of cake onto a plate and handed it to him. "Here you go. I thought you might like the second slice."

Jacob took the plate and planted a quick kiss on Lilly's cheek. Then he hurried from the room before she recovered from the shock of his actions. The cool evening air hit his cheeks and he laughed. He'd been wanting to kiss her for several days now. That wasn't the sweet kiss he'd thought about but it had been fun to see her reaction to his lips on her cheek.

Caleb waited in the barn. "Did you remember to bring me dessert?" he asked, eyeballing the plate in Jacob's hand.

"Sure did. Carrot cake." Jacob walked to his room. "Let's eat it in here."

Caleb laughed. "I'm glad you remembered my cake but you forgot your hat." He followed so close that Jacob feared the boy would step on the heels of his boots.

Jacob pulled a plate from his cupboard and dished up the larger piece of cake onto it. Then he pulled a fork from the crock and handed both to Caleb. "Here, eat this. I'll go back for my hat."

He didn't have to tell Caleb twice. The boy had already slid into the chair beside the bed and begun eating.

Just before he left the room, Jacob ordered, "Don't eat that second piece, that's my breakfast."

Caleb nodded and kept chewing happily.

If he wasn't heading to town early in the morning, Jacob would have been tempted to leave the hat and get it at breakfast. His heart felt light as he thought about his plans. He'd been thinking a lot over the last week about women, mostly about his own mother, and had decided he couldn't judge all women based on her.

Lilly was a sweet woman. She'd laughed and teased with him. It felt good. Almost like they were a family.

He heard her voice as he walked up to the back door. Jacob decided to just listen to the sound for a moment before entering. Leaning against the door frame he listened. He had to admit Lilly's voice soothed him. Jacob knew he was beginning to care for Lilly but told himself he was in control and wouldn't allow her into his heart.

"How about a cup of tea?" Lilly offered Willow, dropping her hand from her cheek.

"I'd love a cup." She slipped into one of the kitchen chairs. "So what's with you and Jacob?"

Lilly laughed nervously, wondering if Willow had seen Jacob kiss her before he'd left. "What do you mean?"

Willow's eyes shone with pleasure. "You know what I mean. You two seem pretty friendly and he's the only ranch hand that is allowed to have meals at the house. Now why is that?" She steepled her fingers and raised an eyebrow.

Lilly waved the question away. "Oh, it's not what you

think." She carried both cups of tea to the table. Lilly pulled out a chair and joined Willow. "I guess I should tell you, especially since you are taking care of Daisy." Maybe she should wait until breakfast when Jacob would be there, too. But if she did wait, then Daisy would be there and they didn't want to tell the little girl yet.

"Tell me what?" Concern filled the widow's voice.

Lilly made the decision to tell the nanny everything. "You have to promise not to tell anyone. Daisy doesn't even know what I'm about to tell you." She searched the other woman's face.

"Of course I'm not going to say anything. Would you stop being so dramatic and just tell me already." The irritation in Willow's voice came through loud and clear.

Lilly decided it would be best to tell her now. "Jacob is Daisy's brother."

Willow gasped. "So Jacob is your brother, too?"

Lilly shook her head. She didn't think of Jacob as a brother. "Oh, no. I should have said he's Daisy's half brother. Daisy and I share the same father and Jacob and Daisy share the same mother."

Willow dropped her voice. "So why is this a secret?"

Lilly sighed, really wishing Jacob was there to help her explain what happened and why they felt the need for secrecy. "A couple of weeks ago, someone took Daisy from her bedroom in the early morning hours, while she was sleeping, and left her in a ravine. Jacob saved her from the cattle that were stampeding through the gorge."

Willow's gasp filled the kitchen. "Someone is trying to hurt Daisy?"

"It would seem so but no further attempts have been made." Lilly was thankful for that. She sipped at her warm tea.

Willow stared at her. "I'm still confused. How did Jacob know where she was and how come you didn't take whoever took her to the sheriff?" She ran her hands through her hair, looking perplexed.

"Jacob was at that very moment on his way to the ranch to work as the Pony Express stock tender. He hadn't arrived yet and he didn't even know that Daisy was his sister at the time. He just saw her and saved her from the cattle. We didn't see anyone else there so that's why we haven't said anything to the sheriff. Oh, and it wasn't until later that we discovered they are related." Lilly felt as if she'd made a shambles out of her explanation. It was no wonder that Willow looked like someone who'd just suffered a tragic moment in their life.

Willow ran her hand over her face. She looked at Lilly with concern in her eyes. "And you don't want anyone to know because if they figure out that Jacob is her brother they might do something to hurt him, too, and then have the freedom to get to her again with him out of the picture." Willow sighed. "That's a tough one." She started to take a drink of her tea but lowered the cup instead.

Lilly could tell the woman was working out the details in her mind. She waited and listened.

"And if you tell Daisy, she'll probably tell everyone and put herself or him or both of them in further danger." Willow took a drink.

Lilly nodded. "Right, she's such a talker and likes

Jacob so much she'll let it slip even if we tell her to keep it a secret."

Willow nodded. "Yes, I'm afraid she would."

The two women sat in silence for a few minutes. Lilly knew she had to ask. "So, now that you know that someone has tried to hurt Daisy, do you want to quit watching her?"

Willow shook her head. She looked insulted when she asked, "Why in the world would I want to quit? Me being here might keep her safe."

"Thank you, Willow. I was just worried you'd be afraid and want to quit. I realize now we should have told you earlier." Lilly felt tears fill her eyes. It felt good to talk to another woman about what had been weighing so heavily on her shoulders.

Willow reached across the table and took her hand. "No, I'll protect that little girl with my own life if I have to. No child should ever be threatened like that." She patted Lilly's hand. After a moment she continued, "I'm surprised Daisy hasn't told me."

Lilly tried to smile instead of cry. "I don't think she understands what happened. She was asleep and didn't wake up until the cows woke her up."

"I have noticed that she's a heavy sleeper." Willow released Lilly's hand and carried her empty cup to the washbasin.

"That she is," Lilly agreed.

Willow turned with a teasing grin. "But that still doesn't answer my question."

Lilly scrunched her face much like she'd seen Daisy do when trying to remember what the original question was. Hadn't she answered all of Willow's questions? Her brow furrowed.

Willow laughed. "What's with you and Jacob?"

"Nothing." She raised her hand and touched the spot where his warm lips had met her cool skin.

"You sure?" Willow asked, crossing her arms and leaning her hip against the sideboard.

Lilly got up and carried her empty teacup to the basin. "Of course I'm sure. Jacob is a nice man who works hard. He's here at the house because of Daisy. Nothing more is going on. Jacob is Daisy's brother. He's nothing to me." Lilly hated that she'd just repeated herself, as if she had something to hide.

Chapter Seventeen

The next morning, Lilly's words still cut through Jacob like a sharp westerly wind. He didn't feel much like riding to town and decided instead to eat the slice of cake for breakfast and go take care of the horses in the small pasture.

He watered the horses and fed them fresh grain. His supplies should be arriving any day. Jacob's mind ran over the conversation he'd overheard the night before. He shouldn't have been eavesdropping, but now that he knew how Lilly really felt about him, Jacob told himself he'd not lower the guard around his heart.

Halfway through the morning, Caleb arrived. He dismounted, tied his horse to the fence and then hurried to meet Jacob in the pasture. Jacob had been checking the horses' hooves, making sure they were still in good condition. "Jacob! Guess what happened this morning?"

Jacob had forgotten that Lilly had said she was going to exchange Caleb and Asher's duties. He grinned. "You fell out of bed and bumped your head. Why else would you come yelling into a corral with half-wild horses?"

Caleb shook his head. "No, that's not it." He eyed the closest horses. "Miss Lilly came to the barn and told me to get Asher and Sam and come to the house. When we got there she told us that Asher and I were going to exchange duties."

"Really?" Jacob released the horse he'd been working on and let it return to the rest of the herd.

"Yep, she said that if I like taking care of the pigs, chickens and cows, I can keep the job." Caleb puffed out his chest.

"How does Asher feel about the arrangement?" Jacob asked, walking to the gate.

Caleb followed. "He's as pleased as I am." The grin on Caleb's face grew wider, if that was possible.

"And Sam?" Jacob held the gate open for Caleb to pass through.

The young man sobered. "He wasn't happy at all. For one thing he didn't appreciate being summoned up to the house with Asher and me. After Miss Lilly told us the news, we were dismissed. On our way out, Daisy stopped me just outside the door and I heard Sam talking to Lilly."

Jacob realized that Caleb had done just as he had the night before and eavesdropped on Lilly and Sam. Neither of them should have done that. He wanted to hear what the foreman had to say but didn't want to ask. "I imagine he wasn't very happy."

"Nope, he told her that she'd been giving you more and more of his job and asked her if she thought she could run the ranch without him." Caleb shook his head. "I have to admit, Miss Lilly didn't take kindly to that line of questioning."

"I'm sure she didn't." Jacob walked over to where he'd tied off his horse that morning.

Caleb followed. "Nope. Miss Lilly told him she didn't want to find out, but she was still the owner of the ranch and could move the men around as she pleased." He sighed. "And then she told him that she valued him as a family friend and didn't want to lose him."

Jacob led his horse to the trough. "So that must have made him happy."

The boy shrugged. "I suppose so. Daisy asked about the kittens and I told her that if Lilly didn't mind, I'd show them to her later. When she ran in to ask, I left."

"It sounds like she worked it all out." Jacob stretched his back.

"Well, I haven't got to tell you the best part yet."

Jacob laughed. "There's more?"

"Yep, guess who mine and Asher's new boss is?"

He sobered. "It's not Sam?"

Caleb rocked back on his heels. "Nope."

An uneasy feeling settled in Jacob's stomach. "Then who is?"

The boy laughed happily. "You are."

That explained why Sam felt Jacob was taking over more of his job. "But why?"

"Miss Lilly said it was your idea to move us and thought since you are always close to the house and Sam is usually out in a pasture or attending to business in town, that it was the perfect solution." He walked to his horse.

Jacob really wished Lilly had talked to him about all this before appointing him boss over her ranch hands. He pulled himself up on his horse and rode up beside Caleb. "Has Asher said how many cattle and pigs you'll be taking care of?" he asked, aware he had no idea what Lilly owned as far as livestock was concerned.

Caleb straightened in the saddle. "After I got back to the barn, I spent about an hour with Asher. He says that right now we have about a hundred cattle on the ranch. Sam took most of the herd to market." He rubbed his chin. "Since you're my boss, I need to tell you that Asher thinks about fifty head of cows are missing. They've been missing since before the cattle drive."

Jacob frowned. "Does Sam know they are missing?"

The young man looked at him. Worry filled his eyes. "Asher didn't tell him. He was afraid Sam would fire him for losing them. You aren't going to fire him for losing them, are you?" Caleb asked.

Maybe Sam already knew that the cattle were missing. Didn't he keep up with the livestock? Or did he just take it for granted that Asher wouldn't lose them? Even though Jacob didn't know Sam well, he felt like he knew the man well enough to know that Sam knew everything that took place on the ranch.

He realized Caleb was staring at him. "No, I'm not going to fire him, but I would like to talk to both of you when we get back to the barn."

"That's what I told Asher you'd say." Caleb's happy grin was back in place.

Asher met them in the yard when they got back to the barn. He grinned. "Hello, boss."

Jacob swung down from the saddle. "Asher."

Caleb and Asher followed Jacob into the barn. Jacob tied his horse to one of the stall doors and motioned for the two young men to follow him to his room. He held the door open for them to enter and then told them to sit down.

Caleb took the chair and Asher sat down on the edge of the bed. Asher looked about the room with interest. "Nice place you have here," he said, still smiling as if it was his birthday.

"Thanks." Jacob shut the door. He decided to treat the men like he would his younger brothers.

Although if truth be told, Jacob had a feeling that Asher might be older than himself. It was in the way the man acted. He let on that he was younger but there were signs in his facial expressions that said he had wisdom, and wisdom usually came with age.

Jacob pushed those thoughts away and crossed his arms over his chest and focused on Asher. "Caleb tells me that you have several head of cattle missing."

Asher's Adam's apple bobbed. "Yes, sir."

Jacob shook his head. "Don't call me 'sir.' I'm not angry, I just want to get to the bottom of this. When did you notice them missing?"

Asher nodded his understanding. "A few days before the cattle drive."

"Did you tell Sam?"

He shook his head. "No, not this time."

This time? Jacob stood a little taller. "This has happened before?"

"Yep."

Jacob didn't like getting one-word answers. "Look, Asher, I'm not angry with you. I just need to find out what has happened in the past. We're both at new jobs. I'll help you with yours but you have to help me with mine, too. So no more one-word answers." He waited for Asher's nod. "Did you tell Sam about this when it happened before?"

In his thick Irish brogue, he answered, "I did."

Jacob grinned. Well it wasn't a one-word answer. "What did he say?"

Caleb spoke up. "Come on, Asher, just tell him."

Asher took a deep breath and blurted, "He said not to tell Miss Lilly, that it would only upset her. Said he'd take care of it." Asher exhaled.

Jacob sighed. "I'm guessing you never saw those cows again."

Asher shook his head. "I didn't tell him this time because it didn't do any good the other times and the last time I told him he threatened to fire me, if I lost more cows."

"All right, now we're getting somewhere." Jacob didn't like what he was thinking and he didn't want the young men in his care to get fired. "Well, let's start fresh."

Both men nodded their agreement.

"Caleb, I want you to do a head count on the cattle we still have. Also, count the pigs and chickens. I want to know exactly what we have."

Caleb stood to leave.

Jacob stopped him. "Don't discuss our meetings with any of the other men. I have a feeling we three are on our own, especially since Sam and I are at odds." He had to find the cows that were missing. Jacob's gut told him Sam was setting him up.

"I think you're right. I've already been told that if I was smart I'd move my bedroll out to the cow shed. I'm not welcome in the bunkhouse anymore." Caleb shook his head. "And I cleaned the place up for that man. You'd think he'd be more grateful." A grin pulled at Caleb's lips.

"You'll bunk here in the tack room with me. And I'm going to have you take care of milk cows only, not the herd." It was his understanding that Asher took care of only the milk cows. Until today he hadn't realized it had been the whole herd.

Caleb nodded.

Asher asked, "What about Sam? He's not going to like that Caleb's workload will be lesser."

Jacob had a feeling Sam wouldn't mind. If he was right, and he thought he might be, Sam would welcome having the herd back in his care. "I'll take care of Sam. Asher, I want you to move in here, too. Make yourself familiar with the barn, the horses and all the tack."

"All right, boss." Asher seemed pleased to be moving out of the bunkhouse.

Caleb looked around. "It's going to be crowded with three of us living in here."

It was Jacob's turn to nod. In one morning he'd been

given two men to worry about, along with the horses, cows, chickens and pigs.

With the added responsibility, Jacob figured he'd be too busy to spend extra time with Lilly. Maybe that was Lilly's thinking, too.

Jacob decided to start taking all his meals but the evening meal in the barn. He wasn't about to give up his time with Daisy. Reading to her in the evenings was the only bright spot in his day. If he kept busy enough, maybe he could forget he was unlovable.

Lilly pushed the hair off her forehead and swiped at the sweat running down the side of her face. Just one more row she encouraged herself. She'd been hoeing weeds since dawn this morning. If she went by the sun's position in the sky, it had to be close to eleven o'clock. But pride in the tiny plants poking their heads through the soil fed her resolve for an abundant harvest in a few months. She had squash, cucumbers, tomatoes, onions, corn, potatoes, green beans, pinto beans, sweet potatoes and lettuce. When summer was almost over she'd plant turnips, pumpkins, cantaloupe and popcorn. With the few apple trees on the property, plus the walnut tree in the backyard and the persimmon trees down by the pond, she would have dried fruit and nuts to go with her vegetables.

She finished the next row and hurried to the tool shed to store her hoe and gloves. When she entered the house, Willow motioned for her to go to the bedroom. There Lilly found the tin tub filled with warm water and suds almost running over the top.

A grin split across her face and she shouted back to the kitchen, "You're a doll, Willow."

A little later, Lilly was dressed in her favorite day dress and in a better frame of mind than she'd been in for a while, she headed back to the kitchen armed with a plan and her sewing basket. The smell of something cinnamony wafted through the house, with a touch of something else Lilly couldn't quite identify.

"What's that smell?" she asked as Willow removed something from the oven side of the cookstove. "And thanks for the bathwater. It was lovely."

"It's a molasses cake. I found the recipe in the front of one of the novels in my bedroom. It called for cloves and, oh, my, I hope it tastes as good as it smells." She set the cake on a slice of wood on the kitchen table. "By the way, who reads novels?"

"Daisy's mom, Gertrude. She loved to read and spent many hours in her room doing just that. Since Daisy's birth I haven't had much time for reading but maybe now that you are here, I'll find more time." She picked a crumb from the edge of the cake pan and popped it in her mouth. "Willow, that tastes wonderful."

"Oh, good. I'm glad. Now I need to finish the chicken and dumplings and lunch will be ready." She turned back around and questioned Lilly. "What are your plans for the rest of the day?"

"I'm going to make Daisy a new bonnet and I have to hem the new dress I made her from one of her mother's dresses."

"I can help you with that."

"No, I really need to finish it myself so it can be a

birthday gift from me. But I sure could use help with the party and decorations."

"We're having a party? And decorations?" Willow barely contained her excitement and Lilly laughed.

"We sure are and since it's the first party we've had since my father's passing, I want it to be outstanding."

"And when is the big day?"

"In two weeks."

"Oh my stars! That doesn't give us much time." Willow poured the chicken and dumplings in a big bowl, then followed with a bowl of green beans cooked with quartered potatoes and bacon. She set one of the last home-canned jars of pickled beets on the table. "If you'll ring the bell, lunch is served."

Asher and Caleb showed up for lunch, Asher appearing uncertain to his welcome and ready to run at the first sign of trouble. "Jacob said Asher could eat in his stead since he wasn't going to be here in time. Is that fine with you, Miss Lilly?" Caleb lost no time in taking his place at the table.

"That's fine with me. Come on in, Asher, you can sit by Caleb." Lilly wondered what kind of a ruckus it would stir up with Sam, but it couldn't be helped at this point. "What's taking Jacob's time right now?"

Caleb could barely restrain his aggravation at being kept from the delicious food in front of him. Lilly hid her smile but shared a knowing look with Willow.

"Don't rightly know what's keeping him. Seems to have something stuck in his craw, but ain't sharing no input with the rest of us." He placed his hands on the table and Lilly had barely slid her chair close to the table when he said the prayer himself. Three sentences. "Lord, we sure are mighty thankful for this food. Bless it. Bless us. Amen."

All through lunch Lilly pondered Caleb's words about Jacob. They were in the middle of cleanup when Willow touched her lightly on the arm.

"I'm sorry, Willow. What did you say?"

"Well, I've talked the legs off a chicken and you've heard none of it so I'm thinking only one thing steals a woman's mind like that. A man. And you're making up all kinds of reasons why he didn't come for lunch and it's obvious he could have since he's in the barn."

"It's that obvious?"

"I'm afraid so." Willow watched Lilly lay out the material on the table for a bonnet for Daisy. In less than five minutes she had it cut out and ready to pin together for sewing.

"Any advice?" Lilly figured since Willow had been married she knew about these types of things. She basted the fabric together, then prepared to add the chain stitching.

"Just don't go making a mountain out of a molehill. Sometimes a man has to work things out in his mind, come to a conclusion on his own before he knows which direction to take. Give him time."

Lilly nodded then looked up. "Thanks, Willow. That sounds like good advice."

Willow smiled but there was sadness in her eyes.

"You know you need to add a thicker ribbon to her bonnet like that advertisement in the almanac. Did you see it?" Willow looked around the kitchen, searching for the book.

Lilly tied a knot in the final stitch then broke the thread with her teeth. "Yes, I saw it. Who would have thought to put two strings to tie a bonnet, one for use and the other for show? I think I might like it on mine but it would get in the way on Daisy's. She'd have it in her food and the hay in the kittens' bed." She held up the newly sewn bonnet for inspection.

"That color is beautiful. What did you say it was again?"

"The tag said magenta. Can you believe the carpet-bagger didn't want to sell it to me? He wanted to keep it to promote the color for more orders next time he comes through. It matches the fabric from her mama's dress. It's not exactly the same color but close. I had to pay a pretty penny for it, but this is definitely Daisy's color."

"That it is. With the white-and-yellow daisy embroidery it will be fit for Sunday best."

"Willow, did you add frosting to the grocery list?"

"Yes, but I don't see why you won't let me make it. Homemade is much better."

Lilly laughed at the accusatory tone in Willow's voice. She sounded as if Lilly had committed a great crime.

"I only want it on Daisy's small cake. She saw it the last time we were in the mercantile and I could almost see her licking her lips. And it's such a wonderful way to add to her day."

"I reckon it is." Willow softened immediately at the thought of making Daisy's birthday a special day. "I never had a birthday cake growing up. In fact, most of the time I didn't even know it was my birthday. Only after Walter and I married did I even celebrate."

"That's sad, Willow. But it was the same with my father. I only found out his birthdate while going through papers after his death. He always said he stopped having birthdays after the twentieth and I believed him. Wish now that I had known. Everyone deserves to celebrate their own special day."

Willow nodded. "That they do. Now what else can I help you with?"

"Well, I still have embroidery to do on the bonnet trim and while I'm doing that, could you make a paper chain? I think I hear Daisy moving around in her room. She can color stripes on paper and never realize what we're really going to do with it. Let her hang some in her room and she'll not think to ask about the rest. I hope." Lilly smiled, knowing Daisy would ask and also knowing Willow would have a good answer.

"I'll get right on it. Good thing we bought colors the other week."

"What made Daisy decide to nap so early in the day? We usually have to make her take a nap after lunch. Even then, sometimes she just rests on the bed and doesn't sleep."

"Her eyes looked a little weak this morning and she sneezed a few times. I thought it was because she was right beside me when I cut the strips of burlap you asked for. The dust was heavy in the air from that stuff." Willow placed a tablet and the new colors on the table. "I think I'll go check on her."

Lilly waited a moment then curiosity got the better of her and she followed Willow to the small hallway off the kitchen. They found Daisy sitting on the floor playing with the rag doll Willow had made her, but when she looked up Lilly gasped.

"Oh, Daisy. What's wrong, pet?" Lilly kneeled in front of her sister and picked her up from the floor. The tip of her nose was red and running and her eyes were a bleary, watery pink.

"I don't know, Lilly. My eyes feel scratchy and my nose is leaking away."

Willow chuckled and held a hand against Daisy's forehead. "You mean running. No fever, so that's good."

"Does your throat hurt?" Lilly held Daisy away from her to examine her better.

"No." Daisy squirmed to get down. "Just my eyes and my nose." She headed to the door. "But my nose is not broke cause it smells something good."

Both women laughed. Lilly looked at Willow with her eyebrows raised in question.

"Since there's no fever and there's been no symptoms of sickness, let's not assume the worst. We'll keep a close watch on her. She could be having a reaction to the burlap. It wouldn't hurt to put her in the bath as well."

"That sounds good to me. First lunch, then a bath."

They heard a commotion on the porch and Jacob burst through the door just as they entered the living room. Lilly's heart leaped to her throat as thoughts ran riot through her head. Someone was hurt, bleeding or dying.

"What is it, Jacob?"

"The boys said Daisy wasn't at lunch and they didn't hear her chatter at all. Where is she?"

"I'm right here, Mr. Jacob." Daisy stood in the doorway to the kitchen, and in the light, Willow and Lilly saw something they hadn't earlier. A light red rash lay along Daisy's neck and inside her arms. Jacob all but ran to her and carried her out of the house into the sunlight, with Lilly on his heels. She pulled up Daisy's shirt and looked at her belly, but there was no rash on her stomach or back.

"What's wrong with her?" His voice sounded strained and worry shone in his eyes.

"Willow seems to think it's a reaction to the burlap they worked with this morning. As soon as she eats, we're going to bathe her and see if it clears up."

"Put me down, Mr. Jacob. I need to eat."

He lowered her to the ground but Lilly noticed his eyes followed her until she disappeared into the house. When he looked back at Lilly his expression shut down and she couldn't read his thoughts. "Jacob?"

"I'd like to build two partitions in the barn if you have the funds available to buy the lumber and nails. The boys need their own space...so do I."

"They're causing the lack of sleep I see under your eyes?" Lilly teased him, chuckling at his look of surprise, but he neither smiled nor teased back.

"It shouldn't cost much. We have most of the supplies in the barn loft. Just some nails and a few studs."

Lilly felt the subtle shunning right to her soul. Jacob was upset with her and she had no clue why. What had happened between the time he left the house last night and this morning?

She studied him a moment but he wouldn't meet her eyes. "Of course, you can build whatever's needed, Jacob. Just charge it to the ranch account."

He turned to go and she called after him. "I have two rolls of fence wire I'd like you to pick up if you would."

He nodded and then entered the barn, hiding his expression from her, causing a pain to start somewhere in the upper region of her chest. The light seemed to have gone out of her day. She floundered a moment until she remembered she had a sick sister inside the house to care for. She turned and walked up the porch steps, the short distance seeming a mile long. Daisy met her, molasses cake crumbs on her dress and in the corner of her mouth.

"Guess what, Lilly? I get to help Willow color a bunch of paper and we're going to make a paper chain." She turned back when Willow called her name. "I'm coming, Willow." She grabbed Lilly's hand and skipped back to where Willow hurriedly added hot water to a smaller tin tub than the one Lilly had used. "But first, I have to take a bath."

Lilly chuckled. Even though she didn't feel merry. Jacob's rejection smarted. She didn't have romantic feelings for the man, but she'd thought they were friends. All right maybe a little more than friends. Was that the reason his shunning her hurt so much? Had he somehow wormed his way into her heart? Lilly tried to reject the thoughts, but if the sadness in her heart was any indication, he had. Now what was she going to do about it?

Chapter Eighteen

Jacob returned from town at a quick clip. His mind whirled with what he'd learned. It seemed the fencing wire Lilly asked him to pick up had already been picked up by one of the men on the ranch. It seemed odd that no one had told Lilly.

A yawn overtook him. After spending a couple of nights with both the young men snoring, Jacob decided to build two smaller rooms off his room. They didn't need a lot of space, mainly a bed and a place to store their clothes. With Lilly's permission, he'd gone to town to get wood and nails.

Jacob glanced over his shoulder to see how his horse faired at the back of the wagon. Lumber and bags of nails filled the bed and his horse snorted as if to say it belonged at the front, not the back, of this cart. Jacob laughed then turned again to face forward.

His mind went to the lost cows. When Caleb had given the count for the cows, Asher had said that was forty-five less than he'd counted a few days earlier.

Jacob couldn't help but wonder if the lost cows were still on the ranch.

Thankfully, Caleb was no longer accountable for all the cattle, only the milk cows. Lilly had thought it wise to have the young man take care of the milking and leave the rest to Sam and his men.

In the distance Jacob noticed a cloud of dust coming his way. He pulled the wagon off to the side and waited to see who would round the bend.

A few minutes later, Sam and four of his men rode up. The foreman pulled up when he recognized Jacob. "Well, well. Looks like you just come from town."

"Yep, Lilly asked me to pick up some fencing wire, but Zac over at the general store said one of your men picked it up last week. What do you know about that?" Jacob tightened his hold on the reins. He stared back at Sam.

Sam grunted. "That's possible."

Jacob nodded. "Well, I'll tell Lilly that's what you said when I report back to her." He clucked his tongue and gently shook the reins over the horses back. The wagon lurched forward.

Sam motioned for his men to go on, but turned his own horse to ride beside the wagon. "What's the lumber for?"

He was tempted to tell Sam it was none of his business, but since he was the foreman of the ranch, Jacob answered. "The boys and I are going to build a couple of rooms off the side of the barn."

The older man laughed. "Getting too crowded for you all in the barn?"

"You could say that."

Sam spun his horse around. "Well, have fun. While you are working hard to build another bunkhouse, I'll be having a good time with the boys in town." He laughed and rode away.

With Sam off the ranch, Jacob decided to ride its fences. He continued on to the barn. Asher and Caleb were there to meet him.

Jacob jumped from the wagon. He untied his horse and climbed into the saddle. "Unload the wagon, boys. I'm going to go check something out." He spun the horse around before the young men could respond.

His first stop was the back pasture, where he did a quick head count. Five more cows were missing. Jacob got down from his horse and walked around. He noticed fresh tracks and that the fence looked newly repaired.

After a few minutes studying the ground, Jacob climbed back on his horse and followed the tracks. He found himself in unfamiliar territory but continued on. The sound of cattle bawling had him cautiously pressing on. Jacob followed the sound until he came to a canyon that he'd never noticed before.

Unsure if the cattle were being guarded or not, Jacob stayed low to the tree line and scouted out the area. The cows were fenced in with new wire. He was sure this was Lilly's wire that he'd been going to pick up in town. There were no men around, so he rode down and counted them. Fifty head, exactly the number that were missing.

Working quickly, Jacob rounded up the cows. He pushed them as fast as he could back to the pasture. Had

Sam and the other men just left the cows? Deep down, Jacob believed they had. What would they think when they discovered the cattle they'd taken were now back where they belonged?

As he closed the gate on the last cow, Jacob realized he couldn't accuse Sam of stealing them. He had no proof. Other than telling Asher and Caleb that he'd found the cows and putting them back where they belonged, Jacob wasn't going to say anything to anyone about what he'd done.

When he arrived back at the barn he hurried inside the house to check on Daisy. She was in the kitchen, setting the table. Her tongue caught between her teeth as she stretched to place the last plate on the mat. There was no sign of a rash and only a little pink remained in the corners of her eyes.

Jacob felt the breath he'd been holding swoosh out of him. He looked over her head into beautiful eyes brimming with compassion. Lilly smiled and his heart did funny things. It dawned on him that he might be doomed to love people that never felt the same about him. First his mother, now Lilly.

Daisy wrapped an arm around his leg. "Let's eat, Mr. Jacob. I'm starving."

He grinned down at her. Jacob knew that whether she returned his love or not, Daisy had stolen his heart and he'd do anything for his little sister.

Lilly carried the cake out to the side of the house, where the party was already in full swing. They'd hung colored chains from tree limb to tree limb, the effect creating a surrounded room with two tables in the center. They found a lace tablecloth in Gertrude's trunk and Lilly had placed a purple sheet underneath the lace. The result looked elegant and princess like.

Daisy stood by the lace-covered table loaded with presents. The men had each brought her a gift. Jacob had presented her with a new pony that morning. It had taken all Willow could do to get the little girl to leave the barn and get dressed for her party.

Thankfully, Daisy had given in and now stood with several youngsters. The children and their parents from town had been invited and they all came to wish her a happy birthday. The little girl was thrilled with all the attention.

Lilly still couldn't believe that Daisy was five years old today. Her heart sang as she looked over all her hard work.

"Need a hand with that?" Jacob asked, coming along beside her.

Other than evening meals and when he read to Daisy, she'd seen very little of him lately. And he seemed to always be busy when she went out to get her mare for a daily ride. "No thanks, I have it," Lilly answered with a smile.

He nodded and walked away.

Lilly missed the days when they worked on the yard and garden. It had been nice to have free time to work on the party decorations and menu, but at times she found herself wanting to share with him. Was he angry that she'd given him more duties? He never brought it up and neither had she. Come to think of it, Lilly was sure that the Johnson ranch owed Jacob money for the work he'd taken on. She made a mental note to talk to him about it after the party.

Daisy thanked each person for her many presents. She raved about her cake and other treats.

Lilly watched her play games with the kids and share the gifts she received. She was proud of her little sister, who was growing up much too fast.

Her gaze found Willow sitting with Gabe in the shade under one of the many trees. Was it too hot outside for the baby?

Lilly walked over to Willow. She asked the question she'd just thought of. "Is it too hot for Gabe?"

Willow smiled up at her. "No, he's fine here in the shade."

Gabe kicked his little legs and waved thin arms. He was a cute baby, but then again all babies were cute, Lilly thought.

Lilly leaned down and whispered for Willow's ears only. "If he gets too hot, please take him inside. There are enough people here watching Daisy that I'm sure she's safe."

"I will," Willow agreed, watching Daisy play a game with the other kids. "Lilly, has Jacob seemed distant to you lately?"

"You noticed it, too?" Lilly stood and searched for Jacob. He sat with Caleb and Asher to one side of the party grounds.

"Yes, he seems more withdrawn. Not exactly unfriendly, but not friendly, either." Willow fanned the baby with her hand. "Has been that way for a couple of weeks now."

Lilly nodded. "I'll have a talk with him. Maybe he's not happy working with the men."

Someone called to Lilly and she smiled at Willow. "Time to go, duty calls." She walked away, feeling both happy that the party was a success and a little saddened at not knowing why Jacob wasn't happy.

The rest of the party went well. Everyone headed home shortly after the cake was cut. Lilly noticed that Sam hadn't attended the party. He wasn't happy, either. She sighed and began cleaning up. Who knew it was so difficult keeping employees happy? She sure hadn't known it to be this hard.

Willow offered to help but Lilly sent her inside with Daisy and the mound of toys. She knew that Willow would soon have a home for each of the new items in Daisy's room. Hiring Willow had been one of the best things Lilly had ever done.

Jacob strolled over to where she busily stacked plates in a wash pan to take inside for a thorough cleaning. "I know you told Willow you didn't need help with the cleanup but we thought we'd help you anyway." He indicated that Caleb and Asher were dismantling a table made of sawhorses and planks of wood.

"Thank you." Lilly smiled at him, happy for the help.

"What would you like for me to do?" Jacob asked, studying her face.

"I have several wooden boxes sitting by the corner of the house—would you mind putting all these center pieces in them and carrying them to the woodshed?"

She picked up the washbasin. It was heavier than she'd thought it would be.

"I'll be happy to do that." He walked to the corner of the house. His shoulders seemed stiffer than she remembered.

With the three of them helping her, the party grounds were cleaned up quickly. She stood looking at the empty space. It was sad—she'd worked hard for two weeks, making decorations, sending out invitations and making Daisy doll clothes for her doll as a gift, and the party had only lasted a couple of hours.

Jacob appeared beside her once more. "Well, if you don't need anything else, we'll be heading back to the barn."

Lilly looked at each of the men. "Thank you for helping me clean up. It would have taken me much longer without your help."

Caleb smiled. "Happy to help." He waved as he ran toward the pigpens.

Asher tipped his hat. "My pleasure." Then he, too, walked away.

Jacob started to follow Asher but Lilly called him back. She saw the weariness in his pretty brown eyes as he turned to face her. "What can I do for you?" he asked.

"I just wanted to talk for a few minutes."

Immediately he became alert. "Is something wrong with Daisy? She seemed fine at the party."

Lilly waved her hand. "Nothing like that. I just noticed that something has been bothering you and has been for a while. Is it the new job? I meant to tell you that you'll receive pay for working with my men."

Jacob sighed. "No, I enjoy working with Caleb and Asher."

She tilted her head and looked up into his face. "Is it something I did or said?" Lilly saw his jaw twitch. Had she gotten her guess right?

He locked his gaze with hers. "I've been keeping something from you and didn't really want to tell you about it because I could be wrong."

Lilly inhaled and exhaled slowly. She didn't want to jump to any conclusions. "What is it?"

Jacob rubbed his hand over his chin. "Has Sam or any of the other men ever told you that there were heads of cattle missing?"

"No. Are there?"

"Not anymore." He pushed his hat back on his head.

Lilly waited him out.

"Two weeks ago, when I went to town for the wire, it wasn't there, remember?" Jacob studied her face.

"Yes, you said that one of the men had picked it up but you didn't know who." She crossed her arms, wishing he'd get to the point.

"Well, at the same time Asher told me that he had about forty-five head of cows come up missing."

Lilly inhaled sharply. "That's a lot of cattle."

"Yes, it is. After I returned to the ranch I decided to go looking for your cows."

"Did you find them?" she asked.

Jacob smiled that tired smile. "Yes, I did. Plus, five more. Someone had corralled them in a ravine on the backside of your ranch. I was able to get them all back into the pasture before the cattle rustlers could get them off the ranch."

She exhaled. "Oh, thank you. That's a lot of cattle, which breaks down into a lot of money. Did you tell Sam?"

"No." He mimicked her by folding his arms, too.

Lilly felt confused. "Why not?"

Jacob licked dry lips. "You're not going to like my answer."

"Probably not, but I need to hear it."

"Because I think Sam is your rustler." Jacob dropped his arms.

"Do you have proof?" Lilly asked, wishing her pleasant day hadn't just been ruined.

He shook his head. "Not solid proof. But I do know Asher has been reporting the lost cattle and was told not to tell you. And that those cattle were never seen on this ranch again."

"Oh, Jacob. I can't go accusing him of rustling cattle without proof." Lilly started walking to the house. Dishes needed doing and she had some serious thinking and praying to do.

He fell into step beside her. "No, I reckon you can't. That's why I haven't mentioned it to you earlier. You don't just go around accusing a man of being a cattle thief."

When they got to the kitchen door, Lilly stood in the way of him entering. "Thank you for the information. I'll think and pray on it but I am asking you not to say anything to anyone else." She saw the hurt in his eyes.

"All right." Jacob turned to leave and then faced her

once more. "Today's Daisy's birthday and I'd planned to read her the birth-of-Christ story tonight, but I just thought of something important I have to take care of. Would you mind reading it to her tonight?"

Lilly shook her head. "You can read it to her tomorrow night. She'll want to play until bedtime tonight. Are you coming for dinner?"

"No, I'll be heading to town in a few minutes. See you tomorrow."

She watched him walk to the barn. She hadn't meant to hurt his feelings by not acting on what he'd told her immediately, but how could she accuse her father's friend of being a thief?

Lilly leaned against the side of the house. She didn't trust Sam. This wasn't the first time something had gone missing and he'd said he'd take care of it, only he hadn't. She'd overlooked those times but now that almost fifty head of her cattle had almost gone missing and he hadn't seen fit to tell her, it made Lilly wonder how many other times she had lost cows and money.

Jacob exited the barn carrying a bag with him. He put it over the saddle horn and then swung into the saddle. It hurt that he didn't even look in her direction as he rode out, headed for town. Lilly sighed.

So much for a perfect day. She pushed away from the wall and opened the kitchen door. As she washed the dishes, Lilly prayed. "Father, help me to make the right decision."

Chapter Nineteen

The decision to go to town had been an impulse and staying at the boardinghouse for the night even more so, but the next morning Jacob was glad he had gone to town. He'd simply needed an evening away from the ranch so that he could think. It hurt that Lilly didn't trust his judgment, but he could understand her needing proof that Sam was rustling cattle off her land.

He picked up his horse at the livery after a big breakfast and was now heading back to the ranch. Jacob had asked Asher to take care of the Pony Express horses and wasn't expecting a rider until tomorrow so he felt he could take his time.

The sound of a hammer drew his attention and he followed the sound to the neighbor's house. It was a nice two-story house with wild roses climbing the front porch, creating a natural shade.

The old man wheezed. "Good morning."

Jacob stopped and nodded. "Good morning. Need

help fixing that fence?" he asked, looking down on the feeble man, who appeared to be having trouble breathing.

"Naw, I'm about done." He leaned on the fence.

"I'm Jacob Young," Jacob said, sliding off his horse and looking at the repair the man had done. "Looks good."

The man held out his hand. "Robert McConnell. I'm glad you approve."

Jacob shook his hand and laughed. "Well, if you don't need my help I'll be on my way."

"Where you headed?" Robert asked.

Jacob pulled himself up into the saddle. "Over to the Johnson ranch. I work for the Pony Express station there."

This information caught the man's attention and he stood up straight. "Those boys are doing a good job getting the mail through."

"Yes, sir. They are." Jacob started to turn his horse back to the main road.

"Jacob."

He turned at the sound of his name.

"Would you tell the owner of the Johnson ranch that I'm putting this place up for sale? She could use it to extend her ranch, if she has a mind to." He began gathering up his nails.

"You're selling?" Jacob turned his horse back around.

Robert nodded. "Yep, and cheap, too. Health ain't what it used to be and the doctor seems to think I'll do better back east."

Jacob leaned on the saddle horn. "I might be interested if the price is right." How cheap was cheap to the old man?

The old-timer shook his head. "I promised Lilly's papa that I'd give the Johnson ranch first crack at buying the place, if I decided to sell it. If she's not interested, I'll offer it to you next."

Seemed fair enough to Jacob. "Care if I take a look at what you got?" he asked, sitting back in the saddle.

"Not at all. The property is fenced off; it borders the Johnson ranch down by the river. You are welcome to look around all you like. Just be sure and tell Miss Johnson I'm ready to sell."

Jacob nodded. "I'll be sure and tell her."

The man picked up his hammer and nails and headed for the house. Jacob took that as his dismissal and gently kicked his horse in the sides to get him to go. He followed the fence down to the river and then continued on until he'd made a complete, if not perfect, square. His heart soared. If Lilly didn't want to buy the land, he'd put in an offer.

As he rode back to the ranch, his mind worked on adding money in his head. He'd not spent much money and had some saved. Would it be enough to buy the little farm? If so, Jacob would be able to live close to Daisy and still have his own place.

All day he thought on the possibilities of the farm. He watched the time, eager to go to the house and tell Lilly about the farm over dinner. Would she want it? He hoped not. And if she didn't, could he buy it? Would he quit his job as a Pony Express man to work the land? Or stay on until spring so that he could plant some crops and maybe raise livestock?

When the dinner bell clanged, Jacob was more than ready. He had missed Daisy's morning riding lessons and wanted to see her. He also wanted to tell Lilly about the neighbor's land and the fact that he was selling it.

It didn't take long for everyone to find their places at the table. Jacob smiled across at Daisy. "I'm sorry I missed your riding lesson this morning but tomorrow we'll get back on schedule."

"That's all right." She swirled her bowl of red beans around with her spoon. "I got to see the kittens today with Mr. Caleb."

"You did?" He spooned the bacon-flavored beans into his mouth. They tasted much better than Cook's.

"Uh-huh. Lilly said I'd been so good that she'd shorten my time away from them and let me see them today." The smile on her face melted Jacob's heart further.

Jacob turned and grinned at Lilly. "Well, that's good."

Willow looked at Jacob with a frown. He quirked an eyebrow at her and looked at Lilly again. Willow shrugged her shoulders.

"You seem awful deep in thought, Lilly," Jacob said, tearing up his cornbread and dropping it into the steaming beans.

Lilly looked up, confusion lacing her features. "I'm sorry. What?"

"I just said you looked lost in thought." He stirred his beans like he'd seen Daisy do moments earlier.

"Oh, well, now that you are here I guess I should tell

you that I fired Sam about an hour ago." She worried her bottom lip between her teeth.

Daisy looked at her sister with wide eyes. "Really?"

Lilly nodded. "I just don't feel he can be trusted."

"Did he give you a hard time about it?" Jacob asked.

She shook her head. "No, that's what has me worried. He simply nodded and went to the bunkhouse."

Jacob studied her. Had she fired Sam because of what he'd told her yesterday? Now what was she going to do for a foreman?

Lilly felt as if she'd been sick for days. Exhaustion hit her hard. She had expected Sam to protest but he hadn't. Her mind kept questioning what she was going to do for a foreman now.

"On what grounds did you fire him? We have no proof that he was rustling your cattle." Jacob took a bite of his beans.

"I simply told him that he'd been hiding the fact that cattle had come up missing and never found, and as the foreman he should have told me immediately." Lilly stared out the dark window. "I really thought he'd justify not telling me but instead he simply shrugged. At that point, I told him that he needed to find a new job. I needed a foreman I could trust."

Willow spoke. "You did what you had to do." She buttered a piece of cornbread and handed it to Daisy. "What did he say when you said that you needed someone you could trust?"

Lilly shook her head. "Nothing. He just walked away."

"Has he left the bunkhouse?" Jacob asked. He pushed his chair back and stood.

She motioned for him to sit back down. "I've asked Asher to come tell me when Sam leaves. I'm giving him until tomorrow to get off the ranch."

Jacob eased back into his chair. He picked up his spoon and began eating. Lilly wondered what he was thinking. Instead of asking that she asked, "How was your day, Jacob?"

He lowered his spoon and a soft grin covered his face. "I've been thinking a lot about buying a small farm to the east of you."

"You mean the McConnell place?" Lilly asked, nibbling on her cornbread.

"Yes. I happened by there this morning while he was repairing the fence around the house and he told me he's moving out east." His warm brown eyes met hers. "Course, he said he'd promised your pa first chance to buy if he ever planned to sell."

Lilly nodded thoughtfully. "Probably because it connects with the river on our side."

"Willow, can I please play in my fort tomorrow?" Daisy asked, wiping crumbs off the front of her shirt.

"No, I told you. It needs to be cleaned up under there first." Willow's stern look caused Lilly to grin.

"I know. Might have snakes or spiders." Daisy spooned beans into her pouting mouth.

Lilly turned her attention back to the McConnell farm. Did she want to add more land to her place? She already had the problem of having no foreman; taking on more land meant even more work.

Jacob pushed back his bowl. "What do you think?"

Daisy answered. "I think we need to get someone to clean out my fort." She sat up straight in her chair and looked to Lilly.

Lilly decided to answer Jacob first and then deal with Daisy and her fort problem. "I don't think now is a good time for me to buy more land." Then she turned to Daisy. "I'll ask Edward and Lewis to work on that tomorrow."

"In the morning?" Daisy asked quickly and then grinned at Jacob. She was probably aware that he, too, had questions to ask her sister.

Lilly sighed. "Yes, in the morning."

She turned to Jacob. "Would you ask the men to come for breakfast in the morning? I want to tell everyone at once what is happening on the ranch. We need to work as a team to make the place run smoother."

"I'll be happy to do that for you," Jacob answered. He started to stand again.

Lilly's words stopped him leaving. "Don't you want to talk about the McConnell place?"

He eased back down. "Well, I suppose so."

"You said you'd been thinking about buying it," Lilly reminded him, feeling as if she really didn't need to, but not knowing how else to get him to talk about it.

"If you are finished, Daisy, let's get you ready for bed," Willow said to the little girl.

Daisy crossed her arms. "I don't want to go now. I want to see if Jacob is going to move away."

Willow stood and crossed her arms over her chest. "Well, then I guess we're at odds. I want you to get ready for bed so you can hear your story tonight, but if you want to stay and listen in on Jacob's private business then I guess we'll skip the story."

Lilly tried to hide her amusement. Willow knew just how to handle her sister. Daisy might think she was making the decisions, but in reality Willow knew that the girl wouldn't pass up a Bible story.

"Oh, all right." Daisy climbed down from her chair. "I want to hear the story more than stuffy ol' business." She looked up at Willow. "Mr. Jacob will tell me in the morning if he's going to move."

As soon as they were out of the room, Jacob chuckled. His warm laughter touched Lilly's heart. "Willow knows how to handle children. I wasn't sure what the outcome was going to be there for a few moments."

Lilly smiled. "You do realize that tomorrow she's going to have loads of questions for you, don't you?"

He sobered. "True, and I'm not sure what my answers are going to be."

"I thought you wanted the McConnell place." She put her hands on her chin and waited for his answer.

Jacob smiled. "I do. If I buy the farm, I will finally have my own home and I'll be closer to Daisy. She can visit me anytime."

Sorrow suddenly flooded Lilly as she realized that Jacob would probably be leaving her ranch and that she'd not see him nightly. He'd become a big part of her routine. Thanks to Daisy they'd spent lots of time together.

"It's not a large farm but I think I can raise pigs, chickens and maybe a few head of cattle. I was thinking of starting an orchard on the back part of it. Lots of good farmland back there." Jacob's eyes turned caramel as he envisioned what he could do on the land.

"What about your job with the Pony Express?" Lilly asked.

Seriousness filled those eyes now. "Well, I'd have to give it up. I'll let the supplier know next time he comes that I need to talk to the division supervisor."

Lilly hoped her smile was sincere but she really dreaded Jacob leaving. She knew it was selfish but she'd have another man on the ranch that she'd have to get to know on top of a new foreman.

"But, if it's all the same to you, I'd like to buy the place and stay on a while." He lowered his voice. "I'm not sure Daisy is out of danger. I'd like to find out first who put her in that ravine." He grinned. "I've kind of started thinking of myself as her protector."

Her hand snaked across the table. She placed it on his forearm and said, "Thank you. With Sam gone I don't know who I can trust."

He patted her hand. "Trust yourself and God. Having the breakfast in the morning is a good start."

Since Jacob was going to stay on anyway, Lilly wondered if he might be interested in being her new foreman. "Thanks. I'm curious about something." Aware they were still touching one another she slowly pulled her hand away.

"What's that?" He frowned and looked down at his arm.

"What is Mr. McConnell asking for his farm?" *And*

can you afford it? She didn't verbalize the last part but thought it.

Jacob shrugged. "I don't know. He said he was going to offer it to you and didn't answer when I asked the price. But he did throw out the word *cheap*," he answered with a grin.

"That sounds promising." She smiled. "I'd like to offer you another job. The extra money might help in purchasing the place."

"What kind of job?" Jacob asked, looking as if he had already guessed her thoughts.

"Ranch foreman." She leaned back in her chair and waited to see what he'd say. Having him as her foreman would keep him on the ranch. Lilly smiled at her own cleverness.

Jacob stood and walked to the coffeepot, where he refilled his cup. "I will help out but I'm wondering if you need a 'real' foreman. I know all your men and they do their jobs and they do them well."

"I'm sure they do but I have to know where and when money is being spent and on what. I need to know how many calves were born and…well, lots of stuff." She waved her hands in front of her as if all those things were coming at her at once.

"I agree you do, but what if you put each of your men over one section of the ranch. Say Caleb over the pigs, chickens and milk cows. Cook over the cooking and bunkhouse duties. Also tell him each man has to have a weekly bath. That house stinks." He grinned after he said that, but he pressed on. "Asher could take care of the horses, Hank could take care of the branding and fences and...well, you get the idea. Make the men responsible for their own sections of the ranch. They could report to you and you could oversee everything." Jacob stopped again.

Lilly thought about what he said. It did make sense and might give the men pride in what they were doing, but still, what if one of them wasn't doing his job? How would she know for sure?

"If you want to give me the title of foreman, that's fine. But please stress that they all have their own jobs and duties and that I am there only to assist them. That way I can make sure that each of them are doing their jobs and still work the Pony Express without having to do the full foreman job." He leaned a hip on the counter and took a sip of coffee.

Lilly nodded. "That's a wonderful idea."

Daisy ran into the room with her favorite rag doll and a blanket.

Jacob laughed. "It's a little warm for a blanket, isn't it?" he asked, scooping her up into his arms and giving her a big hug.

Lilly watched and listened to them. Was she being selfish in wanting Jacob to stay on the ranch? Was she doing it for Daisy? Or herself?

Now that she knew for certain that Jacob didn't want her ranch, but was intent on a small farm of his own, Lilly felt she could remove the wall around her heart. But should she?

Chapter Twenty

The next morning Jacob went to the house with the rest of the men. He knew they thought the worst and he tried to cheer them up. "Come on, fellas, you don't have to eat Cook's breakfast this morning."

"I'd eat Cook's food any day, if it meant I still had a job," Lewis grumbled. He was a man in his late twenties with broad shoulders, narrow hips and hair that hung to his shoulders. His high cheekbones hinted at his Indian heritage.

"Who said anything about getting fired?" Jacob asked, feeling bad for the men but not wanting to speak out of turn.

Caleb spoke up. "She fired Sam. None of us were expecting that. Not that I mind, but still." He ducked his head and watched the tips of his boots as they continued to the house.

Jacob shook his head. Surely Caleb didn't think she'd fire him. Lilly doted on him like a little brother. Didn't he see that? "She invited me, didn't she? And, I work for the Pony Express. Unless I take a job with her, she can't fire me. So I doubt she's going to fire all of you."

Just as they got to the washbasin by the back door, Asher said, "Oh, well, I feel better already. She's only going to fire some of us."

"My adoptive mother says, 'Don't count your chickens before they're hatched.' So stop worrying. You'll find out soon enough what this is all about." Jacob washed his hands and face and then hurried inside.

The kitchen had been changed to accommodate everyone for breakfast. Instead of the small table, Lilly had brought in a longer one made from sawhorses and wooden planks. There were four chairs on each side of the makeshift table and one at each end. Lilly sat at the head of the table. Willow sat on the left side of her and Daisy on the right.

A long sideboard covered one wall, where the coffeepot and platters of eggs, bacon, sausages and biscuits, and a bowl of gravy, awaited them.

Jacob felt the other men begin to come in at his back. He decided to start the self-serving. He picked up a plate from the stack and loaded it with food. At the end, he flipped over a cup and poured himself a cup of coffee.

"Jacob, come sit by me," Daisy called.

Lilly stopped him. "No, Jacob, please sit at the end of the table. Everyone else can sit wherever they wish." Her voice was firm but tender.

He liked that about Lilly. She was strong yet tender. He'd spent most of the night dreaming his farm with Lilly by his side. Jacob knew it was a dream because Lilly would never leave the ranch to live on his small farm. And even if she did, why would she stay when she already had a big ranch with lots of men working for her? She wouldn't. Realizing he was standing and staring at her, Jacob cleared his throat and said, "All right."

Caleb had followed him in line and sat down by Daisy. "I'll sit by you. I went by the barn this morning and your kittens' eyes are fully open now and they are running around everywhere."

"Can I go see them?" She looked to both Willow and Lilly.

Willow looked to Lilly.

The rest of the men sat down with full plates and cups.

Lilly answered. "I suppose so, if it's all right with Willow."

Willow smiled broadly. "I think it will be a fun outing."

Daisy started to climb down from her chair.

"I meant after breakfast," Willow said, halting the little girl's escape.

Jacob noticed the men had gone completely silent and were just sitting there waiting to see what would happen next. Lilly also seemed to be aware of them and said, "Will everyone bow your heads for a quick word of thanks and then we'll all eat."

She said a short prayer of thanksgiving and then said, "Amen."

The men raised their heads but none of them reached for their silverware. Jacob understood their hesitation.

He looked to Lilly. "Maybe you could tell us why you called us all to breakfast."

Lilly smiled. "Well, first off I want to give you all a raise."

Shock, surprise and happiness filled the men's faces. They slapped each other on the back and started talking all at once about how silly one or the other had been. He cleared his throat much like he would have done to his brothers back home to get their attention. As soon as they quieted down, he suggested, "Why don't we let the boss lady finish."

All heads turned to Lilly.

She smiled her thanks. "As you all know Sam left yesterday."

Jacob admired the fact that she didn't say Sam was fired. He watched the men's heads bob in unison.

"Well, I thought about hiring a new foreman, but have decided to do something different here at the Johnson ranch. I would like to give each of you your own section of the ranch to run."

Again the room burst into excited chatter.

Daisy clapped her hands and laughed. Willow shook her head at the antics of the men and Jacob decided to eat his breakfast. All the while Lilly waited patiently for the men to quiet down again.

He watched with a lowered head as Lilly motioned for Caleb to calm down the men. He elbowed Asher in the ribs, and Asher did the same to the man beside him and so on until they were all quiet once more.

"After breakfast, I'd like to meet with each of you. We'll go over your duties and what I expect from you as far as reports and such." At their understanding nods, she added, "I've asked Jacob to help me out."

All eyes turned to Jacob. Cook said. "So he's our new foreman?"

Lilly answered, pulling their attention back to her. "No and yes. No, he's not like Sam. Jacob has agreed to help you out if you need something done in your section. Either by doing the work himself or, if his Pony Express duties won't let him do that, he'll get one of the other men to help you. But for the most part, you are your own boss. All I ask is that you remember that I'm the one who pays your salaries and that I'm the one you need to bring the big problems to. Such as missing cattle or poisoned water holes." She watched the faces around her.

Jacob did, too. He'd expected anger from the more experienced men, but all he saw was smiles and nods. "I hope you all recognize what an honor this is. Miss Johnson has placed her trust in you. Don't let her down." There was a warning in his voice that he hoped each of them recognized.

"Can we eat now?" Daisy asked, hugging her doll close.

Lilly patted Daisy's hand. "You sure can."

Jacob hoped Daisy had learned something from Lilly this morning. She'd shown poise and grace to the men who worked for her. Lilly had immediately lessened their fears with the promise of a raise instead of the threat of firing. She was quite a woman. It was no wonder he dreamed of her at night.

* * *

Lilly sighed as the last man left the kitchen. She stretched out her back and yawned. Each man had expressed his thanks to her for the raise and the new responsibilities she'd given him. Jacob had left shortly after her announcements were complete because he was expecting a Pony Express rider this morning.

Caleb had been the first one she'd spoken to about his new duties and responsibilities and Asher had been second. She'd asked Asher if he'd clean out from under the rosebush while Daisy had her riding lesson with Jacob. The little girl would be happy to have her play area back.

Willow had cleaned the kitchen and retired to her room with the baby, something she did every morning while Jacob taught Daisy about horses and how to ride and take care of them.

Lilly suspected Willow enjoyed reading the Bible because she'd often catch her reading it while Daisy and Gabe napped. The thought reminded Lilly that she needed to pray and thank the Lord for the successful morning.

A howl of pain tore through the house. Lilly thought it came from the side of the house where Asher was cleaning out from under the rosebush.

Willow rushed from the bedroom with her Bible in hand. "What was that?"

Lilly answered as she walked to the door. "I don't know but I think it was Asher."

"Oh no!" Willow ran behind her.

Jacob and Daisy were running toward the house as

well. He stopped in the yard and looked to Daisy. "Go inside and stay in your room," he ordered.

"Lilly, do I have to? I want to see, too."

Willow grabbed Daisy's hand as Lilly said, "Yes. You do."

Daisy dug her heels into the dirt. Willow picked her up and said, "Now is not the time, Daisy." She hauled her into the house.

Lilly felt her insides shaking as she hurried around the side of the house. What would they find? Had Asher been bitten by a snake?

Jacob raced ahead of her calling out his name. "Asher! Where are you?"

His voice sounded faint. "In here." It came from under the rosebush.

Jacob dropped to all fours and proceeded to climb in with the man.

Lilly watched helplessly. She had no idea how both men were going to fit in that small space. "Be careful." She needlessly warned. Then after waiting all of five seconds, she asked, "Is he all right?"

She heard Jacob say. "Hold on, buddy. This is going to hurt."

"It already hurts," Asher answered.

Something popped and Asher groaned.

Jacob crawled out of the bush. He held in his hand some kind of wicked-looking rusted trap. It had steel jaws covered in blood. "Cook!" he yelled.

The cook came out of the bunkhouse wiping his hands on his stained apron. "Yeah!" he called back.

"Go get Caleb. He's at the pigpen," Jacob called back.

Hearing the urgency in Jacob's voice, the cook took off at a run for the young man.

Jacob turned to Lilly. "Asher passed out from the pain. I'm pretty sure his wrist is broken. We'll send Caleb for the doctor on one of the Pony Express horses."

Lilly nodded, but she couldn't take her eyes off the ugly trap. How had it gotten under the rosebush? And why would anyone set it there? Unless they knew it was a place Daisy loved to play.

Caleb came running, followed more slowly by Cook.

Lilly stepped back and let Jacob take control.

"We need to get him out of there," Jacob said to both men. "Caleb, you're smaller. I want you to go in and support his head while Cook and I pull on his legs. Watch his right hand, it was caught in this trap. Put it on his chest before telling us it's okay to pull." Jacob slung the trap to the side and watched as Caleb slipped through the entry of the rosebush.

"Who would have set a trap there?" Cook asked, voicing Lilly's earlier thoughts.

Jacob moved to the rosebush opening. "Don't know. I'll pull him to the entry and then when I get out, we'll both pull Asher out." He crawled inside the small space to grasp Asher's boots.

Lilly watched helplessly. She hadn't realized how big the rosebush was. There were now three grown men under its branches. No wonder Daisy enjoyed playing under there.

With all three men working, Asher soon lay on the ground in front of her. His wrist was bleeding pretty badly and she wondered how much blood he'd lost.

Large puncture holes lined his wrist and a wicked-looking gash, split almost to the bone, traveled down one side.

"Bring him inside," she ordered and then ran to the house. She needed hot, soapy water to clean the wounds and rags to bandage it up until the doctor could get there to sew him up.

Willow met her at the door. "I started water to heating as soon as I got Daisy settled in her room." She fell into step behind Lilly. "What else can I do?"

They were in the kitchen. Lilly pulled a clean kitchen towel out of the drawer and handed it to Willow. "Tear this into strips that can go around a man's wrist."

"It's bad, isn't it?" Willow asked, moving to the table. She used her teeth to start the tear, then proceeded to make bandages.

Lilly pondered how much soap to use. The trap had been rusty, making it even more deadly. She scraped off a good portion and slowly mixed it with hot water.

The sound of the men bringing Asher inside had her running to the sitting area. "Put him in the spare bedroom. This way." Lilly led them down the hall and to the last door on the right.

They worked together to lay down Asher. "Miss Lilly, this is going to ruin that fine quilt."

She waved him away. "Its fine, Caleb."

Jacob turned to Caleb. "I've got a Pony Express horse saddled and ready to go. Do you think you can control him and get to town fast?"

"Yes, sir," Caleb answered.

"Get Doc and then get right back here," Jacob ordered, turning worried eyes on Asher.

Lilly noticed red lines already running up the young man's arm. He groaned and moved his arm closer to his side.

Willow entered carrying the rags, soap and water. "We need to get that cleaned up as quickly as possible. Hopefully the lye will kill the infection."

"Will Mr. Asher be all right?" Daisy asked from the doorway.

Jacob turned to the little girl. "Weren't you told to stay in your room?" His words sounded strict.

Daisy ran from the doorway. The sound of her bedroom door slamming echoed through the house.

Lilly knew Jacob's thinking followed the same path as hers. Someone had set that trap for Daisy. In his fear he'd spoken harsher than he'd intended. Did he feel as helpless as she did right now? Why would anyone want to hurt the little girl? If she'd been playing alone, Daisy could have died in the time it would have taken to find her. Why? Why would anyone want her dead?

Chapter Twenty-One

Jacob paced the hall as the doctor examined Asher. Fear and anger warred within him. Fear for Daisy and what could have happened and anger that it had happened to Asher. And so close to the house. How could he protect Daisy? Who was trying to hurt her? Maybe it was time to reveal that he was her brother and that someone was going to answer to him.

Lilly had gone to the kitchen to make a pot of fresh coffee for the men and tea for herself. News had traveled fast that Asher had been hurt. The men sat or stood out on the porch. Their voices were low and full of concern.

Jacob walked to the kitchen. Lilly sat at the table with a cup cradled between her hands. Her eyes were closed and her lips silently moved in prayer. He turned and left her to her prayers.

Willow stood in the sitting room rocking Gabe. The baby fought sleep. He'd doze off and then he'd shake himself awake and cry. "Babies can sense when something is wrong," she told him.

He nodded.

"So can little girls," Willow gently said. She looked down at her sleeping baby.

Jacob sighed. Yes, he'd spoken too sharply to Daisy and needed to make amends. He walked to her room and knocked.

Daisy opened the door and looked up at him. Her hair was down and tearstains marred her little face. Brown eyes the same color as his swam in fresh moisture that threatened to spill over once more.

Jacob scooped her up and held her close. She placed her little head against his shoulder. "I'm sorry, Mr. Jacob."

He walked to her bed and sat down with her on his lap. "No, I'm the one that's sorry. I was upset that Asher got hurt and I didn't want you to get hurt, too, so I spoke meaner than I meant to."

She patted his cheek. "It's all right. I still love you." Daisy pressed her face deeper into his neck.

If he was going to tell the men he was Daisy's brother, Jacob decided he needed to tell her first. "Let's go see if Lilly has a cookie hidden in the kitchen somewhere." He stood, keeping her in his arms.

Daisy pulled back her head and looked at him with a smile. "I like cookies."

"Me, too."

Lilly looked up as they entered the room. She smiled. "Did you two make up?"

Jacob lowered Daisy to the floor and she answered, "Yep, and we need a cookie to make us feel better."

"Oh, you do, do you?" Her pretty blue eyes met his.

Daisy walked to the cookie jar. "Yep."

"Put some on a plate, Daisy, and bring them to the table." Lilly nibbled at her lip, a sure indicator that she had something to say but didn't know how to approach the subject.

Jacob pulled out a chair and waited. He wasn't disappointed. "Jacob, I've been praying and I think it's time we tell Daisy and everyone."

He grinned. "I was thinking the same thing."

"Tell me what?" Daisy asked, sliding a plate of sugar cookies onto the table.

"Do you want to tell her or want me to?" Jacob asked.

Lilly pulled Daisy onto her lap. "I will." She brushed the hair from Daisy's face and smiled. "Daisy, how would you like to have a brother?"

Daisy blinked. "I already have a brother."

She pulled back so that she could look into Daisy's face. Jacob leaned forward. Fear traveled up his spine. Had someone told the little girl they were her brother? Is that how he was getting so close to her? "You do?" Jacob asked. "Who is he?"

The little girl giggled. "You, silly."

Lilly looked at him. "How does she know that?" Then she turned Daisy around in her lap. "How do you know that?"

"I heard you two talking. It's a secret so I haven't told nobody," Daisy answered. She picked up a cookie and bit into it happily.

Jacob looked to Lilly. "She knows."

"I heard that."

"Well, now that the family discussion is over. I'd like

to talk about that young man in there," the doctor said as he walked the rest of the way into kitchen. "Can a body get a cup of coffee?"

"How is he?" Jacob asked.

Lilly put Daisy into the closest chair. "I'll get you that coffee." She grabbed two cups, poured coffee into them and walked back to the table.

"He's going to be all right. Whoever thought to wash out the wound did a good job." He took a sip from the cup Lilly handed him.

Jacob took his cup also. "That would be Lilly."

"I'm not sure but I think at least one of those teeth must have had some type of poison on it. Thankfully you cleaned it up real good. We still need to keep a watch out and make sure that the rust doesn't cause more infection to take place. I'd hate for the boy to lose that hand." The doctor shook his head.

"Would you like a cookie?" Daisy asked, pushing the plate toward the doctor.

"Thank you, little miss." He picked up a cookie.

Lilly smiled as the doctor took a bite and winked at Daisy. "What do you want us to do for him?"

"Is it possible for him to stay in the house tonight instead of that noisy bunkhouse?" the doctor asked.

"He doesn't stay in the bunkhouse. Asher has a room of his own in the barn," Jacob answered.

"But he's welcome to stay here, if he needs to," Lilly quickly added.

The doctor finished his cookie and drank more of his coffee. "Don't matter where he stays as long as it's quiet and someone can look in on him from time to time."

Jacob nodded. "We'll make sure he's taken care of."

"In that case, I suppose I'll be on my way. The Cooper baby should be arriving any time now. I was on my way to their place when young Caleb insisted I come here first." He walked to the door and then turned to smile at Daisy. "Thanks for the cookie, it sure hit the spot." He pulled his hat from the hat rack and stepped onto the porch.

Jacob followed him out the door and shut it behind him. The doctor looked at all the worried faces and laughed. "You all sure are good people. Your friend is going to be fine." He pulled himself up into his buggy and waved goodbye.

Lilly hurried out the door. "Doc! What do we owe you?"

He laughed. "A couple of frying hens would be nice or you could just have me out for dinner."

She laughed. "I'll see that you get both." Lilly waved at him and then turned to the men.

Jacob laid a hand on her shoulder. "We have something we need to tell everyone. You want to do it out here or bring them inside?" he asked Lilly.

Caleb yelped. "I knew it! You two are getting married."

Lilly felt her face flush. "No, we are not getting married. We're not even courting." She spun on her heels and hurried into the house.

Willow stood by the fireplace laughing. "Well, you can't blame them for jumping to that conclusion the way Jacob announced that you have something to tell them."

Daisy stood beside Willow eating another cookie. "Daisy, no more cookies. You're going to spoil your lunch."

"I didn't get no lunch," Daisy answered.

Lilly realized the child was right and it was closer to dinnertime then lunch. She sighed. How had such a wonderful day gone so wrong?

A thud sounded in the hallway. She turned to see Asher with his hand bandaged, leaning against the wall. "What are you doing out of bed?" she demanded.

"Doc said I could get up," he answered.

Jacob entered the house with the other men behind him. He pushed Caleb toward her. "I beg your pardon, Miss Lilly."

She smiled. "Oh, that's all right, Caleb. It's Jacob that made the blunder, not you."

"How did I blunder? I didn't announce we were getting married." He motioned for the rest of the men to step inside. Then he caught sight of Asher. "What are you doing out of bed?" he demanded.

Daisy hurried to Asher's side. "Doc said he can get up. Stop being mean."

The men behind Jacob snickered. Asher put his left hand on Daisy's shoulder. "Thank you, Miss Daisy." He leaned heavily on the wall. "Caleb, would you mind helping me to the sofa? I think I need to sit down." His face went from white to almost translucent.

Caleb hurried to his side. When the two men were seated, Jacob turned to everyone. "Now that we are all here there is something Daisy and I would like to tell you."

Lewis snickered in the back. "Don't tell us he's going to marry the little girl, now."

Jacob shot him a hard look. That seemed to quiet him down. "Daisy is my half sister. We share the same mother." He looked at all the dropped jaws.

"Daisy, will you help me put Gabe down for his afternoon nap?" Willow asked.

Daisy nodded. "I'm hungry, Willow."

Jacob smiled as they left the room. Then he turned to the men, and in a soft, dangerous voice he said, "Someone is trying to hurt or kill Daisy."

The room grew deadly silent. Lilly studied each man's face. Anger shone from their eyes. Was it anger that someone would hurt the little girl? Or anger that one of them had been caught?

She couldn't believe that one of them was out to hurt Daisy. The only alternative was that it could have been Sam. Now that Sam was no longer welcome on the ranch, maybe the threat would pass.

But why would Sam want to hurt Daisy? He wouldn't. Regardless of his past actions, Lilly couldn't bring herself to think that Sam would ever hurt her or Daisy.

Lilly motioned for them to move closer to the couch so that she could speak softly. "We are not accusing anyone here of wanting to hurt Daisy. We are asking you to help us protect her." She looked to Asher. He'd regained a little color in his face.

The young man surprised her by raising his injured hand. "This was no accident. If I hadn't been cleaning out from under the rosebush, this could have been that little girl in there."

Lewis stepped to the front of the men. "Let's go to the sheriff. He'll find the low-down dog that is trying to hurt one of ours."

Lilly's heart swelled at the words *one of ours*. She smiled at him. "And tell him what?"

Edward spoke up for the first time. He was normally very quiet and kept his thoughts to himself. "That someone stole her from her bed and then sent a stampede of cattle after her."

"Who? We have no proof that's what happened," Jacob said just as softly.

This time Lewis stepped forward. "Well, we know that trap didn't set itself and none of us set it."

"Again, we don't know who did set it." Lilly also spoke softly. "Jacob and I have been over this several times, we just have nothing solid to tell the sheriff. It's up to us to keep her safe."

The men nodded. Each saying with his eyes that he'd protect her no matter what.

"Caleb, I'm feeling a little sleepy from the medicine that Doc gave me. Would you mind walking with me to my room?" Asher asked, pushing himself up from the sofa.

"Sure." Caleb helped him stand.

The other men followed them out, each promising to keep an eye on Daisy. When the last one left, Jacob ran his hand over his face. "That went well."

"How about a sandwich?" Lilly walked toward the kitchen.

"Sounds good."

"I want a sandwich, too," Daisy announced, running up behind them.

Willow's laugh filled Lilly's ears. "I think we could all use a sandwich."

The two women worked together. Willow sliced the bread and meat. Lilly sliced cheese and then opened a jar of pickles. Jacob and Daisy talked at the table.

"Are you going to move into the house now?" Daisy asked.

Lilly kept her back to the two of them. She felt Willow's eyes upon her, but ignored her, too.

"No, I have to stay in the barn with the Pony Express horses," Jacob answered.

"Oh." Daisy played with the hem of her doll's dress. Her little face looked sad.

Lilly carried the plate of cheese and pickles to the table. "Here we go." She returned to the sideboard for the dinner plates. Maybe she could distract her sister with another subject. "Jacob, would you mind helping me bring a couple more shrubs to the house?"

Willow carried the bread and meat to the table. "I didn't know you were going to add more. Maybe Daisy and I can help plant them this time."

Lilly smiled her thanks. "I think that would be wonderful."

"When did you want to do this?" Jacob asked as he put together a sandwich.

"In the morning." Lilly continued standing as she made up four sandwiches.

Jacob watched her with a frown. "Hungry?"

She smiled. "A little. But these aren't for me. They're

for Asher and Caleb." Lilly added a few pickles to the plate while Willow took her seat at the table.

He pushed back his chair. "I'll take them out to them."

"No, you stay put. I want to make sure Asher is keeping that arm up." She picked up the plate. "Go ahead and say the blessing."

Jacob did as she asked.

As soon as he was finished, Lilly picked up the plate and headed out the door. She needed space from him. He'd shown today that he cared and loved Daisy. His warmth and strength put a new beat in her heart.

For the first time Lilly wished that a man—Jacob— would show her the kind of love that he showed to their sister. His eyes had softened, his voice had taken on a loving tone. What would it be like to have him look and talk to her like that?

She knocked on Asher's door. Lilly told herself to put such thoughts out of her mind. Jacob had made it clear he didn't trust women and right now, Lilly knew that included her. Her heart wanted someone to love her. Not just anyone, but Jacob.

Chapter Twenty-Two

Jacob propped both hands over the shovel handle and grinned at the woman staring back at him in disbelief. "Are you telling the truth?" Lilly's voice held a note of surprise.

"I most certainly am."

"But…" She held two strings together, ready to tie them around the stakes Jacob positioned in the ground close to the new plants. "I've never met anyone who didn't like green beans. My dad would turn over in his grave."

Jacob's great knell of laughter rippled through the air. Lilly reached out and smacked his arm. "You let me feed you green beans time after time and never said a word."

He quickly caught her hand and carried it to his lips. His eyes clung to hers, analyzing her reaction. Her expression stilled and grew serious. Expecting her to shy away, his confidence soared when she moved closer and lifted her hand to his cheek. The mere touch of her fingers sent a warming shiver through him.

"You're a nice man, Jacob Young. You make me feel…"

His voice came out throaty and low. "How, Lilly? How do I make you feel?"

She cast her eyes downward but he wasn't having that. He needed to gauge her feelings and to do that he had to look into those beautiful blue eyes. He gently tipped up her chin. A vague shift of the earth passed between them. He knew by the widening of her eyes she felt it, too. He squeezed her hand. "Tell me, please, Lilly?"

Her breath quickened and a slight flush crept into her cheeks. But her voice was calm and her gaze steady when she replied. "You make me feel as if I matter."

She thought she didn't matter? How could that be? "You do matter. You're important to a lot of people."

"And to you, Jacob? Am I important to you?"

His heart sang with delight. This felt right. He decided to jump in with both feet. "Being near you, working side by side, brings great peace and satisfaction to me." He swallowed and forced the butterflies to settle down. "I'm not sure what is happening—this is new to me—but I do know you're more important to me than any other woman alive."

They studied each other; the urge to take her in his arms battled with his desire to kiss her. What amazed him even more was his satisfaction at just being with her. Contentment wrapped around them like a warm blanket.

Lilly laughed gently. "Even when I feed you green beans?"

In spite of himself he chuckled. "I've staked them for you, haven't I?"

Lilly pulled her hand from his face and heaved a sigh. "That you have." She bent down and picked up the strings that dropped when she caressed the side of his face. She tied them into a double knot then brushed dirt from her hands. "Four rows worth that you will have to eat at least two times a week all winter long." Her laugh was infectious and he chuckled as he followed her to the tool shed.

A whistle split the air and Willow stepped onto the porch. She held a tray with two glasses and something cold to drink if the dew on the glass was anything to go by. Jacob appreciated the gesture. He suddenly felt parched.

"Now that's shaping into a great-looking garden." Willow handed them each a glass of blackberry tea, which she'd kept cold in the mouth of the spring.

"And it's because all of us have worked on it and stayed above the weeds, bugs and animals." Lilly always shared the praise with others and Jacob loved that about her.

"Are y'all bringing up any more fruit vines or shrubs?" Willow seemed to have something on her mind but was reluctant to say it.

"We can, Willow. Was there something you wanted?"

Willow sat beside them on the step and rubbed her hands down the front of her dress. She hadn't adopted Lilly's habit of wearing pants, but she didn't seem averse to it, either. "Well, I know that the three blackberry vines you replanted have taken root and will most likely produce next year, but Gabe will be a toddler so I won't get far from the house. I just thought if more vines were planted with the others out back of the tool shed, I could do the berry picking and keep an eye on him and Daisy here in the yard at the same time."

Willow cleared her throat loudly, startling Jacob. She raised her head with a cool stare in Lilly's and his direction. "Unless you don't want me here next year."

Lilly placed both hands on her hips, stood and faced Willow and Jacob. He could barely keep from laughing out loud, but failed to hide the grin he felt curling the sides of his mouth.

"Now, Willow, don't go upsetting the applecart after painting such a pretty picture. You just made me feel like I had a family and I looked forward to the future more than I have in a very long time." She reached for Willow and Willow stepped into arms opened wide for a tight hug.

"Aw, Lilly. You're going to make me cry. It's been a long time for me, too."

Jacob stood and stepped around the ladies. "Mmm, it's getting a little mushy for me. Think I'll go get the tools and head down to the pond for some blackberry vines."

Lilly took her time getting to the pond. Jacob had gone ahead while she and Willow had a good old-fashioned crying fest. Lilly had been bursting inside with so many emotions she had no idea how to handle. Willow shared some of the changes she'd like to make in the house but needed approval from Lilly. It seemed Willow had hidden talents with paint and decorating and had been champing at the bit to try her hand in the kitchen. Lilly told her to go right ahead. Her only stipulation had been that Willow taught her, too.

Lilly shared with her the turn of events in the garden with Jacob.

"Do you love him?" Willow asked.

"I don't know what love is. When I'm with him I like how I feel."

"And how's that?"

Lilly had difficulty explaining. "Like things are right with the world. I feel protected."

"Then just relax and enjoy your time together. When it gets to the place where he's the last thing on your mind at night and the first thing when you wake, then you're ready for the next step."

"What's the next step?"

"Marriage."

"Oh." Lilly thought she would have recoiled from that idea, but instead it beckoned to her like it never had before. Now as she walked the path to meet him, she savored this new knowledge and hoped against hope that Jacob was the one God had chosen for her.

Then she saw him, standing at the end of the path, waiting for her. He quite openly studied her and started to speak, but then turned away, his muscles tense and his head cocked to the side as if listening.

Was something wrong? And if so, what? She stopped, wondering what had caused him to turn from her like that.

* * *

Just when he was about to accuse Lilly of daydreaming, Jacob heard someone approach behind him. He turned and saw two men ride up on the other side of the pond. He didn't recognize them or the horses.

Lilly joined him. "Do you recognize them?" she asked.

"No, you?" He purposely lowered his voice.

"No," Lilly whispered. "I suppose we should find out what they are doing on Johnson land." She started to walk into the clearing up to the water's edge.

Jacob reached out and touched her arm, keeping her partially hidden. "Hold up. I should be the one to confront them. Not you."

She opened her mouth to protest. Jacob laid a hand over her lips, encircled her with his arm and motioned for her to look back toward the men. Lilly watched as a third man rode up to the other two.

Slowly, Jacob removed his hand. "It's Sam."

"I can see it's Sam. What's he doing here? I fired him."

"I don't know but I intend to find out." Jacob walked to the wagon. Thankfully he had brought his own horse as well as the one that pulled the wagon.

"Be careful."

He swung into the saddle. "I will. Keep out of sight."

Had he seen concern for him in her eyes? He wanted to think so. Lilly hadn't said whether he mattered to her or not, and though he felt she reciprocated his feelings, it would be nice to know for certain. He shook his head. He didn't have time for such thoughts.

He splashed in the water's edge as he rode around the pond toward the three men. As soon as they spotted him, all three men turned their horses and took off. Jacob hadn't expected Sam Hawkins to turn tail and run.

It just proved that the man had something to hide. Sam had been up to no good since Jacob had met him. He wanted to give chase but feared they'd circle back and hurt Lilly.

Jacob turned his horse around and rode back to her. "Get the wagon and let's head back to the house." He didn't give her time to protest but continued on to the wagon.

Lilly did as he asked. She climbed aboard the wagon and started back toward the house. "Why do you think they ran?"

"Probably weren't expecting me, or anyone for that matter, to be around. They are up to something and it's not good." Jacob's anger poured from him like mud down a slide.

When they entered the yard, Willow and Daisy came from the house. Jacob stopped beside the wagon. "I'm going into town and let the sheriff know that Sam and a couple of men have been prowling around on your ranch. I'll be back as fast as I can."

At her nod, Jacob turned his horse and took off for town at a hard run. His family was in danger and he wanted to do all he could to stop whatever Sam and his men were up to. Jacob realized he might have waited too long to involve the sheriff.

Chapter Twenty-Three

Lilly climbed down from the wagon. She watched as Jacob sped from the yard. She'd known he was upset the moment his warm fingers had covered her lips. His jaw had been tight when he'd returned.

It had surprised her that Sam and the two other men had run from Jacob. As long as she'd known him, Sam Hawkins had never run from a fight. So why had he today? A shiver ran down her spine.

"What's happened?" Willow hurried down the stairs to meet her.

"Sam and a couple of men were on our land. They ran when they caught sight of Jacob."

"Mr. Sam came back?" Daisy climbed into the bed of the wagon.

"He did."

Caleb and Edward had come from the barn and heard the conversation.

"What's he doing here?" Edward asked in a hard tone.

Lilly shrugged. "Don't know. When Jacob rode out to ask him, he ran."

"Sam Hawkins ran?" Caleb's eyes were the size of a small dessert plate. "I've seen him face rattlesnakes."

"And poachers," Edward said. "Maybe one of us should ride into town with Jacob."

Lilly's looked down the road. "It's too late, he's probably halfway there by now."

Edward nodded. "Maybe so, but if it's all the same to you, I'd like to go after him. Two men traveling is better than one against three."

She didn't have to be told that Edward feared the trio might ambush Jacob either on his way to town or back. "Thanks, Edward. Just be careful."

"Will do, ma'am." He turned and ran for the barn.

Caleb looked to Lilly. "According to the schedule Jacob keeps on the barn wall, there should be an Express rider coming through here in an hour or so. I reckon he forgot."

Lilly hadn't thought about the Express riders until now. "Do you know what needs to be done?"

"Yep, I've watched him do it lots of times." Caleb turned to go to the barn. "I don't imagine it matters who saddles the horse as long as it's done."

"Thank you, Caleb." Lilly turned back to Willow and Daisy. "I'm going to put the wagon up, then let's get a cool drink and sit a spell." Willow raised her arms to Daisy. "Come on, little miss. We'll check on Gabe and then come sit out on the porch with Lilly before we have to get back to work."

"Aw, Willow, he's just sleeping. He's always sleeping.

Can't I go to the barn and play with the kittens?" She leaned down and let Willow lower her to the ground.

Lilly answered. "No, they are busy at the barn. Maybe before supper we can go and we'll take the horses out for a ride, too."

The promise of riding the horses had Daisy running to the house. She flew her doll in the air and raced up the steps. The door slammed behind her as she continued into the house.

Willow grimaced. "Well, if he was sleeping before, I doubt he is now."

Lilly offered a sympathetic smile. "Sorry." She started to the barn but Caleb took the reins from her.

"I'll put the wagon up. Might as well kill two birds with one stone."

"Thanks, Caleb. Today I will let you with no argument."

The two women continued toward the house. Willow asked, "What do you think Sam is up to?"

"I've no idea." He hadn't acted angry the day she'd let him go. If anything he'd been very nonchalant.

Willow stopped on the porch. "I know you don't want to think about this, but is it possible he was the one stealing your cattle?"

Lilly certainly didn't want to think that, but deep down she knew it was a good possibility. "Anything's possible." She opened the door.

The smell of roasting meat filled the air along with the high-pitched cry of a baby. Willow grinned. "Duty calls." She headed down the hallway to where Daisy and the baby waited.

Lilly chuckled when she heard Daisy say, "I was wrong, he's awake." Her humor fled almost as fast as it had arrived.

She continued to the kitchen, where she grabbed a glass and filled it with cool water from the water bucket. Lilly didn't want to stay cooped up in the house so she went back outside with her drink.

"Afternoon, Miss Lilly." The Irish brogue alerted her to who was sitting on her porch.

But what was he doing there? She turned to Asher. "You shouldn't be here." She noted he had a hand gun lying in his lap.

"This is exactly where I should be." His red hair looked ruffled without a hat on it. "Caleb tells me Sam is lurking about on your land."

She leaned against the porch rail. "He is. We saw him out by the pond." Lilly looked at the gun. "Do you think that is necessary here at the house?"

His green eyes bore into hers. "I do. I promised Jacob I'd take care of his family. If Sam comes anywhere near here, that's exactly what I'm going to do."

"Asher, I know you have good intentions but with that hand bound up as it is, I'm not sure you could hit the broad side of the barn."

White teeth flashed. "I'm left-handed, Miss Lilly. I can shoot the whiskers off a rabbit out in the pasture from here." The smile on his face said he was confident but it was his eyes that spoke volumes. There was no doubt in Lilly's mind that Asher would shoot anyone who threatened Daisy.

"I'm glad you are here to protect Daisy. Thank you,

Asher." She took a sip of her water, wishing that Jacob might care for a woman like he did his sister. This afternoon she'd seen concern and something more in his eyes for her. He said she mattered to him. He hadn't mentioned love, but then again, neither had she. There might be another reason he said he cared. Maybe it was for Daisy.

A warm chuckle drifted from Asher. He gazed out over the yard, his eyes moving constantly back and forth. "I'm not here just to protect Daisy. Jacob loves you both."

Lilly frowned. "I don't know where you and Caleb get these ideas."

"From Jacob. He looks at you differently when you aren't aware." Asher smiled up at her. "The man cares about you. But—" he grinned wider "—you didn't hear it from me."

She felt her face flush. Was Asher right? Did Jacob truly care about her? She had felt their talk in the garden bordered on romantic—her heart whispered to trust that it was so. But should she hang her hopes on the words *important* and *matter*? Jacob hadn't made it perfectly clear. Maybe that's the way men were. Maybe Asher and Caleb were seeing things that weren't there.

Jacob returned to the ranch discouraged. The sheriff had listened to him but said unless Sam did more than just meet a couple of men on the property, there wasn't much he could do. He promised to talk to Sam and remind him that Miss Johnson didn't want him on her land.

Edward met him on the outskirts of town. "Mind if I ride back with you?" he asked, looking as if he'd just arrived.

"No, I'd appreciate the company." He looked sideways at the man. "Did Lilly send you?"

Edward spit off to the right-hand side of the horse. "Nope, came up with the idea myself. Got to thinking that those fellas might be braver around one man, but two might make them think before they started anything."

"Good thinking."

They rode in silence for several long minutes. Jacob couldn't stand it any longer and said, "So, who's watching the ranch house?"

"Caleb and Asher. I'm sure by now Lewis has come in from feeding and is keeping a watch out, too." He rubbed his nose.

"Good." Jacob relaxed in the saddle. Maybe he was being overcautious. Why would Sam attack Daisy and Lilly now? He'd had years to do so. But if it wasn't Sam that had attempted to hurt Daisy twice, then who was it?

Jacob caught himself glancing uneasily over his shoulder. His gut told him Sam was at the root of all the problems at the ranch and the nagging in the back of his mind refused to be stilled. There had to be a way to prove it, but how? His mind floundered.

Edward was a quiet man so Jacob wasn't surprised when they rode into the ranch yard with hardly ten more words between them. "I appreciate you riding back with me, Edward."

The other man nodded. "I hope Cook fixed something besides beans and fatback for dinner tonight." He slid off his horse and walked him the rest of the way to the barn. "Every now and then a man needs a little meat added to the menu."

"I hear you." Jacob walked his horse to the house. He tied his reins on the railing. Dusk descended and a cool breeze rustled through the honeysuckle and shrubs. Jacob sensed someone standing in the shadows of the porch.

"I take it you didn't run in to Sam again."

He relaxed as he recognized the Irish lilt in Asher's voice. "Nope."

Asher stepped from the shadows. "What did the sheriff say?"

"Just that he'd check on Sam and remind him he's not welcome here." Jacob walked up on the porch. "You been out here long?"

"All afternoon."

"Come on inside. We'll grab some grub and head to bed."

Asher put his gun in the holster at his hip and followed him up the porch. "Caleb took care of your rider this afternoon."

Jacob stopped. He pulled his hat from his head and slapped it against his thigh. "I forgot all about him."

Asher sidestepped to keep from running in to Jacob. "It's a done deal, Jacob. Caleb handled it. He got the horse ready and took care of signing off on the stop."

Jacob turned to retrace his steps. "I better go check and make sure he did it all correctly."

Asher stopped him with a hand on his shoulder.

"There's no need to skip dinner. The boy did fine. Your rider was here and gone in record time."

"Boy?" Jacob found it humorous that Asher called Caleb a boy when he was most likely the same age. "How old are you, Asher?" Jacob figured Asher might be a bit older than he appeared, but thought it wouldn't hurt to know for sure.

"Thirty. But that's our secret. I don't want these youngins calling me old man and such."

Jacob laughed, barely able to control his gasp of surprise. Asher didn't even have the shadow of a beard this late in the day, and he sure didn't have lines around his eyes from squinting in the California sun. Of course he always wore a hat for protection. "Your secret's safe with me." He turned back around and opened the door for Asher. It felt good to know there was someone on the ranch older than him, but Jacob wasn't about to tell Asher that.

The smell of peach pie filled the air. Jacob's stomach growled in anticipation. It had been ages since he'd had the dessert and couldn't wait to sample it.

"Jacob? Is that you?" Lilly called from the kitchen.

"Who were you expecting? Sam?"

She smiled. Her gaze moved to Asher and a pretty pink filled her apple cheeks. "No, I just wanted to make sure it was you."

He looked from her to Asher. Asher grinned and headed for the table.

"Sit down. I've saved you both a plate." Lilly pulled two covered dishes from the back of the stove.

Jacob didn't know what to think. Had Lilly and

Asher realized they liked each other while he was gone? He eased into his chair with a tired sigh. The thought troubled him more than he cared to admit. To his way of thinking, the special moment in the garden meant something was happening between him and Lilly. He'd thought she understood that.

She sat the plates in front of them. "I'll get you a cup of coffee."

"I'll just have water, Miss Lilly," Asher said, picking up his fork and digging into the meal.

Jacob said a silent prayer over his dinner and then started eating, too. Why had she saved a second plate for Asher? Hadn't he been the one to invite the man in?

Lilly handed Asher his drink and then set a coffee cup in front of Jacob. "What did the sheriff say?"

"That he'd look into it and remind Sam he wasn't welcome here." Jacob wondered how many times he'd have to repeat himself.

Asher continued to eat but a knowing look had entered his eyes. Jacob studied the man. Would women find Asher attractive? He had grass-green eyes—not a lot of men had eyes that green. And his hair was a deep red. Again not many men had that color of hair. A dimple winked in his cheek when he smiled. Did women like dimples?

His gaze moved to Lilly. She busied herself at the sideboard. "Asher, I told Willow about your love of peach cobbler and she baked you one this afternoon." She carried the dessert plates to the table and sat them down in front of them.

Asher looked up with pure joy on his face. "That

smells and looks good enough to eat, Miss Lilly." His gaze met hers and Lilly flushed crimson.

Jacob wanted to pound his fist on the table and ask what in blue blazes was going on. But he knew that would be ungentlemanly of him so held back. A bitter jealousy stirred inside him. He recognized the emotion and felt guilty and selfish. He'd felt the same emotion when kids in the orphanage were adopted and he remained. Unloved and unacceptable. He'd thought he'd never experience these feelings once he was an adult.

"Well, I'm going to go check on Daisy. Take your time, men, and enjoy your meal." She left skittish like a newborn colt entering the pasture for the first time.

He turned to look at Asher. "What was that about?" Asher shrugged.

Why didn't he believe him? Jacob couldn't help but dislike the thought of Asher and Lilly being sweet on one another. He knew he cared about her but did he care enough to get this jealous?

Jacob sat in shock. He loved her. The thought of her caring for Asher tore his heart deeply. He did what he knew he had to do. Jacob silently prayed. *Oh, Lord, please help me to work through these emotions and not be jealous of Asher and Lilly. I waited too long. Judged her against my mother's actions. Oh, how wrong I was.*

Chapter Twenty-Four

The next morning, Jacob skipped breakfast. He couldn't face Lilly knowing she and Asher were planning a future together. He'd ridden the fence lines and turned his mind to the danger that Daisy was still in. Deep down, Jacob felt Sam was the one that had tried and failed at harming the little girl.

Instinctively, he headed to the canyon where he'd found the fifty head of cattle weeks earlier and returned them to the pasture. Jacob looked down into the ravine. Just as he figured. Cattle bawled and pushed against each other. He couldn't be sure but figured there were at least a hundred head.

A fire pit sat off to one side and three men rested on the ground around it. Jacob watched as the noon sun beat down on his back. Sam stood and stretched. Slowly, Jacob backed his horse up until he felt it was safe to swing into the saddle. He needed to get to town and tell the sheriff where the rustlers were holding the cattle.

Jacob thought about returning to the ranch and telling Lilly what his plans were, but if he did, he'd lose valuable time and Sam might get away with the cattle. He turned his horse toward town and rode hard.

Lilly clanged the dinner bell and waited for Caleb and Jacob to arrive. Caleb stepped out of the shadow of the barn but she saw no movement that indicated Jacob was there as well.

She turned back to the house, worry lining her gut and mind. Where was Jacob? He'd been gone all day.

Asher had been sitting on the porch. He placed a hand on her shoulder. "He's fine. Probably riding the fence line again." He entered the house and took his seat at the table.

"Green beans, again?" Daisy whined as she pulled herself into her chair.

Lilly nodded. She'd hoped to tease Jacob about them, but felt disappointment at his absence.

The two men chatted about the animals in their keep while Willow tried to persuade Daisy to eat her vegetables. Lilly half listened but mostly worried about Jacob. He'd not come to breakfast or lunch. Had she said something to keep him from the house?

Chairs scraped against the wood floor as the men rose. She looked to their plates and saw where they'd eaten and were leaving the table. How long had she stewed about Jacob's whereabouts? She felt the screams of frustration at the back of her throat. A person could go insane with all the uncertainty she'd experienced lately.

Everyone looked to her as if waiting for an answer

to a question. "I'm sorry. I guess I wasn't paying attention," she confessed.

"With Jacob gone, we were wondering if you wanted us to stay close to the house," Caleb said.

Lilly shook her head. "No, go ahead and do your evening chores. I'm sure we'll be fine."

Caleb nodded. "I've got a sow about to drop a litter. Kind of wanted to stick close to the pen tonight." He headed out the back door with a grin on his face.

"Tonight is Lewis and Edward's night off. I think they've gone into town." Asher scratched his chin. "I think I'll take care of the horses and then take up space on the front porch." He smiled at Willow. "Maybe you'd like to join me in a half hour. I've something I want to show you."

Willow nodded. Her cheeks turned a pretty shade of pink. "I'll get Gabe down for the night." She looked at Daisy and frowned.

Lilly realized her sister sat with a pile of green beans still on her plate. "Go ahead, Willow. I'll clean the kitchen and see that my sister eats all her vegetables."

"Thanks, Lilly." Willow and Asher left the room with the baby.

She placed both hands on the tabletop opposite Daisy and leaned across, eyeball to eyeball with her little sister. "You're not getting down from this table until all those beans are gone. You hear?" When Daisy nodded Lilly picked up the dirty dishes and started to scrape them into the slop bucket.

"Can I take some milk to my kitty?" Daisy asked, pushing the green beans around on her plate.

Lilly carried the plates to the washtub. "No, you can eat." She filled the pan with hot water and ignored the whine in her sister's voice. As Lilly washed the dishes it dawned on her that Gertrude hadn't cared much for green beans, either. Funny how both Jacob and Daisy shared their mother's dislike of the vegetable.

"I really want to see my kitty."

"Well, eat your green beans and maybe we'll both go see your kitten." Lilly knew it was wrong to bribe the child but thought she could use a breath of fresh air, too.

"I don't like them." Stubbornness filled Daisy's voice.

Lilly sighed. "I know." She pulled the cookie jar toward her and filled a small plate with them. Willow and Asher would appreciate the treat and it gave her an excuse to see what Asher had for Willow. "I'll be right back," she told Daisy as she carried the dish out of the kitchen.

Their voices drifted through the open door.

"Oh, Asher, it's beautiful," Willow exclaimed. The sound of a soft creak filled the night air.

His voice sounded gruff as he said, "I'm glad you like it."

"It's the prettiest rocker I've ever seen."

Lilly leaned against the doorjamb and smiled. How long had Willow and Asher had feelings for one another? Had she been so wrapped up in her own thoughts that she'd overlooked their obvious interest in each other?

Willow continued. "But I can't accept it."

His voice sounded hurt. "Why not? You and Miss

Lilly sit on the porch steps every morning and evening. Ta my way a thinkin', a lady should have a chair to sit in and one with a baby should get to rock."

"But Asher, it's not proper."

Relief filled his voice. "Sure it is. I'll make one for Miss Lilly, too. That ways you two can sit on the porch and talk to your hearts' content if you want to."

Softness and a faint tremor filled Willow's voice. "That is so sweet of you. Thank you."

Lilly decided not to interfere in their conversation and happiness. She retraced her steps back to the kitchen. Her gaze moved to Daisy's chair. It was empty and her milk glass gone. The green beans remained untouched.

"That little scamp." Lilly put the cookies back in the jar. She hung her apron on the hook and headed out the back door. "I'll skin her alive," she muttered as she walked to the barn.

Asher and Willow's voices drifted on the night air but she couldn't make out what they were saying. There was no reason to alarm them. Daisy had simply snuck out to give her kitten milk.

Lilly entered the dark barn and stopped just inside the doorway. There should have been some kind of lantern lit. She hadn't expected the complete darkness that enveloped her. Before she could call out Daisy's name a sweaty palm clamped over her mouth.

"If you want to keep that brat alive you will do as I say and not make a sound."

Sam's voice rang in her head as if he was yelling instead of whispering hotly into her ear. Lilly nodded her understanding. Her heart beat in her chest and her mouth felt as dry as cotton. The force of his grip caused his fingernails to indent the sides of her cheek. She flinched and he tightened his grip.

Sam's strong arm circled her waist and he almost lifted her off the ground. He stumbled behind her, pushing her and half dragging her. Lilly knew they were headed to the side of the barn that was seldom used. The smell of horses and hay didn't have the soothing effects it had in the past. Where was Daisy? What had they done to her?

Once outside under the moonlight she knew she'd been right. Sam turned her toward a pile of hay that rested against the side of the barn. A small form lay still and silent on the hay. To the right of where Daisy lay, two men stood holding the reins of horses.

Lilly cried out as she lunged toward Daisy. The muffled sound tore from her throat. Sam's arms tightened and he prevented her from going to her sister.

"Jacob should have let her die in that ravine," Sam growled in her ear.

Lilly struggled to get to Daisy. A black and frightful fear that the little girl was dead caused an acute sense of loss. Nausea rose in her throat.

"She's not dead but if you don't come quietly, she very well can be." Sam motioned to one of the men. "Show her."

He was a big man. The giant picked up a pitchfork and started toward the hay. Lilly shook her head and grew as still as her trembling body would allow her to.

"That's better. Let's go." Sam motioned for the man

to back up and they all quietly left the barn, leaving Daisy and the ranch house behind.

Lilly walked in front of Sam. His hand remained over her mouth as he pushed her along in the shadows until they were far enough from the barn to safely mount the horses. The two men got up on one of the horses while Sam and Lilly watched.

"I'm going to remove my hand so we can get on the horse, but if you make one sound, O'Reilly is going to shoot you and then we'll go back to the ranch and kill Daisy. Understand?" Sam hissed against her ear.

She nodded. Fear for Daisy consumed her. Lilly climbed up on the horse and realized it was one of the Pony Express horses. It flicked its ears nervously as Sam tucked himself into the saddle behind her. His hot breath fanned against her cheek.

They walked the horse until they were past the pasture that housed the Pony Express corral and then took off at a dead run. Lilly wondered where Sam was taking her and what he wanted. If he'd wanted her dead, he would have already killed her. No, he wanted something else. But what?

Chapter Twenty-Five

Jacob rode back into the ranch yard. Frustration ate at him. He tied his horse off at the front porch. He'd spent too much time in town waiting for the sheriff to come back. Unfortunately, the man never had returned and Jacob didn't have any more time to wait for him.

"You've been gone all day," Asher said in way of greeting.

"Where's Lilly?" Jacob looked from Willow to Asher.

Willow answered. "In the kitchen."

Jacob heard them follow him into the house. "Asher, where are the rest of the men?" He walked into the empty kitchen. He turned to look at Willow. "I thought you said Lilly was in here."

Confusion laced Willow's face. "She was." She turned around. "I'll go see if she's getting Daisy ready for bed."

"Caleb is at the pigpens. Lewis and Edward rode to town, tonight's their night off, and Cook is in the bunkhouse." He leaned against the doorjamb. "What's going on?"

"Sam has stolen about a hundred head of Johnson cattle. He's camping in the canyon on the south side of the ranch. The sheriff is out of town so we have no one to catch him."

Jacob studied the kitchen. Lilly's apron hung on its hook by the back door, but the table hadn't been cleaned off. That was so unlike Lilly.

"They aren't back there." Willow raced into the kitchen, panic filling her voice.

Asher and Jacob exchanged knowing looks. Jacob's heart jumped into his throat. What would Sam do with his sister and Lilly? Why had he taken them? What did he have to gain?

"I'll check the barn. Daisy wanted to give her kitten milk earlier. We may be panicking for no good reason."

Jacob nodded at Asher.

Asher was gone in a flash.

Jacob covered his face with trembling hands. He tried weighing the whole series of events, but all he managed was a tumble of confused thoughts and feelings. He swallowed hard and lifted his chin. He had to get his thoughts together and not panic. Jacob hurried to the dinner bell and began clanging it. Over and over again, the bell rang its sound, shattering the evening quiet. He hoped Cook and Caleb would realize it was a call for help.

Then he turned to Willow standing behind him. "When Caleb gets here send him to town for the sheriff. Hopefully the lawman is back by now. If the sheriff is not back, tell Caleb to round up Edward, Lewis and some of the men from town. I'm pretty sure Lilly and Daisy have been kidnapped by Sam."

He started to untie his horse.

"Where are you going?" Willow twisted her skirt in her hands.

"I'm going after them. I have a hunch Sam has taken them to the south canyon." Once more he questioned in his mind why had Sam kidnapped Lilly? He strained to find that elusive thought just at the edge of his mind. It flickered, disturbing him, but he couldn't grasp what his mind tried to tell him. He began to catalogue his thoughts one by one. First Daisy, now Lilly. How would getting rid of either of them profit Sam? The answer came, and he groaned, his voice hoarse with frustration. He should have known what the man wanted. Sam wanted the Johnson ranch. Anger boiled in his stomach like a volcano ready to erupt.

Willow dropped a shaking hand over his. "At least wait for Asher. If Lilly and Daisy aren't in the barn, he can go with you."

She looked over Jacob's shoulder and gasped.

He turned to see Asher coming toward them carrying Daisy's small form. The anger dissolved to icy fear as Jacob ran to them. His baby sister was gagged and tied up, her little hands at awkward angles and he could see how the rope had cut into her tiny wrists. He rubbed the back of his hand across his mouth. Lightly he fingered a curled tendril of hair on her cheek. "I'll take her."

Asher laid Daisy in his arms. Her eyes remained

closed, her face pale as death. Jacob hurried to the house. He needed light to see if she was breathing.

Willow rushed ahead and opened the door. "Take her to her bedroom," she instructed in a calm voice.

Jacob did as she said. He laid her on top of the little Dutch girl quilt. Her chest rose and fell. His knees sagged. Thank the good Lord she was alive. He gently removed the gag from her mouth while Willow worked on the twine that bound her feet.

Asher stood in the doorway. His jaw worked with anger. A few moments later the front door banged closed, alerting them that the other man had left the house.

Willow gently pushed him out of the way. "Let me look at her." She ran her hands up and down Daisy's arms and then her legs. "Nothing feels broken." Then she moved her hands to the girl's head. She felt around. "Help me get her into a sitting position."

Jacob picked up his sister and held her in his lap as he sat back down on the bed. Her head rested against his chest. She felt so small. "Why isn't she waking up?" he asked.

Willow's hands were back in Daisy's hair. "She has a large lump back here." Her concerned eyes met his. "She must have bumped her head. Go ahead and lay her back down on the bed."

Scuffling boots in the hallway told Jacob that the men had arrived. Caleb and Cook stuck their heads into the bedroom doorway. "What's going on?" Caleb asked without entering the room.

Jacob hugged Daisy and then laid her back down on

the bed. "Daisy has been hurt and Lilly is missing." He turned to face the men. "Caleb, go into town and get the doctor and the sheriff. The sheriff may not be back yet. If not, round up Edward, Lewis and any other men that will come and meet me in the south pasture. Sam is holed up there and if I'm not mistaken he's taken Lilly with him."

Caleb headed out the door. "I'll be back as quick as I can."

Jacob called after him. "Take one of the Pony Express horses and ride as fast as you can."

The young man didn't answer but simply raced out.

"What can I do, boss?" Cook asked.

"Go with Caleb. I don't know if Sam has anticipated that we'll go to the sheriff or not. But if he has, he'll have men waiting outside of town to stop the boy." Jacob's gut knotted. What kind of danger waited for the men? What kind of danger was Lilly in? How far would Sam go to acquire the Johnson ranch?

Cook was an older man, much too old to ride a fast horse into town in the fading light of the day. Yet, he didn't protest. He simply nodded and hurried from the room.

Jacob turned to Willow. "Is she going to be all right?"

Willow nodded. "I think so. We'll know for sure when the doctor has a look at her." Her hand shook as she wiped the hair from Daisy's face.

"Take care of her, Willow. I'm going after Lilly." He turned to leave.

Asher stood in the doorway. "I'm going with you."

Jacob shook his head. "No, I need you here."

Anguish filled Asher's face. "You don't trust me to have your back," he accused.

"That's not it." Jacob realized Asher blamed himself for Daisy's being hurt and Lilly missing. He walked up to Asher and placed a hand on his shoulder. "I need you here to protect Daisy. There is no other man I trust to do this for me."

Asher's tormented green eyes looked up at him. In a thick Irish tone, he whispered, "I should never have let it happen in the first place."

"Asher, this has been planned for a long time. They just chose today to carry it out. This isn't your fault." He held up a hand to silence Asher's protest. "I need you to take care of Daisy. If Sam kills Lilly he'll be back for Daisy and anyone else that stands in his way. I trust that you will be here to protect her." Jacob looked deeply into the other man's eyes.

New resolve entered Asher's face. "I will. You can count on it, boss."

"Thank you." Jacob looked back at Daisy's still small form once more before heading out the door. He didn't know how much time he had so he ran for his horse. As he rode to the south pasture, Jacob prayed. "Lord, we need You. You know the circumstances. Please keep Lilly safe. Let Daisy be all right. Father, I love them both so much." Jacob stopped praying. He loved Lilly. He knew it as well as he was breathing. Life without her would be an empty vastness of waste.

Lilly sat with her hands tied behind her back on the hard ground. She shifted, trying to ease the ache in her back. The tightness of the ropes had cut the circulation to her hands. She studied the area, searching for a landmark or a familiar tree that might tell their location, but the light from the small fire wasn't sufficient to see by.

She listened to the men arguing in front of her.

"I didn't sign up to hurt women and children." A young man with brown hair and blue eyes confronted Sam, his brow pulled into an affronted frown.

Sam paced in front of him both hands on his hips, drops of moisture clinging to his forehead. "Too late for regrets now, Parker. You are in this up to your neck."

A third man, short and built like a barrel, slapped his hand on Parker's shoulder. "Stop whining, Parker. What are we going to do now, boss?" His brown gaze made Lilly's skin crawl as he looked at her.

Sam marched back to where Lilly sat. "This would have been so much easier if you would have married me after your pa died. But, no you wanted to run the ranch on your own. Took that brat in and pushed me away." He shook his head. "And for what?"

Lilly didn't answer him. His eyes blazed and anything she might have considered saying would have earned her another slap to the face. She licked her cracked lip and looked away.

"Why didn't you just marry me? I wouldn't have had to run off all those men." He laughed cruelly. "Not that any of them were really interested in you. I just wanted you to think they might be and that they wanted the ranch. It worked, too. You grew to not trust anyone, didn't you?" He kneeled in front of her and pulled her chin up to look him in the eye.

The man was crazy. How long had he wanted the Johnson ranch?

He dropped her chin and slapped her hard across the face once more, knocking her sideways. Lilly barely managed to stay upright. "I thought if I killed your pa you'd be easy to manipulate. But no. You have his same stubborn pride."

"You killed Pa?" Lilly felt tears burn the back of her eyes and slowly find their way down her cheeks.

"I wondered how long it would take you to put that together. It's too bad I had to tell you now. The ranch would have been mine, too, if Gertie hadn't up and died after having the brat." He frowned. "Of course, poor Gertie and the brat would have died later anyway."

Lilly felt like she was in a great fog of heartbreak and fear. "Why?"

"I want to build my own legacy. Not live off your papa's." He laughed. "Gertie kept talking about her boy. 'When we get established, I can go get my boy.' I didn't want that boy on my ranch. No, I am going to start my own legacy. Find a wife who is timid and will do what I tell her to do. All I have to do first is get you to sign the deed over to me; kill you, go back and kill the brat and the place will be mine." He laughed hysterically.

Lilly tried to block out his cold words. She watched the younger man ease toward his horse. To distract Sam from noticing she said, "Gertie wanted Jacob to come here and live?"

Sam's gaze returned to her. "That's what I said, wasn't it?"

His eyes narrowed. "Imagine my surprise when I

found out that Jacob Young was really Jacob Fisher and that he'd actually arrived at the ranch. I knew then he was after my land. And you fell for him hard, didn't you?" He paced madly back and forth in front of her.

The young man eased himself and the horse into the trees. "Jacob didn't even know his mother had lived here when he arrived," she answered, looking down. Had Jacob known all along? Deep down Lilly knew Sam was spinning lies.

Sam stalked over to his horse and pulled out a piece of paper. He looked about. "Where's Parker?"

The other man shrugged. "Probably went to check on the cows."

"The cows are here, fool." He waved his hands around. "Go find him."

With a grunt, the barrel of a man pushed himself away from the tree he'd been leaning against. "All right, boss." Then he left, too.

Having him there hadn't been comforting, but having them both gone now left Lilly in Sam's care alone. She wiggled closer to the base of the tree.

He turned his attention back to her. "This paper is the deed to the Johnson ranch. All you have to do is sign it and I'll let you go."

Lilly shook her head. "I'm not sure that will hold up in court. Did you get the paper from the bank?" Fear caused her voice to shake.

Sam looked down on the paper. "No, I didn't get it from the bank. I had a man in Sacramento write it up. Looks real, too." He held it out for her to see. "Don't you think so?"

In the dim light, Lilly couldn't tell if it looked real or not. "I don't know. There's a smudge in the ink, the banker might question it." She couldn't see any smears but thought Sam looking might stall him long enough for her to work her hands free.

He bent his face over the paper. "Don't see no blotches." Sam looked up at her. His long legs walked the short distance between them and he leaned down.

Lilly braced for another slap to the face. A large crack sounded but she felt no pain. Opening her eyes, she saw Sam looking behind him. "What was that?" she asked, praying he'd go investigate.

Sam turned to look at her. "Don't know." He stood slowly and called out for his men. Neither answered.

Lilly watched him stomp off into the darkness. She struggled to undo the rope that held her hands together. As she struggled with it, she silently prayed. *Lord, please help me.*

Chapter Twenty-Six

Jacob hurried to the tree where Lilly sat. Her head was down but her arms were working and he could hear her breathing hard. He kneeled down in front of her. "Shhh, it's me."

Lilly's head snapped up. "Jacob?"

One eye was nearly swollen shut and her lip was cracked and bleeding. Jacob reached out and touched her puffy cheek. "It's me. Can you turn around so I can untie you?" he whispered.

She nodded and turned. "Hurry," Lilly whispered to him. "It's Sam and he won't be gone long."

"Ya got that right. Move away from her."

Jacob slowly raised his hands and turned to face Sam. "What are you doing, Sam?"

Sam laughed. "Not, 'how are you doing?'" He shook a pistol at Jacob, indicating he should move away from Lilly.

"No, I couldn't care less how you are doing but I'm a mite upset at what you are doing and am trying to understand what it is that you are doing." He hoped that the way he spoke would confuse the other man.

"That don't make a lick of sense," Sam said, scratching his head with his gun. He focused on Jacob. "What did you do with my men?"

Jacob inched away from Lilly. He hoped Sam would follow his movement and ignore Lilly. Her hands were almost free, maybe she'd be able to get them loose and then run for it. "Last time I saw the big guy, he was sporting a knot on his head and was sitting under a tree taking a little rest."

Sam shook his head. "That one always did like his naps. But for some reason I don't think he meant to take the one you are describing."

This was all senseless chatter. Jacob hoped that Caleb and the men would return before Sam totally lost his mind and started shooting. Jacob grinned. "I reckon not."

"Where's Parker? Did you knock him in the head, too?"

"Nope, can't say that I did. Saw him ride off down the valley there. Thought you'd sent him on an errand." Jacob slowly began to lower his arms. From the corner of his eye he could see Lilly struggling with the rope.

A string of curses filled the air. "I should have known that boy would hightail it out of here. Boy doesn't have the stomach for this kind of work." He spit on the ground.

"What kind of work is that? I mean aside from the cattle rustling?"

Sam studied him then looked to Lilly, who stopped

moving. "So are you going to sign the deed or not?" He growled and looked down on her.

"Don't sign anything, Lilly. He'll kill you before the ink is dry, if you sign it." Jacob moved to stand beside her, but Sam quickly retrained the gun on him.

"You just want the ranch for yourself. I've seen the way you've been romancing her." He waved the gun in Lilly's direction. "Planting bushes and working in the garden. Talking to the brat like she was special or something. You have them both thinking you are an honorable man."

Lilly spoke up. "He's more honorable than you. Jacob doesn't want my ranch, he's buying the McConnell farm."

"That right? Didn't know it was up for sale."

Jacob could see the man mentally calculating how he could add the small farm to the ranch. He wasn't surprised when Sam turned his attention back to Lilly.

"You gonna sign this?" He waved the paper in her face.

Lilly swallowed. "I can't sign anything with my hands tied up like this."

Sam grinned. "True, but you're almost free. I can wait while you get them free of the rope." He shook his head and laughed. "You two thought I didn't know what she was doing. But I did."

Slowly Lilly pulled her hands from behind her back. She searched Jacob's face as she did so.

"You know, I been thinking. You sign this paper and I'll let Jacob go. We'll have to ask him to get off our ranch, but I think he'll do it in exchange for his life."

Sam sounded smug. He still pointed the gun at Jacob. "Or I can shoot him now, if you don't sign."

"He's going to kill us both if you sign that paper." Jacob kept his gaze on Sam. If the man lowered the gun, he'd rush him.

"Nope. I'll kill him. You've known me a long time, Lilly. You know I'll put a bullet through him if you refuse one more time." He cocked the gun.

"No! I'll sign it." She pushed herself off the ground and reached for the paper.

Jacob hated the fear he heard in her voice. "Lilly, don't do it."

She took the paper from Sam. "I'd rather lose the ranch than watch him shoot you. I can't live without you, Jacob Young."

"Now ain't that sweet." Sam dug in his pocket and pulled out a pencil stub. "Here." Sam thrust it into Lilly's hand.

Jacob took his chance. He rushed toward Lilly and shoved her behind him. "I won't let her sign it. You will kill her anyway."

"What if I said I wouldn't?" Sam lowered the gun. "What if I said, you fight me for her and if you win, I'll let you have her and the ranch. But if I win, I get to kill you and I'll get the girl and the ranch." He grinned evilly as he tucked his gun in his gun belt.

Jacob ground through his teeth. "Lilly is a woman, not a possession to own."

"Maybe not to you." Sam rushed forward and slammed his fist into Jacob's ribs.

Jacob pulled out of his grasp and sidestepped the second blow. He threw a few punches of his own, catching Sam off guard.

Sam stumbled backward and then ran forward with his head down.

Jacob grabbed him by his arm and then drove his fist into the man's face. He released Sam's arm as he fell back.

Sam stumbled but caught himself just before falling. He rushed back in. This time he hit Jacob in the mouth, smashing his lips against his teeth. When he pulled back for another strike, Jacob twisted to the side, avoiding his fist.

The two men went at each other like barroom brawlers. Jacob hit Sam a few times and was hit a few times. He focused on the gun at Sam's belt as they fought.

Sam came at him again but this time Jacob caught his arm and twisted it behind Sam's back. He reached with the other hand and pulled the gun from Sam's belt, then shoved Sam away from him.

When Sam turned he saw the gun pointed at his face and stopped. He leaned on his thighs, breathing hard. His face was battered and bruised.

Fighting didn't solve anything. Jacob hated that he'd been forced to use his fists, but was thankful that Lilly was alive.

The sound of several horses running toward them down the middle of the ravine caught his attention. He recognized Caleb in the lead and sighed with relief.

The sheriff jumped from his horse. "What's going on here?" he demanded. He pointed his gun on Sam and looked to Lilly.

Lilly ran to Jacob and threw her arms around his neck. "Is Daisy all right? Did you find her?"

"Yes, she's with Willow." Jacob laughed. "You really should answer the sheriff."

She released Jacob and glared at Sam. "This man stole my cattle, hurt my little sister and tried to kill us. I want him off my land."

"Let's get him on a horse," the sheriff said, motioning for two of the men to grab Sam.

Sam growled. "You can't get rid of me, Lilly Johnson. I'll be back."

The sheriff shook his head. "Not where you're going. If the judge don't hang you, you'll go to prison for the rest of your life."

Sam tried to grab Lilly as they pulled him past her. Caleb stepped up and knocked the man out cold. "That's for hurting Daisy."

Lilly's voice pulled everyone's attention back onto her and away from Caleb. "Sheriff, do I need to come with you to the jail?"

He took off his hat and shook his head. "No, Miss Lilly. I'm sorry we arrived late. Jacob has warned me several times about Sam. I should have listened."

"You came when we needed you most, Sheriff." Lilly turned to Jacob. She wrapped her arms around his middle. "Right now all I want to do is go home and check on my sister."

The sheriff nodded. "I'm glad Jacob was here."

She smiled then winced from the cut on her lip. "Me, too."

Jacob picked up his hat and then hugged her close

to his side. "Sheriff, one of his men is in that grove of trees over there. He shouldn't give you any trouble."

The sheriff nodded. "We'll pick him up on our way back. If you two can come in to town in the next couple of days, we'll take care of them both." He turned and motioned for his men to follow.

Edward, Lewis and Caleb stayed behind. Jacob asked, "Can you three get these cows where they belong?"

Lewis answered. "We sure can."

Asher came out of the trees leading his horse. "I'll help them."

"I thought you were guarding the women at the house," Jacob said.

"The doctor is there and he says that Daisy is going to be fine. Other than the lump on her head she is well. So I thought I'd come help here while he has a piece of Willow's pie." He ducked his head.

Lilly pulled away from Jacob. She walked over to Asher. "Please don't blame yourself for what happened. If anything it was my fault, I didn't tell you I was going after Daisy and I should have."

Asher nodded then looked to the other three men. "What are you three waiting for? Didn't you hear me say Willow is serving pie at the house?"

Lilly laughed and walked back to Jacob. "I'll make sure you all get a piece when you're done with the cattle."

Jacob put his hat on and then tucked Lilly against his side. He didn't want to lose her again. They walked toward the trees, where he'd tied off his horse. She seemed quiet but after all she'd been through, Jacob imagined that she'd want to think on what had happened. He helped her onto the horse and then climbed on behind her.

Lilly laid her head back on his shoulder. "Thank you for coming for me, Jacob."

His arms slipped around her waist. He laid his chin on top of her head. For the first time in his life, Jacob felt truly loved. Lilly had been willing to sign that paper and give up her ranch for him.

Jacob felt the ice around his heart melt. It no longer mattered that his mother had deserted him. Lilly hadn't. He had known for a long time that he loved her now he felt free to tell her so. But how to do so? Was now a good time with Daisy lying in a bed at the house? Should he wait?

Lilly said just above a whisper, "You came back for me."

She felt his chin bob on the top of her head. "Why?" she asked.

"You don't know?"

Lilly thought she did but wasn't sure. "Why don't you tell me?" She held her breath, waiting to see what he'd say. "Jacob, I need to hear you say it."

Jacob pulled the horse to a stop. He swung her into the circle of his arms. Her hand rested against his heart. She felt the rapid hammer and hope blossomed.

"I love you, Lilly." A twinkle of moonlight caught her eyes as he looked at her.

"Really? You love me?" She tried to keep the smile

off her face. Every time she smiled her lip hurt. Her whole being seemed to be filled with waiting.

"For the first time in my life, I know that I love someone besides myself. It consumes me." He hesitated, his expression serious. "I don't have the right words except to say, I love you, Lilly Johnson. You and Daisy are my world. When I thought I had lost you…" He stopped and inhaled a deep breath. "I felt gutted.

Lilly felt humbled in the face of his vulnerability. Yet she was blissfully happy, fully alive. Jacob gave her a newly awakened sense of life and purpose. She wanted him to understand. She struggled for words to share with him.

"I thought you loved me, too. Was I wrong?" The need for reassurance filled his lowered voice. His chest heaved as if he couldn't get enough air in his lungs.

A cry broke from her lips. "Oh, I do love you, Jacob. More than anyone in the world. When I thought Sam would kill me, my only regret was that I hadn't told you."

He gathered her tightly against him, his face buried against her neck. She felt the shudder that racked his body.

"I was scared out of my mind. Life would be miserable without you, my precious Lilly." His voice broke with huskiness.

Lilly withdrew slightly from his embrace, unable to see clearly she watched the stars disappear and his face grow closer. She knew he was going to kiss her and raised her face closer to his.

His kiss was soft and caressing, yet she inhaled

sharply at the contact. "I'm sorry, darling. Did I hurt you?" Jacob's hand cupped the side of her face and his lips brushed her hairline.

"You didn't hurt me. Sam did."

Jacob rained kisses along her jaw; she kissed his chin. Her heart sang with delight.

Jacob raised his head. "Lilly Johnson, will you marry a stock tender who works for the Pony Express?"

"No, but I will marry Jacob Young, my protector." She reached up and touched the cut next to his eye. "We really should get you to the house and let the doctor have a look at you."

He gently nudged the horse forward and they headed home. "He'll want to look at you, too."

"I know." Lilly turned in the saddle and faced forward once more. "Jacob?"

"Hmm?"

"Are you still going to buy the McConnell farm?"

"Yep."

"Why?"

He rubbed his chin against the top of her head. "Because I think it will produce a nice orchard."

"I can put your name on the ranch, too."

"There is no need for that. The ranch is yours and Daisy's. I'm happy to own the farm next door. Besides Daisy might want to keep her family on that ranch someday. You and I are going to need our own place."

His lips brushed the top of her head. "Lilly?"

"Yes?"

"I'd like to invite my family to the wedding."

Lilly leaned against him. "I'd like that, too."

"Do you mind waiting until September or October to have a wedding?"

Joy bubbled in her laugh and she placed her arms on top of his as he held the reins. "Not at all." Lilly sighed contently. For the first time since her father died, Lilly looked forward to the future. She'd known all along that Jacob wasn't like other men. God had sent someone just for her and she felt blessed.

Daisy would be thrilled to learn that Jacob had asked her to marry him. She couldn't wait to share her happy news with her little sister. At last they could all be a family. A real family.

Epilogue

Lilly couldn't believe it was her wedding day. She stared into the mirror and admired herself in her mother's dress. It was made of a soft cream-colored, satiny material with gold round buttons from her neck to her waist in the front. A wide gold belt encircled her narrow midriff. From there the dress flowed out into a beautiful cream-colored train. Lilly loved the lace on the sleeves. It looked more country than citified and that's why she loved it so. That and the fact that her mother had worn it on the day she married her father.

Tears filled Lilly's eyes as she realized how much her mother would have loved to have been here on her special day. She refused to let the tears flow and instead focused on her hair.

Willow had pulled a part of it up and left the rest flowing around her shoulders in soft ringlets. A pretty gold comb sat on top of the curls. It had taken what seemed like hours to get it to stay in place. Dogwood petals were tucked into the tresses not only making her hair look elegant, but they also put off a sweet fragrance.

A soft knock sounded at the bedroom door.

Lilly had hoped to have a few more minutes alone but knew Daisy was as antsy to see her as a puppy for a new bone. She assumed the knock came from Willow since her sister would have pounded on the door. She laughed. "Come in."

A young woman that Lilly had never met before entered and shut the door behind her. She was of average height with light brown hair. Her blue eyes shone brightly with unshed tears, but the wide smile on her face said they were tears of joy. Twin dimples winked at Lilly as the woman approached.

"I hope you don't mind my barging in like this. Seth and I just arrived and I couldn't wait to meet you." She didn't offer a handshake, she simply enfolded Lilly into her arms. After the quick hug she stepped back and held Lilly at arm's length. "It is so nice to meet you. I am Rebecca Young, Jacob's mother."

Lilly returned her smile and barely swallowed a happy squeal. "Oh, I am so happy to meet you, too. Jacob was afraid you wouldn't be able to come." Happiness filled her and she moved in for another hug. "Jacob loves his family and wanted you all to be here for the wedding."

Rebecca laughed. "I almost had to light a fire under that dear man of mine, but at the last minute he picked up the pace and here we are." She released Lilly's hands and stepped back a little farther still. Her blue gaze took in the wedding dress and Lilly.

She didn't know what else to do or say. Lilly nervously ran a hand down the front of her dress. "I'm glad you and your husband could come." She wet her lips.

In an awe-filled whisper, Rebecca said, "Your dress is beautiful and so are you. I was really worried about Jacob when he left Wyoming, but now I see that God knew what He was doing all along." She came forward and touched one of the curls that lined Lilly's face.

Lilly swallowed. "Thank you. I am so nervous." Her hands began to tremble to prove her point. She clutched them in front of her.

"That's to be expected, after all it is your wedding day."

Why did she suddenly feel so nervous? Was it because Jacob's family had arrived? Or because she was about to marry someone who took her breath away and made her feel special?

"Can I come in now?" Daisy yelled from the hallway.

Rebecca laughed. "We better let them in."

Lilly nodded, glad that her sister had arrived.

As soon as the door opened, Daisy ran into the room. She slid to a stop and looked up at Lilly. "You are beautiful. Is that really you, Lilly?"

All nervousness disappeared. Lilly kneeled down and met Daisy's gaze. "Yep, it's me. Do you think Jacob will recognize me?"

Daisy nodded. She went into Lilly's outstretched arms. "I love you, Lilly."

"I love you, too," Lilly whispered back, tightening her hug.

After a moment Daisy pulled back. She pointed at a

little girl about her age. Blue-green eyes stared back at Lilly, aware that all attention was now on her. The child tucked her face behind Rebecca's dress.

Lilly remained kneeling. "You must be, Joy. Jacob has told me all about you. He loves you very much and I know I will, too."

Joy peaked out. A small grin parted the little girl's lips.

"She doesn't talk as much as me. Her mama says she's shy. I'm not shy, am I, Lilly?" Daisy said.

Lilly laughed. "No, you are not, sweet girl."

Rebecca laughed, too. "Come on, children. Let's give the bride a few more minutes alone." She took each girl by the hand and walked to the door.

After the girls had exited, Rebecca turned to Lilly and said, "Welcome to the family, Lilly. I'm sure we will all love you, as much as Jacob." Then she shut the door, leaving Lilly alone in the quiet room.

She turned back to the mirror and smiled. "Thank You, Lord for bringing Jacob into our lives just when we needed a protector. You knew I didn't trust men and he didn't trust women. I still don't know how You managed to make us fall in love, but I'm so glad You did." Lilly ran her hands down the front of her dress one more time.

She straightened herself with dignity and walked to the door. A sense of strength came to her. Today was her wedding day and she couldn't wait to see her groom. Lilly resolved to make Jacob the happiest man alive; to be the best wife she could. In just a few moments she would vow to love and cherish him all the days of her life. She wanted to savor every detail of her wedding. Lilly yearned for success in this new chapter of her life with Jacob. With God's help and blessing, they would have many years together.

With dazzling determination and anticipation, she entered the small church and walked straight toward her groom, a tall, dark-haired man, eyes brimming with tenderness and passion and a curious deep longing that echoed in the very depths of her heart. Her Jacob. Proud, tall handsome Jacob.

And when the preacher said, "What God has joined together, let no man put asunder," she lifted her face for Jacob's kiss, giving herself freely to this man who'd stolen her heart, body and mind.

His lips captured hers like a whisper. Lilly thanked the Lord for bringing the perfect man for her into her life. She realized if it hadn't been for the Pony Express, then Jacob may never have arrived at the ranch. With a smile, she also thanked the Lord for the Pony Express.

He whispered in her ears the words she'd longed to hear all day. "I love you, Lilly Young."

* * * * *

Dear Reader,

I hope you enjoyed *Pony Express Hero*. The Pony Express has always fascinated me and when I wrote *Pony Express Courtship*, the book before this one, I fell in love with Jacob. The 1860s were an exciting time for our country and the Pony Express added to the excitement in a big way. There were many boys that were orphaned and most had no idea why their parents gave them up for adoption or left them in orphanages, much like Jacob. When Lilly entered the pages of my mind, I immediately saw her as a Cinderella-type character, only she had no fairy godmother to help her out but I knew she had a Heavenly Father who would change her life and that He'd use Jacob to bring love into that life. Writing about Jacob and Lilly enriched my life and I hope their story has touched yours, also.

Feel free to visit me on my website and blog www.rhondagibson.net.

Warmly,
Rhonda Gibson

REQUEST YOUR FREE BOOKS!

2 FREE INSPIRATIONAL NOVELS
PLUS 2 *FREE* MYSTERY GIFTS

Love Inspired® **HISTORICAL**

YES! Please send me 2 FREE Love Inspired® Historical novels and my 2 FREE mystery gifts (gifts are worth about $10). After receiving them, if I don't wish to receive any more books, I can return the shipping statement marked "cancel." If I don't cancel, I will receive 4 brand-new novels every month and be billed just $4.99 per book in the U.S. or $5.49 per book in Canada. That's a saving of at least 17% off the cover price. It's quite a bargain! Shipping and handling is just 50¢ per book in the U.S. and 75¢ per book in Canada.* I understand that accepting the 2 free books and gifts places me under no obligation to buy anything. I can always return a shipment and cancel at any time. Even if I never buy another book, the two free books and gifts are mine to keep forever.

102/302 IDN GH6Z

Name	(PLEASE PRINT)

Address	Apt. #

City	State/Prov.	Zip/Postal Code

Signature (if under 18, a parent or guardian must sign)

Mail to the **Reader Service:**
IN U.S.A.: P.O. Box 1867, Buffalo, NY 14240-1867
IN CANADA: P.O. Box 609, Fort Erie, Ontario L2A 5X3

Want to try two free books from another series?
Call 1-800-873-8635 or visit www.ReaderService.com.

* Terms and prices subject to change without notice. Prices do not include applicable taxes. Sales tax applicable in N.Y. Canadian residents will be charged applicable taxes. Offer not valid in Quebec. This offer is limited to one order per household. Not valid for current subscribers to Love Inspired Historical books. All orders subject to credit approval. Credit or debit balances in a customer's account(s) may be offset by any other outstanding balance owed by or to the customer. Please allow 4 to 6 weeks for delivery. Offer available while quantities last.

Your Privacy—The Reader Service is committed to protecting your privacy. Our Privacy Policy is available online at www.ReaderService.com or upon request from the Reader Service.

We make a portion of our mailing list available to reputable third parties that offer products we believe may interest you. If you prefer that we not exchange your name with third parties, or if you wish to clarify or modify your communication preferences, please visit us at www.ReaderService.com/consumerschoice or write to us at Reader Service Preference Service, P.O. Box 9062, Buffalo, NY 14240-9062. Include your complete name and address.

LIH15

SPECIAL EXCERPT FROM

Love Inspired HISTORICAL

*When a bachelor rancher abruptly gains custody
of his twin nieces, he needs all the help he can get.
But as he starts to fall for the girls' widowed caretaker,
can love blossom for this unexpected family?*

*Read on for a sneak preview of
STAND-IN RANCHER DADDY,
the heartwarming beginning of the series
LONE STAR COWBOY LEAGUE:
THE FOUNDING YEARS*

At last, CJ thought. Help was on the way.

With each step Molly took in his direction, he felt the
tension draining out of him. She was a calming influence
and the stability they all needed—not just Sarah and Anna,
but CJ, too.

If she ever left him…

Not the point, he told himself.

She looked uncommonly beautiful this morning in a blue
cotton dress with a white lace collar and long sleeves. The cut
of the garment emphasized her tiny waist and petite frame.

He attempted to swallow past the lump in his throat
without much success. Molly took his breath away.

If he were from a different family…

"Miss Molly," Anna called out. "Miss Molly, over here!
We're over here."

Sarah wasn't content with merely waving. She pulled her
hand free of CJ's and raced to meet Molly across the small
expanse of grass. Anna followed hard on her sister's heels.

Molly greeted both girls with a hug and a kiss on the top
of their heads.

"Well, look who it is." She stepped back and smiled down

at the twins. "My two favorite girls in all of Little Horn, Texas. And don't you look especially pretty this morning."

"Unca Corny picked out our dresses," Sarah told her.

"He tried to make breakfast." Anna swayed her shoulders back and forth with little-girl pride. "He didn't do so good. He burned the oatmeal and Cookie had to make more."

Molly's compassionate gaze met his. "Sounds like you had an…interesting morning."

CJ chuckled softly. "Though I wouldn't want to repeat the experience anytime soon, we survived well enough."

"Miss Molly, look. I'm wearing my favorite pink ribbon." Sarah touched the floppy bow with reverent fingers. "I tied it all by myself."

"You did a lovely job." Under the guise of inspecting the ribbon, Molly retied the bow, then moved it around until it sat straight on the child's head. "Pink is my favorite color."

"It's Pa's favorite, too." Sarah's gaze skittered toward the crowded tent. "I wore it just for him."

The wistful note in her voice broke CJ's heart. He shared a tortured look with Molly.

Her ragged sigh told him she was thinking along the same lines as he was. His brother always made it to church, a fact the twins had reminded him of this morning.

"Pa says Sunday is the most important day of the week," Sarah had told him, while Anna had added, "And we're never supposed to miss Sunday service. Not ever."

Somewhere along the way, the two had gotten it into their heads that Ned would show up at church today. CJ wasn't anywhere near as confident. If Ned didn't make an appearance, the twins would know that their father was truly gone.

Don't miss
STAND-IN RANCHER DADDY
by Renee Ryan, available July 2016 wherever
Love Inspired® Historical books and ebooks are sold.

www.LoveInspired.com

LIHEXP0616

Reading Has Its Rewards

Earn **FREE BOOKS!**

Register at **Harlequin My Rewards** and submit your Harlequin purchases from wherever you shop to earn points for free books and other exclusive rewards.

Plus submit your purchases from now till May 30th for a chance to win a $500 Visa Card*.

Visit **HarlequinMyRewards.com** today

MYR16R1